Praise for Bianca D'Arc's *Sweeter Than Wine*

Rating: 5 Angels and a Recommended Read "Bianca D'Arc, has in my humble opinion, out done herself with this book...this one is outstanding...the fabulously written plot, the intriguing supporting characters, the emotionally wrought erotic scenes, and the battle against an ancient evil has made it one that I highly recommend."

~ *Hayley, Fallen Angel Reviews*

Rating: Recommended Read "Sweeter Than Wine will take you on an erotic and loving journey, which has an element of danger...it will leave you hoping and wishing for the next story."

~ *Jo, Joyfully Reviewed*

Rating: 5 Blue Ribbons "SWEETER THAN WINE is emotionally deep and had me openly weeping at points...a must have for any paranormal fan."

~ *Jen L., Romance Junkies*

Rating: 5 Kovers "...paranormal romance with a riveting suspense storyline, a chivalrous hero and a heroine who can stand up for herself when the need arises."

~ *Jennifer, CK2S Kwips & Kritiques*

Rating: 5 Red Tattoos"...unforgettable...Heat flares easily and often throughout Sweeter Than Wine...With a fantastic cast of secondary characters you'll just love and plenty of potential antagonists out there I will be waiting eagerly on the edge of my seat for the next installment..."

~ *Megan, Erotic Escapades*

"Hot-blooded vamps, weres, and fey in a fast-paced tale...a series peopled with strong folk who come from vastly differing backgrounds, with various strengths, shortcomings, and quirks."

~ *Julia Clark, ParanormalRomance.org (PNR)*

Look for these titles by
Bianca D'Arc

Now Available:

Wings of Change
(I Dream of Dragons Volume 1 Anthology)

Forever Valentine
(Caught By Cupid Anthology)

Dragon Knights series:
Maiden Flight
Border Lair
Ladies of the Lair—Dragon Knights 1 & 2 (print)
The Ice Dragon
Prince of Spies
FireDrake

Tales of Were series:
Lords of the Were

Resonance Mates series:
Hara's Legacy
Davin's Quest
Jaci's Experiment

Sweeter Than Wine

Bianca D'Arc

A Samhain Publishing, Ltd. publication.

Samhain Publishing, Ltd.
577 Mulberry Street, Suite 1520
Macon, GA 31201
www.samhainpublishing.com

Editing by Angela James
Cover by Scott Carpenter

First Samhain Publishing, Ltd. electronic publication: December 2007
First Samhain Publishing, Ltd. print publication: October 2008

Dedication

To my family, who never seem to bat an eyelash when I say things like "my latest book is about vampires and *were*cougars".

To Serena Polheber, for being a good friend when I needed a sounding board, and to Megan Bamford for her unfailing friendship and support.

Chapter One

"Christy was brought in to Emergency a few hours ago." It was clear that even Jena—a doctor used to dealing with this kind of situation—was struggling to retain emotional control. "The trauma team did their best, but it's just not possible to repair all the damage in time. Her organs are beginning to fail one by one. She probably won't live through the night."

Her soft voice didn't carry beyond the small circle of friends gathered in the hospital waiting room. The old study group from college was reunited in their worry, with some additions. Lissa and Kelly had recently married, so their husbands, Atticus and Marc, were there. As was Sebastian.

He was the odd man out—a single, unattached male—but he was a close associate of both Marc and Atticus, and had a personal interest in Christina, though none of the others realized it. Sebastian had kept quiet about his attraction to Christina. She was still married and Sebastian was old-fashioned enough to want her to be free before making a move on the beautiful young woman.

"What happened to her?" Atticus asked, his arm around his wife, offering comfort.

The women shared knowing looks and Sebastian's senses went on alert.

"She told me a week ago that her husband had been violent with her on a few occasions recently. They've been having problems for a while now and I'm pretty sure she told Jeff she wanted a divorce." Jena's eyes welled with tears. "I heard from the team that brought her in that he'd been arrested."

"Her husband beat her?" Marc spoke in outrage for all the men.

Jena nodded, gulping. "I think he just snapped. He's never been the most stable personality. Even in college, he was a little weird."

Sebastian had heard enough. He moved closer to the women, drawing their attention. "Take me to her."

Lissa and Kelly gave him curious looks while Jena seemed puzzled. He would have repeated his demand but Marc stepped smoothly forward, projecting calm.

"Perhaps if we could see her now?"

Jena nodded, rising. "Yes, of course."

Marc shot him a quelling look as they all started down the hall, but Sebastian ignored it. Christina was dying. That was all that mattered. If he had to disobey a direct order from the Master, he'd do it. For her. To save her.

Sebastian thought he was calm, but when he saw her pale, bruised body lying broken amid the white sheets and bundles of tubes, he cursed.

"And they call us monsters." His breath hissed out between his teeth and his eyes glowed red.

"We can save her, can't we?" Lissa looked up at her husband with hopeful eyes.

Atticus nodded thoughtfully. "We can, but it should be Sebastian, I think."

"Sebastian?" Kelly stepped forward and Sebastian chafed at the delay.

Thankfully, Marc agreed. "If he will agree to take on the responsibility."

"I will." Sebastian didn't have to think twice. This is what he wanted more than anything. Relief filled him at the idea he wouldn't have to fight any of them over who would be her maker. He knew in his soul he was meant to do this. He was meant to bring over this sad, broken, beautiful mortal woman to their world. He would save her, then he would cherish her, for as long as she'd let him.

"What are you people talking about?" Jena planted herself in front of Sebastian, forcing him to look at her rather than stare at Christina as he had since entering the small room. He didn't have the patience to deal with this. His fangs grew as his anger and frustration built. His eyes glowed and the doctor gasped.

"We can save her, Jena." Lissa intervened, much to Sebastian's relief. "We've been keeping a big secret from you since Atticus found me." She looked over at her husband for support.

"What Lissa's trying to tell you—" Kelly stepped forward to Jena's other side, "—is that we were both close to death and our husbands saved us. They made us like them and now we'll never die. At least not by normal means."

"What the hell are you talking about?" Jena repeated, standing her ground, braver than Sebastian would have credited.

He let the tips of his fangs show. "We're not human. We've been changed."

"Are you trying to tell me you're vampires or something?"

Sebastian grinned, showing off his pointy, pearly whites. "Or something. Now, if you want your friend to live, I suggest you stand aside." Sebastian pushed at her surprisingly strong mind, but she would not be swayed.

"I don't believe this," Jena whispered, looking around at her friends as if seeking confirmation that this was some kind of joke. But serious expressions met her gaze.

"Believe it." Sebastian made to move past her, but the doctor grabbed his arm. He could have easily pulled free of course, but her action so surprised him, he paused.

"You think you can save her?" Jena's expression was hopeful, yet leery.

"I know I can," Sebastian answered.

"I don't want her in any pain." Jena stared at his teeth with fascination. Sebastian could almost see the moment when she accepted that this was for real and not a hoax of some kind. Her gaze narrowed. "Will it hurt?"

Sebastian actually grinned at that. "Our kind can make the bite inordinately pleasurable. Would you like a demonstration?" His mocking tone dared her. "I haven't fed and I could use the strength if I'm going to give Christina a good portion of my blood." He stepped toward her in a threatening manner and all four of the other vampires in the room moved to defend her. Sebastian was growing even more impatient. He had to save Christina. Didn't they understand?

"Okay." Jena bared her neck.

"What?" Both Kelly and Lissa objected.

But the doctor squared her shoulders. "I want to know he's not going to hurt her and if his being at full strength is important for her recovery, then I want to help." Sebastian also sensed the good doctor wanted confirmation that they were for real. She was the type who needed proof.

Kelly shook her head with a delicate snort of amusement. "Our very own Florence Nightingale, willing to sacrifice anything for her patients."

"You prove to me this won't hurt her more, and I'll stand aside and let you do what you've got to do to save her. I don't want to see her die any more than you do." She stared at her friends with a hurt expression. "I can't believe you didn't tell me."

Lissa flushed and shrugged. "We thought it was best to keep this a secret."

"What, you didn't want me to know you go around biting people and drinking their blood? Gee, I wonder why not?"

"Sarcasm is unbecoming in a doctor." Kelly chastised her friend in a teasing tone. "Besides, we only bite our husbands. We nourish each other." Marc stood beside her and pulled his young wife close, the love between them obvious.

Jena shrugged. "I still want to make sure this will work. You're not married, right?" she asked Sebastian point blank.

"Not yet."

"Good. Then bite me. Have a snack and prove to me you won't hurt her."

She stepped forward and placed herself only inches away from him. She smelled clean and good, and he was hungry. It wouldn't do to attempt the conversion of a grievously injured mortal without proper sustenance. The process would go better for Christina if he was at full strength when he turned her.

Without further ado, he caught the good doctor in his arms

and clamped down on her speeding pulse, biting deep. He allowed her only a minimal awareness of the pain and focused on the pleasure awakening deep inside her body. She began to pant, her blood rising, her passion heating the warm syrup as it bathed his tongue. He pulled her closer to his hard frame, sliding one muscular thigh between her legs and grinding her against him, bringing her to an explosive orgasm as her blood and lust fueled his hungry being.

She looked flushed and downright shocked as he put her away from him with a slight bow of thanks. She turned crimson as she realized her friends and their husbands had just watched her achieve a fast, explosive orgasm.

"Thank you, Doctor. Now I will attend your patient." With another curt bow, Sebastian lifted her and placed her down behind him in the small room. He hovered over Christina's pale form for a moment, touching her cheek with his fingertips. Her eyelashes fluttered, but she didn't wake. He looked at the mass of tubes running here and there, and started to disconnect the I.V. There would be nothing going into her body but his rich blood, and not through an I.V.

Jena came up on the other side of the small bed and turned off some of the monitors, helping him disentangle Christina from the tubes.

"If you hadn't just bitten me, I'd wonder if I was going insane." She was shaking her head, obviously bemused by the rapid and startling flow of events, but still game to try and save her friend.

"Don't worry, I'll take good care of her."

"Do it now, Sebastian." Marc stepped forward. Sebastian looked up to see the last remaining monitors begin to flash alarmingly. "Doctor, if you would watch the door to keep any of your colleagues from entering?"

Jena went to the door and Sebastian sat at Christina's side. He let one hand trail down her cheek as he moved closer, savoring her soft skin and delicate scent. She was almost gone. He could feel it.

Using one long finger, partially transformed into a sharp claw, he slit his wrist and held it to her mouth. He had to massage her throat to help her swallow. For long minutes he watched her drink from him, the color slowly returning to her cheeks, but he knew she was not out of the woods yet. The conversion would take all night and she would need more time to heal as well, with such extensive injuries. Even vampires could not heal so quickly from such deep wounds.

"I've adjusted the paperwork and removed any evidence from her file." Jena's familiar voice comforted Christy as she drifted up out of the darkness of unconsciousness. Her mind was muzzy with sleep, or maybe it was drugs. She recognized the smell of the hospital.

"Thank you, Doctor."

The second voice was deep and richly masculine. Christy didn't quite understand her reaction to it. Hearing that particular male voice felt like a caress in her mind. In a split second of recognition, she knew to whom it belonged.

But why would *he* be here? And where was Jeff? A shiver of alarm coursed down her spine when she thought about her volatile husband, but this man's presence made her feel somehow safer, though she had no plausible reason for it.

Her heart thrilled at the idea of seeing him again. Tall, dark and mysterious, he'd been in her mind since she'd first seen him at Lissa's wedding. They'd shared a single dance at that meeting, and one other at Kelly's wedding a few months later. He'd swept her around both ballrooms like a dream. He'd fired her imagination for months afterward, though she knew those dances were moments out of time, never to be repeated.

"She wakes." The bed at her side dipped as someone sat down. Christy struggled to open her eyes though they seemed almost glued shut. As her blurry vision cleared, she saw his face.

Sebastian.

He looked so good, his mere presence comforted her starved senses. Had she conjured him from a dream? In reality, they'd only met twice and had barely spoken. Christy had been uncomfortably aware of her husband, Jeff, watching every move she made for later commentary. Even then, their marriage had been falling apart, and soon after, Jeff had taught her to fear his unpredictable moods. But this all made no sense. Sebastian had no reason to be at her bedside with such a heart-stopping expression on his handsome face.

"Am I dreaming?" Her weak voice sounded thin, but overall she felt better than she'd expected physically, though mentally she was still fuzzy.

"Does this feel like a dream?" Sebastian grasped her hand and squeezed with gentle pressure, but she didn't have the strength to squeeze back and her entire body hurt.

"Do you remember what happened?" Jena asked from her other side. Christy looked over at her friend, noting the circles under Jena's kind eyes and the lines of worry on her face. That look brought it all back in a rush. The anger, the fear...the pain. Christy gulped, suppressing a shiver.

"I remember. At least until I blacked out. Where's Jeff?" Anguish blocked her throat as she remembered the last time she'd seen her husband. She hated the debilitating fear he'd instilled in her. The mere thought of what he'd done—and what he could still do to her—made her quake with apprehension.

"Jeff's in jail, where he belongs," Jena was quick to reassure her.

That made sense to her foggy brain, and went a long way toward soothing some of her immediate anxiety, though the fear lived on in her soul. "I saw him being handcuffed and then I remember seeing the grass zooming up at me. I guess I fainted."

Jena clutched her other hand. "You passed out. The ambulance brought you here and one of the emergency room staff called me." Tears gathered in Jena's eyes. It struck Christy because Jena was always so strong. She never showed this much emotion. "Christy, you nearly died."

"I did?" She took quick stock of her body. She was sore all over, but the initial ache was fading. "I feel okay. Just bruised." She remembered the wrenching pain in her side when Jeff had kicked her. "He broke ribs, didn't he?"

Jena nodded. "And punctured a lung."

"Then you must have me doped up pretty good. I don't feel it." She tried to smile at her friend, but Jena's eyes clouded.

"Uh, Christy, there's something you should know."

"Thank you, Doctor. She is my responsibility now." Sebastian's voice was filled with quiet authority, respectful but firm.

"But she should hear this from one of her friends."

"She will, in due time, but it's enough for her to know that you support her, regardless of her state. You have done that already and I thank you."

"What's going on?" Christy grew concerned over the obvious battle of wills between Sebastian and Jena. If she was any judge, even Jena couldn't win such a fight with this formidable man.

"It's all right, Christina. Jena was part of what we did to save your life, though she does not fully understand it." Sebastian's fingers stroked her hand with reassuring pressure.

"We? Who's we?"

"Christy, you need to know that Lissa and Kelly were present when the decision was made. They're like you are now."

"That's enough, Doctor. I'll take it from here."

"But she needs to know—"

"She will, soon enough." He motioned toward the door. It was a clear command. "Thank you for your assistance."

Jena left with a doubtful expression. Christy was still out of it, but she instinctively trusted Sebastian. There was no real reason why he could claim so much of her trust, but she knew on some intrinsic level that he was okay. More than okay, actually. He was nothing at all like Jeff. Where Jeff's size intimidated, Sebastian's even broader shoulders comforted. Where Jeff's hands brought pain, Sebastian's brought a gentleness that almost made her weep. And where Jeff's words cut to the bone, Sebastian's whispered across her delicate psyche in gentle waves that made her want to bask in their glow forever.

Sebastian turned his gorgeous eyes back to her after Jena closed the door. Christy felt his penetrating stare as he lifted her hand to his lips in an old-world gesture of respect that touched her heart.

"You will no doubt be surprised by much of what I have to tell you, but it must be said and you must believe." His gaze caught hers, and held. "You wouldn't have lived through the night had we not intervened. Your friends, Kelly and Lissa, petitioned for your conversion and their mates agreed. I claimed the right and responsibility of turning you and I want you to know I'll live up to the duty I assumed when I gave you my blood."

"You donated blood?"

His sexy lips quirked in a semblance of a smile. "You're probably thinking of transfusions and other medical intervention when what I did was much more primitive. No, dear Christina, you drank my blood and now you are as I am. Immortal."

After a moment, she laughed into the tense silence. "You've got to be kidding."

"I'm afraid not." Sebastian shook his head slowly. "Lissa and Kelly have also undergone conversion by their mates and now your friend Jena knows of our existence. She'll no doubt be watched from now on to preserve our secret. Our survival depends on the secrecy of our existence."

"What are you?" She remembered Jena's serious tone. It was obvious Jena believed this odd tale and Jena was the smartest of all her friends. If Jena believed it, it was probably true, incredible as it may seem.

"Some call our kind vampire, though I'm not particularly fond of that term myself."

"You prefer 'undead', perhaps?" She made a stab at a joke, though it wasn't much of one.

Sebastian grimaced. "I don't like that word either. Makes me sound like a reanimated corpse."

"Isn't that what I am? You said I would've died without your intervention." The horror of that was still sinking in.

"No, my dear. You did *not* die. And now, you *will* not. At least not by normal means. Certain things can kill us, but it's rare. In all my years, only one of my acquaintances lost his life through accident."

"And just how old are you?" Dread gathered in her gut.

"I was converted in the year 1702, on the road near Bristol." He shrugged.

"Connecticut?"

He chuckled and shook his head. "England. I was on my way home, traveling from London, when my coach was attacked by highwaymen. We fought back but were outnumbered and I

17

was left to die in the forest. A woman found me that night and turned me to save my life but she was also on the run. She left me to fend for myself and I learned through bitter trial and error what I could and couldn't do with my new abilities. My life as I'd known it was over and eventually I traveled to the Americas to make my way in a new land that was a bit more primitive. I met Marc LaTour in Boston and he took me under his wing, so to speak. That was well before the American Revolution. We've been friends ever since."

"Wow." She was simply stunned.

"I tell you all this to impress upon you how important it is that you learn from me. I took on the responsibility of being your maker. I know, more than any of the others, how important it is to have a maker that will devote time to teaching you the ropes when you are newly turned. Your friends have their mates to look after them, but you have no one. I'll watch over you, Christina. I'll teach you what you need to know to survive and thrive in your new life." His gaze was intent. "It would be my deepest honor."

Christy's mind raced. Jena wouldn't have left her alone with this man if he were an escaped lunatic, would she? No, but that meant the incredible tale he was spinning had to be true. It was shocking. Unbelievable. Scarily true.

"I feel different." She flexed her fingers, noting a strength in her grip that had never been there before.

Sebastian nodded. "You'll be stronger now than you were, able to see clearly in the dark. You won't be able to walk in the sun, though I've heard after a few centuries, some of our kind can take the early morning or late evening sunlight without too much pain. You'll be lethargic during the day, unable to fend for yourself until you get a few decades under your belt, so it's imperative you plan ahead and have a safe place to stay during the hours of daylight. I think your friends will want to help you there, but for now, I'll take you home with me." He stood from her bedside and began rummaging through the closet for what was left of her clothes. "You'll find I take my responsibility for your training very seriously. I'll see to your education and to your needs for the time being."

"But why? You barely know me."

He turned back to the bed and pressed her bedraggled robe

into her hands. His gaze held her immobile, his expression unreadable, but very intense.

"I pride myself on being a man of honor, Christina, but even though you're married, you've been on my mind since the moment I first saw you. As far as I'm concerned, by abusing you so badly, your husband has lost all right to you. That means you're free. And I'm free to pursue the attraction I can no longer deny."

His eyes lowered to study her lips, gone dry all of a sudden, as if heated by his gaze. Her tongue peeked out to wet them and he groaned, leaning downward as if mesmerized. She knew he was going to kiss her and for the first time in a long time, she wanted a man's attentions. She wanted Sebastian's kiss. Not daring to move a muscle, she welcomed him as he lowered his head. Firm, masculine lips traced hers with a butterfly caress before grinding deep and hard.

His tongue demanded entrance and she complied, delighted by the taste of him and the ardor he couldn't hide. Her pulses leapt and her hunger grew. She encircled his neck with her hands, sinking them into his thick hair and dragging him closer. Oh, how she wanted him.

But Sebastian drew back, breathing hard. Flames of passion flickered in his eyes, but he appeared to be in perfect control. It both irritated her and made her feel secure. Of late, Jeff was never in control. He would scream at her as soon as kiss her and it was comforting to know for certain that Sebastian was the total opposite. Sebastian was a man in complete command of himself and those around him. A master. And she feared and hoped she could become his willing slave. At least sexually. She'd missed the active sex life she and Jeff had as newlyweds. They'd been sleeping in separate rooms for over a year, unable to get along in every way.

"We must go. There's little time before dawn."

Ever the gentleman, he helped her into the stained robe. She'd been getting ready for bed when Jeff went berserk, and she had arrived at the hospital in her robe and little else. Sebastian lifted her in his arms as if she weighed nothing at all and strode into the corridor.

"Won't the hospital object?"

"They won't see us. I'm diverting the attention of the

mortals, except for your friend Jena. Atticus and Marc have our escape vehicle ready at the exit."

"You can do that? You can influence people's minds?"

Sebastian shrugged. "Though I'm young when compared to Marc and Atticus, I'm no fledgling. You'll gain many new skills, once you've matured a bit."

"Wow."

Jena met them in the corridor, her eyes worried. "Are you okay?"

Christy tried to find words to reassure her friend, but it was hard to concentrate in Sebastian's embrace. He made her feel so small, yet so protected.

"I'm good, Jena. Thank you for taking care of me."

Jena leaned forward and kissed her cheek, emotion getting the best of her. "I've been so worried for you. Lissa and Kelly assured me that Jeff will never be able to hurt you again and for that, at least, I'm glad. I think Sebastian will take good care of you, and if he doesn't—" Jena's face turned upward with steely determination, "—he'll answer to me." Sebastian nodded in acknowledgement but didn't speak. Jena returned her gaze to Christy. "For what it's worth, I think he's a good guy, and he won't hurt you. I've had a demonstration of what he can do." Jena blushed inexplicably. "I think you're in safe hands." She turned again to Sebastian. "I've fixed the records here at the hospital the way Marc requested, so you should have some time before Jeff figures out where she's gone."

"Excellent." Sebastian's voice dripped with molten steel at the mention of Jeff's name. "You're a very efficient woman, a skilled doctor, and a good friend. I thank you for the care you've given Christina and the assistance with her conversion. Part of you is part of us now. We'll always thank you for your sacrifice."

"What are you two talking about?"

Christy's voice was small, tired and a little miffed. If these two had secrets, she wanted to be let in on them. And why was one of her best friends so chummy all of a sudden with Sebastian? If she didn't know better, she'd think she was jealous, but it seemed impossible to be jealous of a man she'd only met twice before. Christy knew something was odd about the way she felt, but was too tired to ponder it at the moment.

"I'll explain it all to you soon, little one. For now, we must away."

She chuckled. "No one talks like that."

"I do." He smiled down at her, something shining in his eyes she didn't dare name. "There's something about having a damsel in distress in my arms that brings out memories of my former self. You must forgive me if I slip into the speech patterns to which I was born."

He walked on, nodding to Marc as he held the door for them.

"There's nothing to forgive. What woman wouldn't be thrilled to be romanced by a real English lord?"

He paused by the side of a waiting luxury car. "And how did you know I was noble born?"

"Oh, come on, Sebastian. You have aristocracy written all over you."

He raised one eyebrow. "I must endeavor then, to fit better into my present circumstances."

"No need to do so for me," she said, yawning and settling her head against his shoulder. "I like you fine just the way you are."

She thought she heard him growl as he handed her into the wide backseat of the waiting car, but she was too tired to take in much. She had a vague impression of Lissa seated in the front seat with her husband, Atticus, driving. In the darkness before dawn, Christy wanted to ask more questions, but she was too tired and too befuddled by all the amazing revelations of the past hour.

The last thing Christy saw before sleep claimed her was Sebastian's handsome face. She felt warmed by his regard and it lulled her into a deep, healing sleep.

While she slept, Sebastian kept busy, making decisions and arranging things. He placed a difficult call to his good friend Matt Redstone and checked in with Christina's friends to keep tabs on her soon-to-be ex-husband. He also placed a call to his lawyer and had her start looking into every facet of the couple's relationship.

There had to be something more as to why Jeff had snapped and attacked Christina so brutally. From all accounts, the relationship had been going south for a while now. He had to have known divorce was the next logical step. Which led Sebastian to believe there was something Jeff feared would come out as a result of the divorce. Fear of discovery could have set him off on his murderous rampage. Sebastian would bet that money was at the root of Jeff's unpredictable behavior, and Sebastian's lawyer, Morgan, would sniff out whatever it was Jeff was trying to hide.

Jeff was in jail now, but he probably wouldn't stay behind bars for long. The man was too slippery for that. Sebastian had never understood how someone like Christina could have married a snake like Jeff Kinsey in the first place. But knowing of the wealth she'd brought to the marriage from her family, Sebastian suspected Jeff was nothing more than a gold digger. Her friends said Jeff had been a handsome youth when he'd seduced Christina in college, but hadn't worked a day in his life since hooking up with her.

Still, from what he'd heard from her friends, the marriage started well enough. It was only after Christina's parents died, leaving her in control of a great deal of money, that Jeff had started acting like a real jerk. When he'd gone too far during an argument and knocked her down, Christina finally woke up and started talking about divorce—but only to her friends. Jeff had made her afraid of his reactions and it took a great deal of courage for her to speak of her desire for a divorce to him. Her anxieties had proven true when Jeff snapped and beat her within an inch of her life. The very thought of it set Sebastian's teeth on edge. He could still read the horror in her lovely eyes.

Jeff had taught her to fear. Sebastian would teach her the opposite. He'd show her nothing but care and compassion, and give her confidence in her new abilities. He'd strive to help her overcome her anxiety and banish it for all time.

He'd find a way to neutralize Jeff and repair the damage he'd done to Christina's self-esteem. She had a beautiful soul and it was a crime to see her so damaged—both physically and emotionally. It was up to Sebastian to help her. He was her maker. He had to both keep her safe and figure out how to salvage the situation. She was changed, but would she be strong enough to overcome her past and start a new future, stronger than before? It was Sebastian's job to make certain she was ready.

℘

In a hotel room across town, *Altor Custodis* agent Benjamin Steel began filling out his latest series of reports. He'd been sent to check out Kelly LaTour's friends. As the new wife of the Master Vampire of this region, she was most certainly changed now, but she'd been mortal until a few months ago.

Steel's boss at the AC wanted her friends investigated to see if more than one conversion had taken place. This group of bloodletters was notoriously hard to trace. Marc LaTour was an old one, and therefore cagey as hell. It was a tribute to Steel's record that he'd been selected and sent on this particularly difficult mission, but he knew his skills and was comfortable with the idea he was the best investigator the AC had right now. Steel would accept no less from himself. He was a man driven to excel, and since he'd been violently awakened to the real nature of the world, he'd redirected his energies to scouting for the *Altor Custodis*.

It was a far cry from what he'd done in the SEAL Teams, but it was work. And keeping tabs on the freak show supernaturals was as good a job as any for a retired spec ops warrior.

Only he hated the paperwork. Resigned to his fate, Steel dug out his notes and began to compile them into some sort of order. He wouldn't file the report until the mission was completed, but he might as well get started. The paperwork wouldn't do itself.

Chapter Two

Christina woke in slow increments, like a kitten just learning about the world around it. Sebastian watched her from the side of the large bed, waiting for the moment when she'd realize she wasn't alone.

"I bet you're hungry." He was enchanted by the sleepy look in her eyes as she met his gaze. Rubbing her tummy, she looked like she was considering his words.

"I feel strange."

He nodded and moved closer, sitting on the edge of the bed. "That's to be expected when you're newly turned."

"Then it wasn't a dream?"

"No, my dear. It was most certainly real." He dipped his head closer, smiling so she could see his fangs. He was hungry too, it seemed. "You've been deep in healing sleep for more than two days. That's longer than most of the newly turned, but you were gravely injured, so I encouraged your sleep." He tugged at the sheet that covered her, inching it away. "I've decided on a course of action some might consider reckless." He paused. "Do you trust me?"

She seemed to think that one over before answering. "I think so."

"What I'm going to ask of you will seem strange, but I need you to believe it is for your own welfare that I've even considered this." He pulled the sheet a little lower.

"Now you're frightening me, Sebastian."

"That's not my intent. But I need you to know that what comes next is necessary for your future. I want you to be strong enough to deal with Jeff Kinsey on your own. I believe standing up to him—and winning—is the only way to face the rest of your years, now that you are immortal. If you let him win, even the smallest confrontation, it will set a tone for your new life that could prove disastrous."

"Did I mention you'd already scared me enough?"

Sebastian was glad to see a spark of humor in her wary eyes. It made him feel a little better about what he was about to do, though other aspects of his plan still made him uneasy. There was jealousy for one thing. It was likely to eat him alive before long. Good thing the task could be accomplished quickly. He knew he couldn't take too much of this.

"I'm sorry, Christina. What I propose will not hurt. On the contrary, it will bring you great pleasure, but it is somewhat...risqué. I know from your friends that you've never been very adventurous sexually. That will have to change."

She looked wary, but receptive. "What exactly are you talking about?"

"Your body is fully healed now, and its chemistry forever altered. Now it's time for your lessons to begin."

"Lessons?"

"I promised to teach you everything you need to know to survive in your changed state. Those lessons begin now, with our most basic needs—blood and lust. You need to feed." He dipped his head, kissing her savagely. He didn't mean to do it, but her soft lips were so close, so inviting, he couldn't resist.

Sebastian reveled in the sweet taste of her, delving deep with his tongue as her petite fangs began to emerge. He ran his tongue over them, encouraging their arrival. He'd forgotten how it felt to kiss one of his own kind. It was beyond erotic. It was nearly orgasmic in itself.

When she jumped, he pulled back, looking past her beautiful, bare body to see what had scared her. Sebastian understood her alarm when he saw Matt. He'd come in and prowled right up to the bed, taking a seat near the foot as if he belonged there, while Sebastian had been distracted. It was a shock to realize he'd been so lost in her kiss, he hadn't even sensed Matt's arrival. Matt's knowing wink didn't go a long way to soothe Sebastian's self-recrimination, but it did make him smile. The lad was audacious, but Christina needed a little nudge to guide her on this path. Before the night was through, Sebastian knew she'd need to put all her inhibitions behind her and Matt Redstone was just the creature to help her do it.

"I invited a mortal friend to help you learn how to feed both bodily and psychically." He waved one hand toward Matt, releasing her slowly. "He is *were*. You might note the difference in his scent from ordinary mortals. He'll make an excellent first feeding for you to grow strong and he's agreed to let us use him as our guinea pig for this evening. It's a rare honor. You should be thankful."

Christy looked at the gorgeous, muscular man who sat on the edge of her bed and began stroking her legs. "Um, thank you?"

She didn't know what to think. On the one hand, she'd never slept around. On the other, she'd never been this horny in her life. It had to do with whatever Sebastian had done to save her life. She felt different in startling ways. Liquid fire raced through her veins and straight to her womb, making her yearn in a way she never had before.

Cunning topaz eyes smiled up at her. "You're very welcome, sweet thing. It's been a long time since I had vampire pussy." He licked his lips, daring to smack them at her. She liked the sparkle in his gaze and could tell right away this handsome stranger was a bit of a tease. He drew her, but at the same time she was afraid of her own response. She didn't know this man. Was Sebastian going to sit by and let him touch her—perhaps even take her—just like that?

"Sebastian?" Her voice rose along with her distress.

Reassuring hands stroked her back, helping her sit up. "Don't fear anything that will happen here this night. A vampire's first feeding is one of the most important of her existence. That Matt has agreed to let you feed from him tonight is no small thing. A portion of his inherent cunning, agility, and strength will forever be passed on to you. Like I said, it's a great honor."

"But is he going to um..." she felt heat stain her cheeks, "...will he want to have sex with me?"

Matt shifted to sit between her legs. "I'm going to fuck your brains out, sweetheart, and eat this pretty pussy 'til you come in my mouth."

"Sebastian!" The objection came out on a shocked gasp.

To be honest, though, she had to admit the new hunger wasn't only for the blood she could actually hear coursing through this strange, savage man's veins. He was handsome and muscular in a way she'd never seen in person. His golden hair practically invited her fingers to run through it, and he had the most gorgeous, bright, inquisitive eyes.

"It's all right, Christina." Sebastian's hypnotic voice soothed her. "It's only fair that Matt gain something from giving you his blood. By lapping your fluids, he will temporarily attain some of our healing and regenerative abilities to augment his own. It's a fair exchange."

"Who is he?" She was upset both at Sebastian's cavalier attitude and his assumptions about her willingness to sleep with a complete stranger. But even more upsetting was her body's response. She wanted to know how that muscular body would feel over her—inside her—fucking her. The thought was deliciously forbidden and altogether shocking. She shook her head, but clarity refused to come. So she appealed to Sebastian—her lifeline in this world gone wild. "How do you expect me to be intimate with someone I don't even know? That may be normal for you, but it's not for me. Not by a long shot!"

"Sorry, ma'am." Matt grinned and held out one hand for her to shake, still sitting between her thighs. "I'm Matt Redstone. Like Sebastian said, I'm *were*, and the youngest brother of the leader of the cougar clan."

She shook his hand as if in a trance. This was probably the strangest situation she'd ever been in. Bar none.

"What is *were*? What does that mean?"

Matt Redstone shot an amused look up at Sebastian. "She doesn't know anything yet, does she?"

Sebastian shrugged. "She didn't know about us until she woke after being turned. She's got a lot to learn."

"Stop talking about me as if I'm not here."

That earned her a little slap on her pussy from Matt. She yelped in surprise, but it felt so startlingly good, her fangs dropped even further. She began to understand there was some correlation between her new fangs and her level of sexual excitement. If having two sexy men like these staring with palpable hunger at your bare body didn't flip your switch, she didn't know what would.

"To answer your question, I'm a *were*cougar." She had no clue what he was talking about and it must've shown on her face. "You've heard of *were*wolves, right?"

She heard the words, but their meaning seemed preposterous. "You're not trying to tell me you turn into a hairy beast every full moon, are you?"

"Not at all. I can change at will, full moon or no. And I turn into a cougar. We have very soft pelts, if I do say so myself."

He didn't look like a lunatic. And Sebastian seemed to take his words in stride. Then again, Sebastian was an honest-to-goodness vampire! So maybe there were *were*wolves in the world too. Both men seemed to believe it.

"There are other shapeshifter tribes," Matt went on, "that share their souls with different animals. Sebastian has a few friends among them, so you may meet one now and again, though historically the *were* usually don't have much to do with your kind. Just like humans, there are few of your kind we trust, but I've known Sebastian a while. He's okay."

"Glad you think so, cub." Sebastian chuckled, though his eyes followed every movement of Matt's roving fingers playing through the neatly trimmed curls covering her mound.

Christy was glad she'd groomed shortly before Jeff had gone nuts on her. She liked to keep herself tidy, with a little thatch of curls at the top of her thighs. She liked the way it looked and felt, and if she was any judge, the *were*cougar sitting between her legs liked it too. She could smell his arousal. When she inhaled noticeably, Sebastian smiled.

"You are learning his scent differences already, aren't you? Can you differentiate the subtleties? Can you smell your excitement separate from his...and mine? Concentrate, little one. Work out the scent trails in your head. Learning to control and use your newly enhanced senses will help you in the future. Eventually, you'll be able to actually smell a lie, with practice. If nothing else, learning the scent differences of *were* will help you know when you're in the presence of one of Matt's brethren. They're not always easy to spot, since they blend among humans so well, but their subtle scent differences are unmistakable."

She was fascinated as the wafting fragrances filtered through her nose. It felt like she'd never really smelled anything before and only now, her senses were coming to life. She tried to listen to Sebastian's rich voice as he coached her, but it was hard to focus as Matt's shaggy head lowered and his long tongue darted out to lick her clit. Her thighs widened even further, seemingly of their own accord. She'd never felt sensations like this. Matt's skilled tongue rasped along her folds, driving her so high, she felt as if she might take flight. And she wanted more.

"Concentrate now, *cara mia*," Sebastian whispered, nuzzling at her neck. "Listen to the pulse of his blood, the way it flows through his veins. He's got a healthy circulatory system. All *were* do. Sometimes that alone can identify them as *were* and not human to my ears. Do you hear it?"

She thought she understood. If she listened closely, her ears were telling her things they never had before. She could hear the swish of Matt's blood, so different from the gentle gurgle of Sebastian's. She could almost taste the wild scent of Matt's skin, subtle and musky, and altogether inflammatory, so different from Sebastian's enticing male fragrance. If she had to give it a name, she'd say Matt smelled like carnal lust while Sebastian was outright sin.

And she wanted them both. She shocked herself with the thought and with the knowledge that she could have them both. Tonight.

She'd fantasized about such things, but her sex life up 'til now had been rather tame. A late bloomer, she hadn't experimented much in college and married soon after graduating. Things had been good with Jeff at first, though he wasn't very inventive in bed. That had been a disappointment, but one she was willing to live with when she still believed the marriage could be saved. Then the real troubles had begun with Jeff, and they'd stopped having sex altogether over a year ago.

But Jeff was in jail for the moment, and she was...well, she was different. Just how different, she had yet to discover, but she was going to enjoy this freedom from reality while she could. Soon enough she'd have to deal with the fallout of her life and her embattled marriage.

She could never go back to Jeff. It was the one bright thing in this whole sorry mess. Well, that and Sebastian. If she were being honest with herself, she'd admit Sebastian had captivated her from the moment she'd first seen him at Lissa's wedding. He was so tall, dark and mysterious. What woman wouldn't dream of him?

And she had. Night after night, she'd dreamed of Sebastian and the pleasure he would bring her, but he always disappeared with the morning light, haunting her dreams but abandoning her days.

"Sebastian!" She cried out his name as she neared a peak, Matt's tongue seeming to drive right up into her. She clutched at Sebastian's shoulders, dragging him downward.

His lips found hers, his fangs bumping against hers but not breaking the skin. His tongue swept inside her mouth, stabbing in and out much like Matt's did below. She screamed deep in her throat as she came and Sebastian swallowed the primal sound as Matt swallowed every last slick drop of her climax.

As the lethargy of climax filled her, she felt herself being lifted and turned, to lie atop Matt's muscular body. She let her hands roam over his biceps and pecs, amazed at the solid build of the man. She'd never touched a man who was built like this.

"You must work out."

Matt grinned. "My brothers and I own a construction company. I still work with the crews now and again, but running in the woods will keep a body just as fit."

"I can't even imagine." She smiled down at him as he lay beneath her, his hands stroking up her torso to fondle her breasts.

"It's like nothing in the world. But as you age, you might learn to shift. Many of your kind can do it, and you won't be limited to one form. You might be able to fly, sweet thing. I can see you as a graceful little owl, prowling the night. You'd be gorgeous."

She blushed as he played with her nipples. The idea of flying made her think of Sebastian and she looked around to discover where he'd gone. She liked Matt, but she didn't want to be left alone with him. She needed Sebastian near. He was her comfort, her guide and her...well, she didn't quite know what he was, but he was important. She didn't think she could do this without him.

She knew they expected her to bite Matt and drink his blood, but the idea gave her the willies. Sure, she felt the hunger and her fangs were nice and long now, but she had no real desire to bite this man. For one thing, she didn't want to hurt him, and for another, she didn't quite know how to go about biting anyone.

Her fears calmed somewhat when she found Sebastian leaning against the wall at the side of the bed. He had a front row view of their naked bodies as she draped herself over Matt. Sebastian's eyes glowed red and the way he looked at her body made her unbearably hot.

"What now?" She asked Sebastian, but Matt answered.

"Now I get to fuck your sweet pussy." He moved upward, supporting her hips exactly where he wanted them and found her center with his hard cock. He was built big and very solid, and when he pushed her hips down gently, she took him inside with a bit of caution. "Work it down slow and easy, sweetheart. Take me all the way."

This whole experience was moving too fast, but she couldn't stop it. She wanted this, no matter how much it shocked her human sensibilities. There was another side to her now, an earthier side pushing her to take him and mark him, bite him and drink him down. She didn't understand the force driving her, but she was powerless against it.

Christy took Matt by degrees, pulsing to spread her lubrication on his hardness, wanting him inside her in a way she hadn't wanted a man in years, if ever. She'd never wanted Jeff this badly. Certainly not after he'd begun to get irrational. Even before, their sex life had never been this hot. Nothing could compare with this in her admittedly limited experience.

Sebastian's gaze followed all and made her belly clench as she took another man right in front of him. It was wicked and deliciously exciting. She'd never known she had exhibitionist tendencies, but this experience showed her all kinds of new things about herself and her shocking desires. She felt energy coming from Matt in a way she couldn't explain if asked, but she felt it washing over her, warming her and giving her strength. Her eyes met Sebastian's and he nodded as if in approval.

"You feel it too?" she gasped.

"It is what sustains us, Christina. The energy of life." Sebastian's voice drifted across her senses, an additional caress.

She didn't fully understand his words, but now was not the time to ask questions. Matt demanded her attention, sliding home with a definitive shove. Seated fully, she let him steer. Matt was stronger than any man she'd ever known and he seemed content to thrust up into her while she concentrated on just how to go about biting him. Sebastian prowled near, his gaze burning as he watched Matt fuck her. With elegant hands, he positioned Matt's head and moved his shaggy hair out of the way.

"Use your tongue to find the pulse." His fingers traced the beating pulse she could easily see on the big man's corded neck. No wonder Sebastian had enlisted him for her first meal. He was probably easier to feed from than a regular person. "Lick the site where you will bite. Your saliva will act as an anesthetic and sanitizer, to both deaden the area and protect him against infection from the incisions. You can also use your mind to lessen the pain of the bite, though that skill will strengthen in time."

"I don't want to hurt him." She panted as Matt stroked inside long and hard. She was so close.

"I will help you this time, little one. I will cloud the pain from his mind while you find your way. Lick him," Sebastian coached. "Take your time and find the sweet spot."

She leaned in and followed Sebastian's instructions. After a quick search with her lips she felt the one place where his pulse was nearest the skin and thought she knew what Sebastian was talking about. She licked Matt's salty skin, loving the taste, and was gratified to hear him groan. It didn't sound like he was in pain at all. On the contrary, she could feel his excitement and his passion, and she instinctively tugged at it with her mind, surprised when she felt his passion climb higher, as did hers. She was feeling everything this beautiful man under her was feeling and it energized her.

"You are already feeding off his psi energies. Good. Now, you must complete the bond with blood." Sebastian cradled the back of her head while she found the spot with her tongue and then positioned her newly sharpened teeth. "Do it now, Christina."

Sebastian's soft urging spurred her on, while Matt's thrusting pushed her passion to a level she had never before experienced. She bit down.

Her mouth flooded with a sweet, coppery, wild flavor and she wanted more. Matt's blood trickled into her mouth as she lapped at his salty skin. She sucked at the small incisions she'd made with her new fangs so as not to lose a single drop of the rare vintage. She was as gentle as she could be, not wanting to hurt this beautiful man who was giving her his life's blood, his strength, his passion and his lust.

She swallowed once, twice, three times before she exploded into the most intense orgasm of her life. Matt shot into her in hot jets as she collapsed against him, her head buried in his neck, licking at the small wounds she'd made.

Sebastian gave her a moment to calm before he moved. He lifted her head away to inspect his friend's neck. She was a neat eater, but too prim. She'd barely sipped and she needed more for her first real feeding. Plus, she'd been so overwhelmed, she'd neglected to properly seal the wounds, but that would come with practice. For now, he would help her.

Sebastian leaned in and used a slight brush of his healing energy to close and heal the tiny wounds. By morning they would be gone. Matt met his eyes as he pulled back, Christina still cradled to his chest.

"She's special, isn't she?"

Sebastian tilted his head. "You could say that."

"She didn't feed properly. She barely took a sample."

"I know." Sebastian quirked a smile at his friend. "I don't suppose you'll object to hanging around a bit longer?"

"Are you kidding?" Matt ran his hands down Christina's lithe body. He was still inside her, though he was spent for the moment. "She's a sweet fuck. I don't mind having more of her."

33

She stirred on his chest, sitting up. "Keep talking about me like that and you won't get any more."

"Whoa, truce, babe. I meant it in the most complimentary manner. You're incredible, Christy. Truly."

Her eyes flashed with humor. "I suppose I'll forgive you this time. If you'll just make me come like that again." Matt answered her teasing by tweaking one of her rosy nipples.

Sebastian grasped the other and tugged in tandem with Matt. He leaned in to kiss her, sweeping his tongue into her mouth. He loved the taste of her and the tang of Matt's shifter blood flavoring her mouth made the kiss even more exotic. He lapped at her mouth while she squirmed on Matt's cock. Knowing the other man was still inside her made the kiss even hotter.

Sebastian was feeding off their energies. It would probably be all he got this night, but if the next round was anything like the first, it would be more than enough to sustain him. Matt fucked her, already up for more, but Sebastian was directing this little show and he had a different treat in mind.

"Get off him and turn around," he ordered as he drew back. "I'm going to show you an alternate feeding site."

Matt groaned as Sebastian lifted her off him. "You gonna partake, old buddy?"

"Maybe. But only enough to show her how."

With that assurance Matt lay back on the bed and spread his legs, helping Christina kneel over his chest. His tongue zeroed in on her pussy, licking deep and long. Sebastian watched her reactions, knowing Matt was driving her wild.

"Some *were* can shift parts of themselves. Their tongues for example. I'm told it drives their women wild."

She moaned. "Drives this woman wild too."

Sebastian chuckled as he settled opposite her. He could see her struggling for control as Matt's big hands roamed over her body, wherever he could reach. The sight was entrancing, but Sebastian had to focus. He needed to teach her, to watch them, though heaven knew, he'd much rather be the man inside her. Still, watching them brought a kind of satisfaction he hadn't expected and a pulsing arousal he could do nothing about. Not yet, at any rate.

"There is a strong pulse here." Sebastian traced a spot on Matt's inner thigh with one long finger.

"Hey man, that tickles!" Matt chuckled as he went back to licking her pussy.

"So sorry." Sebastian knew he didn't sound the least bit sorry as he took Christina's hand and made her stroke the area on Matt's thigh. He then moved her hand so she could cup Matt's balls. Sebastian tried not to think about how her hands would feel on his own member, or how much he envied his friend at this moment. "Now I want you to suck him, and watch me closely. When he comes, I want you to swallow every last drop. *Were* come will nourish you and make you stronger than most of the newly turned."

Sebastian stroked her hair, looking deep into her eyes, noting the pupils dilated in pleasure. He could see Matt moving under her as he licked her. The sight made Sebastian's temperature rise, but he had a job to do here. He couldn't let their ardor distract him. Not yet.

He pushed Christina's head gently downward, his hand cupping her nape as she moved toward Matt's straining cock. Sebastian felt his own body clench as she took Matt in her mouth. She tongued him shyly at first, her wide eyes looking up at Sebastian as if for approval. The mixture of innocence and passion in her gaze was hotter than anything he'd ever experienced in all his long years.

Her midsection contracted jerkily as Matt did something to push her higher and her eyes glazed over. A moment later, she was sucking in rhythm, so lost to sensation, Sebastian had to tug on her hair, to get her attention. "Now watch."

Sebastian released her and leaned in to lick the area he'd shown her on Matt's thigh. He tried to concentrate on the pounding pulse he could both see and hear, but Christina's soft moans brought Sebastian to a painful arousal. He paused to find her watching him as he prepared Matt's skin for the bite. Her lips were cherry red around Matt's cock and Sebastian knew Matt's tongue was buried deep in her pussy as she squirmed over the man. Sebastian didn't think he could get any harder, but the strong swishing of Matt's *were* blood through his veins was a siren call Sebastian couldn't refuse.

He bit down clean and deep as Christina moaned, holding

his gaze. Rich, red, *were* blood poured over Sebastian's tongue and he swallowed once, gratefully, sharing the intimacy of the moment with Christina. Never before had he felt such a pull, such a sharing. This was all new, and very enticing. Her eyes pled with him as she neared her release. He could also taste the need in Matt's blood and the slight trembling of his limbs. Sebastian knew he had to release them both to ecstasy. He reached for both of their minds, and gave them a gentle push over the edge into orgasm as he drank one more swallow from Matt, then sealed the wounds with a little zap of his healing energy.

Sebastian watched in satisfaction and a bit of envy as she drank Matt's come. Sebastian dreamed of the night she'd lick his cock like that. It would be soon, he promised himself, but first he had to prepare her for her new life. Letting Matt fuck her and feed her was an important first step. It would make her faster and stronger than most vampires. She'd need those skills when the time came to confront her past. That was the only reason he allowed this interlude. He was doing it for her. All for her. So that she would be strong and sure in her own abilities.

Her arms trembled as she came down from the orgasmic high, still licking Matt's big cock and sighing softly. Sebastian gently grasped one of her legs and coaxed her to kneel at Matt's side.

"Now I want you to try it."

She looked up at him, lethargy and satisfaction in her soft eyes. She was tired. He could see it and sense it, but she needed to do this. She'd barely fed from the *were*cougar. She needed his magic blood to make her strong, especially this first time. All they'd done to this point would be for naught if she failed to drink deeply enough this time.

"I don't know if I can do this." Her eyes were wide with apprehension.

Sebastian reached out to cup her cheek. He was deeply touched by this gentle flower of a woman who had been treated so badly by her husband. He never wanted to see her hurt again. Not if he could prevent it.

"You must. I have faith in you. Just do as I showed you. I'll take care of the rest."

"I don't want to hurt him."

Matt surprised them both by sitting up and drawing Christina's face close to his. "Do I look like I'm in pain, sweetheart?" He kissed her forehead, meeting Sebastian's gaze over the top of her head. Both men knew the importance of this first feeding. "I want you to do this. I want you to be strong." He moved back and stroked her hair away from her face. "Sebastian told me what happened to you, Christy." The cougar's voice rumbled low in the dimness of the room. "My sister was killed by her mate before we knew he'd been abusing her. It's the reason I agreed to this. I don't like the idea of any woman being unable to defend herself—especially one that's been hurt so badly, the only way to save her was to change her. You've suffered enough."

She sobbed then, allowing Matt to pull her close against his chest. The men shared a look of understanding across her shoulders, each aware of the hurt this woman had suffered. Jeff Kinsey was a disgrace to mankind. A brute who resorted to violence and attempted murder when he didn't get his way. Neither Sebastian nor Matt would stand for that. They both wanted her to be strong enough to face anything or anyone that came her way in the future.

Sebastian knew they were of one mind where Christina was concerned. He and Matt had talked about this in depth while she slept. Giving *were* blood to a novice was not something anyone did lightly. Only these special circumstances allowed such a rare occurrence.

"Why are you being so nice? You don't even know me." Her words were whispered against Matt's chest.

"I know enough." His eyes were grim as they met Sebastian's. "I know your husband's type and I know what will happen if you feed properly from my blood this first time. I know it will make you stronger than a vamp your age should rightly be." He kissed the crown of her head gently. "And I know Sebastian. He wouldn't have asked this of me if it wasn't important. I trust him with my life and that isn't something any *were* says lightly. Especially about a bloodletter."

She looked up into Matt's eyes. "You're a special man."

Matt's big hands cupped her pretty fanny. "Did I also mention that I get a boost in my own healing abilities and a night of unbelievable sex out of the deal?" His eyebrows waggled, teasing her. "I'd almost forgotten how good being with a vamp could be. My kind has nothing on you guys when it comes to pleasuring your partner. We have to do it the old-fashioned way, but you've got some kind of voodoo that launches your partner into the stratosphere. It's pretty beguiling." He smoothed her hair. "Don't think I'm not enjoying myself, and you won't hurt me, sweetheart. For one thing, Sebastian here is using his mojo to cloud any pain you miss, but if I'm not much mistaken, you're already exerting your own power to dull any pain your magic tongue doesn't already negate."

She looked over at Sebastian, her eyes wide. "I'm not doing anything."

"Yes, you are. Actually, it's rather remarkable. I think your new instincts are kicking in sooner than normal because of your overwhelming desire not to hurt him. I noticed your energies, shielding him from the small pain of your bite when I tried to shield him. You needed a boost, but I think he wouldn't have felt much anyway, even if I hadn't been there to back you up."

"It takes a lot to hurt a *were* anyway. Our pain threshold is pretty high compared to a human or even a vamp." Matt kissed her sweetly before setting her away. "Now bite me, woman. I want to feel that magic tongue of yours on me again." He lay back and positioned the pillows under his head so he could watch everything, a broad, encouraging smile on his face.

It was obvious to Sebastian that she was still unsure, but she moved down Matt's rangy body with purpose as Sebastian encouraged her. She started by teasing Matt some more, licking his balls until he was hard and swollen again.

"You trying to kill me with pleasure, little vamp?" Matt asked, looking at her with indulgent eyes. Her fangs elongated and scraped ever so lightly along the ridges of his big cock as both men watched, entranced at the sight. Sebastian had to shift his legs to accommodate the uncomfortable hardness in his trousers. Watching Christina tease Matt made him harder than he'd been in centuries.

"Mmm." The sound of her moan shuddered through him. "I thought you should enjoy the ride if I'm going to suck your blood."

"That's not all you're sucking." Matt chuckled, then gasped as she took him deep in her throat. "Yeah, baby, just like that."

She felt Matt's excitement rising and she wondered just how to go about this. Sebastian was there, though, guiding her.

"Feel your fangs dropping even more?" Sebastian's voice made her feel shivery inside. "Take a moment now and do what you need to prepare. Then you can bring Matt with you when you go over the moon."

It was easier this time to locate the pulse that pounded through the *were*cougar's strong body. Her fangs dropped all the way as her hunger rose. Christy ran her tongue over the sharp tips as she lowered her head to the area Sebastian had shown her. With a glance up at Matt's approving gaze, she set to work, locating the right spot and using her tongue and mind to block any pain her bite might cause.

Sighing as she found the right place, she sank her fangs deeply, decisively, and felt the welling of his powerful blood into her mouth. It was unlike anything she could have imagined. Christy had been squeamish before, but now, with the hunger riding her and Matt's potent blood flooding her senses, she feasted.

Still, somewhere in the back of her mind, she felt concern for Matt's comfort. She wanted him to enjoy this and if not enjoy, then at least feel no pain from what she was doing. With a glance upward, she reassured herself he was all right. His eyes glowed as he watched her, his cock hard as a rock between them.

With a last long lick of the wound she'd made, she focused a tiny bit of the magic now flowing through her veins and sealed the punctures with a thought, healing them as if they'd never been. Rapacious now, she climbed over Matt, settling herself over his hardness. He slid inside her waiting core, and she loved the feel of him filling her as she began to move.

But it became clear Matt wasn't going to sit by and watch this time. He rolled, taking her with him until she was underneath him as he rocked, gently at first, into her welcoming body.

"You're beautiful, little vamp. And considerate. I didn't feel a thing, except for hunger. For you. If I didn't believe you were already claimed, I'd be tempted to keep you for myself, Christy. You're one hell of a woman."

"Matt," she whispered. "You're sweet. But if you don't move your ass right now, I'm going to bite you again." She smiled and flashed some fang.

The big man laughed and moved more forcefully within her, bringing her to a swift peak that didn't dissipate. It grew. And grew.

"Your wish is my command, sweet thing." Matt reached down to nip at her neck playfully, firing her senses as he moved faster and deeper. His cock slid home over and over, harder and harder, driving her higher and higher. It was bliss.

"Matt!" She was close now. Very close to some point she had never reached before.

"Come now, little vamp. Come for me. Right. Now." He bit off his words as he pounded home.

Christy cried out as she came on command for the big *were*cougar like she'd never come before. Until this night, her husband had been her only lover. Their sex life had been good, in the beginning at least, but he'd never shown her this kind of passion or fulfillment.

Damn.

One more thing to hate Jeff for.

Christy drifted off as Matt rolled away. The last thing she saw before she fell asleep was Sebastian's handsome face, watching her as if he wanted her next climax to be his.

Chapter Three

"Are you sure about this, man?" Both men stood over the exhausted female lying asleep in the bed, looking down on her with varying degrees of indulgence and care. Sebastian had cleaned her and the bed while Matt grabbed a shower and dressed.

"Look at her, Matt. She's so petite. She's been a victim too long. I'm just making sure that when the time comes, she can fight back. She'll never be whole if she doesn't face her past and come out the victor."

Matt sighed and rubbed one big hand over his face. "I hear you. I'll come back tomorrow night. A double dose of *were* ought to help. I just hope she doesn't become too strong for even you to handle."

The *were*cougar left as silently as he'd come only hours before.

A half hour later, Marc called to check on Christina's condition. Sebastian reassured his old friend that she'd responded well to the conversion and was still the kind soul she'd been before, only stronger, though he was careful not to mention the *were*cougar's involvement in her feeding. Marc didn't need to know about that...yet.

"I wanted to let you know we've had some disturbing news from the *Were* Lords."

Sebastian was surprised. "I didn't know you were in contact with them."

"It's a recent development and it's not direct. I got the news from Hiram up in Seattle. He got it from another who apparently had direct contact with the *were*folk a few weeks ago. Regardless, the news is startling. They said the *Venifucus* are back, and that the *weres* recently defeated a mage who claimed to be part of that ancient society."

"You're kidding."

"Afraid not, my friend." Marc's voice was as serious as Sebastian had ever heard it. He was too young to have ever dealt directly with the *Venifucus*, but he'd heard plenty of tales about the evil group.

"So do you believe it? Couldn't it just be a couple of buffoons using the name?"

Marc sighed over the line. "I hope that's all it is, but we have to keep alert, just in case. Sebastian, you've never seen these folks in action. Believe me when I say, if the *Venifucus* are back, we're all in very real danger."

They talked over the possibilities for a few more minutes, but they didn't have enough information to formulate any real plans other than to stay vigilant. Only an hour or so remained before dawn, and sleep for their kind. Eventually, Marc came back to the subject of Christina and her problems.

"What will you do about the husband?"

"Is he still in jail?"

"For now, though he's hired a good lawyer. I expect he'll be out in a day or two."

Sebastian felt a fire in his gut. He wanted to kill the mortal who'd dared lay a finger on the woman entrusted to his care. But it wasn't his fight. Still, he had some ideas of how to work behind the scenes to keep an eye on the mortal.

"Since Christina now has many years before her, I think she needs to stand up to him before I take any action. As her maker, I think it the best course. Hiro is coming over tomorrow to begin her training."

"Wise decision, my friend. I was going to suggest something similar. It's important that she begins her new life from a position of strength instead of as a victim."

"Of course, I'll be standing behind her to help if she has any problems with the man."

"I expected no less."

Sebastian kept vigil at Christina's bedside until morning. Only then did he go to his own room across the hall and let daybreak send him to slumber. When he awoke moments before true nightfall, he made his way to her room, waiting for that magic moment her sleepy eyes would open.

Christy woke as the sun dipped below the horizon the next night. She felt fantastic. Strange, hungry, powerful and sexy. It was empowering. And a little scary.

She remembered what had made her feel that way. Christy could hardly believe the things she'd done—and let the men do to her—the night before. She felt the heat of a blush stealing across her cheeks even as she sat up in the disheveled bed.

"Good evening." Sebastian's voice came to her from the darkness of the room. He stepped forward and she saw him, her eyesight sharper than it had ever been. He was so handsome, so debonair. She'd never met a man quite like him, and likely never would again. He simply took her breath away. "How do you feel?" he asked.

She clutched the rumpled sheet to her breasts, shy now after the debauchery that had come before. She realized that while Sebastian had directed the entire scene last night, he hadn't touched her much at all. He'd kissed her though. Oh, how he'd kissed her.

Sebastian's kiss had felt more intense than any kiss she had ever received. His kiss felt like he wanted to be inside her. Desperately.

But he hadn't done much more than kiss and touch. He hadn't made love to her. He'd only watched and instructed as he let his *were*cougar friend fuck her in varied and exciting ways.

She'd never come so hard in her life. Or so many times. Last night was truly a night to remember and she'd blush every time she thought of it for the rest of her life, she was sure. Just like she was doing now. But Sebastian was waiting for an answer.

Christy shrugged and tried to be nonchalant. "I'm okay."

Sebastian sat on the side of her bed, his eyes kind. No man

should look that good or that understanding. Certainly no man she'd ever dealt with on an intimate level had ever looked at her with such compassion.

"Just okay?" Sebastian's fingers rose to stroke over her cheek.

A tiny shiver of attraction coursed down her spine. "Better than okay, but very...decadent. I can't believe half the things...the things..." she stammered, trailing off, the flush of embarrassment heating her cheeks even more than before.

Sebastian chuckled as his hand slid down to stroke over one bare shoulder. Caressing. Comforting. "The wicked things you did and had done to you last night? Ah, but my sweet, you're immortal now. Sex is life to us."

"But then why didn't you...?" She could have died of embarrassment when she realized she'd spoken aloud.

"Why didn't I partake of your lovely body? Is that what you want to know?"

Cringing a little at how needy the question sounded, she nodded.

"I dare not. For one thing..." he squeezed her shoulder, "...I am your maker. I must be your teacher in these early days until you learn your limitations and strengths, and can stand on your own with no uncertainty." She liked the sound of that. He stroked down over her arm and took her hand. "For another, I greatly fear that once I have you, I'll never be able to let you go." He kissed her hand in a gallant, old world gesture that made her womb clench.

His eyes were hot, his expression tight. "I've watched you for a long time, Christina. Longer than you might realize. And I've wanted you from the first moment we met, but you were already claimed. You'll never know how much I wanted to tear your husband limb from limb when I realized what he'd done to you, but it's not my debt to repay. Not yet anyway. Not until I know for sure whether you could truly be my One." He released her hand and rose, his gaze filled with regret. And promise. "The only way to learn the truth of it, is to fuck and feed. I dare not do either with you until you've gained the strength Matt's blood can grant you. I want you to be strong, Christina. I want you to know that no one will ever be able to hurt you again. Not even me."

"Why?" She was puzzled by his words and nearly overcome by the sexual tension rising like a sudden conflagration between them.

"By feeding from Matt, you'll gain an echo of his *were* traits for the rest of your immortal life. Your senses would have been sharp, but with Matt's blood in your system, they'll be as sharp as the cat that shares his soul. You will probably also gain some of his cougar cunning, agility and strength. Vampires are powerful in many ways on their own, but few have the coordination to be able to use their abilities effectively when first turned. I'm hoping you will. I'm hoping you'll be so fast, agile and wily, you'll be able to evade even me, though I have three centuries of experience on you."

She was amazed. But still puzzled. "Why? Why would you want me to be stronger than you?"

His eyes darkened. "So you'll never be afraid. So you'll know—for certain—that you'll never be hurt again. So you can never *be* hurt again."

Christy's breath caught and tears filled her eyes, but Sebastian moved away, toward the door.

"This room has an attached bath and you'll find some workout clothing that might fit in the drawer over there. Come downstairs when you're ready. We have much to do this evening before Matt arrives." Sebastian walked to the door as he talked in a business-like tone.

"He's coming back?"

Sebastian turned at the threshold and she could see his eyes glint in the darkness. "After tonight, you'll be more powerful than I, Christina. I know in my heart, you will use your abilities wisely."

She was floored. "How can you have such faith in me?"

Sebastian looked away. "I know your heart, little one. There is no other I would trust with such power, but you need it. You now know what it is to be defenseless against those physically stronger than you. Tonight, with Matt's help, that will change forever."

Sebastian left her and she had a moment to savor the new knowledge flooding her mind. She perceived things in much greater detail on a sensory level, but what he'd told her about his motivations and the consequences of what he'd set in motion completely floored her.

But the question remained...why?

Why would he go so far out of his way to make her stronger even than himself? Why would he want that? Why would he send her into the arms of another man to accomplish it?

Did he love her?

Did he pity her?

Did she dare find out?

Christy cleaned up and dressed in the sweatshirt and loose pants she found in the drawer. They were a bit too large, but by rolling the cuffs, she made it work. She headed out of her room and toward the faint sounds in one of the downstairs rooms. Her hearing was so acute it was hard at first to discern one sound in the old house from the next.

The ticking of multiple clocks in rooms all over the large place had her covering her ears before she discovered she could tune them out or turn them down with a thought. She heard the creak of each floorboard as she moved slowly through the space, the swish of water through the pipes, even the soft hum of electricity flowing through the wiring in the walls. It was incredible, and it only got stronger the more she thought about it.

Just as she could turn the sounds down by thinking about it, she discovered. It was like magic.

Then again, she'd done a lot of things that would have been out of character for her just a few days ago. She'd fantasized about some of the sexual excesses she'd participated in last night, but they'd only been fantasies. She never thought she'd have the nerve to try anything like that, but the new fire in her blood seemed to spur her on.

She followed the soft sounds of moving feet on a wooden floor to a room in the lower part of the house that surprised her yet again. Hovering on the threshold, Christy was surprised to find another man with Sebastian. Both were wearing traditional martial arts uniforms that looked as if they'd seen a great deal of use. They were worn, with lighter spots on the elbows and knees, and comfortable looking. The soft swish of cotton greeted her ears as the two men moved side by side in some sort of pattern that took them through various defensive and offensive moves.

She knew a little bit about *karate*, having once taken a semester of it in college. She'd enjoyed the class even though she was bad at it. She'd wanted to take another semester, but right about that time, she'd met Jeff and been dazzled by the young man whom she eventually married.

On trembling legs, Christy stepped forward into the peaceful room she now recognized as a *dojo*—the place to study and practice martial arts. It had smooth wooden floors and beautiful Japanese tapestries hanging on one of the walls along with framed woodblock prints and a few black and white photos. There were mirrors on the entire wall to her left, and to her right, the opposite wall consisted of several glass doors that opened onto a lovely stone garden complete with fluttering bamboo and trickling water. It was beautiful.

Near the door were a few wooden benches. Remembering to bow as she entered, a formality her college *sensei* had insisted upon, she left her shoes outside the door, next to two much larger pairs, and took a seat on the bench. She watched in awed silence as the men spun and kicked in the patterns of the most difficult *kata*—a sequence of defensive and offensive moves done in a choreographed pattern—she'd ever seen.

Their concentration was absolute, but she knew they were aware of her presence. They completed the *kata* and both bowed, signaling the end of the pattern. Sebastian smiled at her as they moved nearer and his expression put her at ease.

"Christina, please allow me to introduce Hiro Yamamoto, a long-time friend and one of those I've asked to help teach you."

Christy held out her hand to the tall, dusky-skinned man. She could tell by his features that he wasn't fully Asian, though his name sounded Japanese. He took her hand with a firm grip, but his strength was tempered and his manner non-threatening. This was a man who knew his own measure and didn't need to prove how strong he was, unlike her husband.

Resolutely, she shook off thoughts of Jeff. She wouldn't allow his darkness to shadow her new life. She'd been given a second chance and she was going to run with it as fast and far as she could.

"It's a pleasure to meet you, Mr. Yamamoto." She smiled and was gratified by the man's return grin. It lit his dark eyes and made him seem somehow less scary.

"Please—" his voice held no trace of accent, "—call me Hiro. You've been in a *dojo* before, haven't you?"

"I took a Shotokan class one semester in college. I loved the history and grace of it, but I was terrible. No coordination at all, and some boy accidentally punched me in the nose during our first sparring practice, so I was a little afraid to do much after that."

Hiro chuckled, though Sebastian looked stern for a moment. She got the impression he didn't like hearing about her little hurts, so she made a mental note not to mention those kinds of things in front of him again. She was his guest. She didn't want to upset him.

"Would you like to try again, if we promise never to punch you in the nose?" Hiro chuckled with amusement, putting her at ease.

Gathering her courage, she nodded. "I'd like to try learning *kata* again. It was so beautiful and such good exercise. I was in terrific shape that semester, even though I was ranked at the bottom of the class."

"There are no rankings here," Hiro said softly as he moved backwards, drawing her into the center of the room. "Only learning. Follow what I do and try to do the same."

Hiro bowed to her and she returned the gesture nervously, noting Sebastian had opted to sit this one out, watching them from the sidelines. The ambiance of the room was calming, but Sebastian's eyes were hot as they followed her hesitant movements. She watched Hiro and tried to follow what he was doing as he started slowly, in a simple pattern that looked like the capital letter I. He stopped a few times to demonstrate the individual movements of blocking, punching, how to make a fist and the proper foot positions for greatest balance.

After a few minutes of his tutelage, she began to feel a little more comfortable. This was easier than she remembered. She didn't lose her balance once, which had always been a problem, and her body wasn't nearly as awkward as she remembered it being when she'd tried so hard before. This time, her movements came almost effortlessly and she felt an increased spring in her steps, her feet and hands answering her commands without much conscious thought. It was amazing.

She followed Hiro, unconsciously mimicking every one of his movements as if it were second nature. She didn't need to think about how to move. She just did it. Before she knew what was happening, Hiro had gone beyond the basics to flying, spinning kicks that she executed with ease. She landed after a particularly high spinning back kick and stopped in shock when she realized she'd been a good six feet off the ground!

Mouth gaping, she turned to find Sebastian watching her.

"What's happening to me?" Panic filled her as the past few moments registered on her conscious mind. She'd been so in the zone, she hadn't questioned what she'd done and now it seemed impossible.

"You're a natural, sweetheart," Hiro said with a satisfied grin. "You're too modest."

"No, I swear..." her breath came fast as panic started to build, "...I was a total klutz the last time I tried this. I have no idea—"

Sebastian came over and took both of her hands in his, pulling them into his chest, sheltering her with his tall body. "Calm down, Christina. This is what I was hoping for. The cat lives in you. You have all the strength of our kind and some of the agility of Matt's cougar. Don't be afraid."

Hiro laughed and shook his head, gaining her attention. "Matt, huh? I should've guessed. He's the only one I've seen jump higher."

"You know Matt?"

Hiro nodded. "I trained him, just as I'll train you."

"But why?"

The half-Asian man shrugged. "Because Sebastian asked. He's my friend and more than that, I owe him my life. You're important to him, so therefore, you're important to me. We'll work together every evening for about two hours. It's a strict schedule, but with the shifter influence, you should advance quickly to the more complex moves. Like I said, you're a natural. I had a much harder time adjusting when I was newly turned."

"Then you're—?"

"Vampire?" Hiro chuckled when Sebastian cringed at the word. "We're siblings of a sort, you and I. Sebastian was my maker too." He bowed slightly to Sebastian and moved toward the doorway. "I'll leave you two to sort things out. Don't forget. Tomorrow evening at sunset. We've got a date in this *dojo*."

A little overwhelmed, Christy could only nod as he left, her hands still held tight against Sebastian's chest as his warmth surrounded her. He moved slightly, keeping hold of one hand while he turned them toward the wall of glass and the moonlit garden beyond. He put one arm around her shoulders, the contact with his warm body comforting her strained senses.

"The night is beautiful, Christina. Let's not waste it in fear." He led her outside to a stone bench in the middle of the meditation garden and they sat, his arm still around her, one hand holding hers. "Never be afraid of what you've become, or what you will yet be. You're a strong woman with a pure soul. You have power now, but you have to train it and grow accustomed to it in order to use it to the best of your abilities."

She couldn't deal with much more. She had the feeling Sebastian was quietly preparing her for something, but she had no idea what. She didn't know what her other friends had been through when they were changed, but she didn't think it involved having wild cougar sex with a stranger, then being trained by a pumped up, devilishly handsome version of Mr. Miyagi.

"You said my friends were turned by their new husbands. How? Why?"

Sebastian sighed, contemplating the stars twinkling above them. "It started with Lissa. When the passenger van wrecked, only she and Atticus were left alive, as you know, but it was a much closer thing than you realize. Atticus was run through by a support beam, close to the heart. He was ready to bleed out— one of the few ways one of us can actually die—but he heard Lissa's heartbeat, and he fought back from the edge to save them both. He needed her blood to be strong enough to heal them both, but she'd already lost almost too much. The only way to save them both was to feed, then give her his blood. To turn her. A dangerous gamble, but one that worked out best in the end. She was his One, his life's mate. She completed him." Sebastian's arm tightened around her.

"They were married soon after, as you know, and Kelly went to work for them at the vineyard. That's where she met Marc LaTour and when he was poisoned by silver—yet another way for us to die a very painful death—she saved him. They knew they were true mates by that point, but Marc was waiting for her to decide if she wanted to be turned. Unfortunately that decision was taken out of their hands by the turn of events. Then Carly met Dmitri—"

"Jeez, Carly too?" she interrupted, surprised. "But she lives way out in Wyoming now."

"Yes, and oddly enough, her new home was right above Master Dmitri's hidden lair. It brought her to his attention and shortly thereafter, he learned she was the One for him. Then she got into a terrible accident, and was forced to choose between never seeing the sun again or death. Luckily for Dmitri, she chose to be turned." Sebastian sighed and she felt his warm breath ruffle her hair. "With you, there was no choice. You were too near death to ask, but I couldn't let you die, Christina. I hope you don't hate me for making the decision without your consent."

"I don't think I could ever hate you, Sebastian." She felt the truth of the words as they left her lips. "And I'm truly grateful for this second chance. When Jeff turned violent, I didn't know how to fight back. I just sat there, taking the beating, like a punching bag. I don't ever want to feel that helpless again." Sebastian squeezed her shoulder, offering comfort.

"That's all over now. You are already far stronger than he, and after tonight, you'll be more cunning than many ancients. He'll never be able to hurt you again. Nor will any other man."

"Is that what the martial arts lessons are all about?"

"You're strong, but you need training in order to master your new skills and abilities. Hiro and I can do that for you, if you let us."

"He's an interesting man."

"He's a true friend and a man of deep conviction."

"Is that why you turned him?"

"I knew Hiro as a mortal, before I found him dying on a battlefield, fighting for what he believed in and to protect the innocent. Knowing him as I did, I couldn't leave him to die. I liked him too much, but more than that, I respected him. He comes from a long line of martial arts masters. His father immigrated to the United States and married an American woman. It wasn't easy for either of them, but it was especially tough on Hiro. Even with that, when innocents were attacked, he stepped forward to help defend the people of his country and for that he nearly died."

"I can tell how much you love him." She patted his arm, understanding.

"He is like a brother to me." Sebastian smiled crookedly. "Sometimes a pesky younger brother, but still a brother. It's nice to have family again. After so long alone, it's good to have family to care for."

"Do you have any other progeny around that I should know about?" She chuckled as she gazed over at the trickling water draining through a series of bamboo pipes. The garden was peaceful and made her more relaxed than she could ever remember feeling.

"No, sweet." He kissed the top of her head as she leaned back against the seat, his arm around her shoulders. "Only you and Hiro. Generally speaking, we don't make many offspring that way. When you turn someone, you are responsible for them, and you risk much if you don't know the measure of the person. If they turn bad—if they kill innocents or act so rashly they threaten the secrecy of our existence—the Master of the region will demand their death for the good of all. Then it falls to their maker, or one of the enforcers to do the deed."

"Enforcers?"

He absently stroked her shoulder with his thumb. "You've met Ian Sinclair, haven't you?"

"Once. At Lissa's."

"Ian is one of Marc's most trusted enforcers. Marc LaTour is Master of this region. The two of them are very old. Ian was a knight during the Crusades, if you can believe it." He tugged her closer, so she rested against his shoulder. "He's been assigned to watch over your friend Jena, since she knows about our kind now. Marc decided she had to be watched, lest she somehow betray her new knowledge to the wrong people. There are those in the world who still hunt our kind, and those who watch us, whose intent is unclear. We have to be vigilant to protect the secrecy of our race and ensure our continued existence."

"They won't hurt her, will they?" Apprehension filled her for Jena, the smartest of her college friends who'd gone on to medical school. She knew Jena had done all she could to save Christy's life after Jeff nearly killed her. She loved her like a sister and didn't want her in danger.

"I doubt it. She didn't strike me as the kind of woman who'd sell out her friends by trying to tell the world about immortal vampires."

"No. She wouldn't. She'd probably do her best to try to figure you out, though. She's a true scientist at heart. She loves riddles and puzzles of any kind."

"Well, she won't get much of a chance to study any of us. She'll just have to be content knowing we're out there."

Christy laughed softly. "That'll drive her nuts for sure, but she's not reckless, and she's a steadfast friend. She'll keep your secret."

"I had to bite her, you know." Sebastian stilled, as if he were holding his breath. "I'm sorry. She wouldn't let me help you until she was sure what I proposed wouldn't hurt you more."

Christy turned to face him, the moonlight gilding his handsome face. "It's okay, Sebastian. Both of you were only trying to protect me." She reached up and kissed his cheek. "Just don't ever do it again, okay?"

He dipped his head and took her lips with a languid kiss. "It's a deal, milady."

They lost track of time as the moon rose higher over the trees shrouding the backyard oasis of calm. Sebastian kissed her with drugging thoroughness, leaving no millimeter of her mouth unexplored, no nerve ending untingling. The man was a talented kisser and a devastating masculine presence.

Dimly, Christy heard a soft rumbling purr and suddenly a warm, furry, and very large body pressed against her legs, rubbing lightly. It startled her enough to pull away from Sebastian's hot mouth. Looking down, she stared into the sparkling topaz eyes of the biggest cat she'd ever seen.

"Don't let him frighten you. It's only Matt."

"Matt?" Suddenly, it all made sense. She knew Matt was a *were*cougar, but before last night she'd never even suspected such things were possible. Soft, tawny fur covered Matt's large body and tickled her hands as he rested his head in her lap and snuffled at her fingers. A long, wet tongue licked out to rasp over her hand, making her laugh. Emboldened, she reached out and scratched behind the cougar's pointed ears, luxuriating in the feel of his thick pelt under her fingers. It was one of the most sensual and exciting things she'd ever experienced.

Matt settled one big paw on the stone bench, right between her legs, forcing them wider. His nose fell unerringly to the juncture of her thighs, sniffing playfully. She pushed him away, but he would not be deterred, sending that long tongue out to press between her thighs, causing almost unbearable pressure as his purr grew louder.

"There are better places for this than outdoors on a hard stone bench, you creature of mischief." Sebastian pushed at the cat with a good-natured shove, freeing Christy. She stood quickly, unwilling to be pinned by the cat again, though she wasn't scared so much as excited.

Sebastian ushered her inside, the cat following close behind. Once indoors, Matt moved up next to her, putting his large body under her hand as he led her through the house to another room she hadn't seen before. This room was as decadent as the *dojo* was austere. A giant sectional couch filled one wall and looked like the most comfortable nest she'd ever seen. The opposite wall was covered with what looked like a movie screen with all kinds of electronic gear set in built-in cabinets all around. This was obviously some kind of high-tech media room and it was built for comfort as well as style.

The colors were bold, but pleasing to the eye and the furniture looked both adaptable and functional. Of course, it would be useful for more than just watching movies. If the building rumble in the cat under her hand was anything to judge by, tonight the main attraction in this movie theater would be her.

Chapter Four

Sebastian watched Matt, in his furry form, hop up on the leather sectional.

"Mind the claws, you mangy alley cat!"

Matt paused to send a disdainful look over his shoulder as he stretched out in a boneless heap. Relaxing on the couch, he let the change take him.

Christina's gasp called Sebastian's attention back to her. No matter how many times he saw the shift from *were* to human, it still amazed him. He could only imagine how Christina must feel, seeing it for the first time. When he looked back at the overstuffed couch, Matt lay there in all his naked human glory, staring back at Christina with lust clear in his eyes. For a moment, Sebastian had to work to hold his temper in check.

He had to remind himself, this was what he wanted. He'd asked Matt to help her. More than that, he *needed* Matt to give Christina some of his speed, agility, and strength. That he'd agreed to do so was unprecedented, but Sebastian had a very special relationship with this particular *were*cougar. Sebastian had been there for Matt and his brothers after their sister's brutal death at the hands of her crazed mate. Sebastian had helped them hunt down the cougar and dispense justice for his crime. Because of his sister's tragic death, Matt had a soft spot for any woman like Christina, who'd been abused and betrayed by a man who'd promised to love, honor and cherish her.

As a general rule, the various supernatural races didn't mix. Most vampires disdained the *were* and vice versa. *Were* blood was a delicacy to vampires, though Christina was too young to realize it. The consumption of *were* blood allowed them faster healing and much more energy than regular mortal blood, but it was damned near impossible to get. The *were* had ample means to protect themselves even from ancient vampires, and it just wasn't worth the trouble for a momentary high.

Unless it was your first meal.

Few knew how crucial a newly turned vampire's first meal was to the rest of their existence, but Sebastian knew the secret because of his own experience. Centuries ago, he'd been left alone in the forest after his maker turned him and left him the same night. When he woke, Sebastian had followed the scent of blood to a wounded animal left for dead. Newly turned, he didn't know much, but instinct kicked in and while he couldn't bring himself to feed from a human, he acknowledged his need for blood. Sebastian drank from the injured wolf he found cowering in the undergrowth. The poor creature had two broken legs—one front and one hind—and would require months of rehabilitation if the wounds didn't fester, which was likely in the murky forest.

Sebastian sank his teeth into the creature's neck, startled when it changed under his hands. He tasted the red copper of blood and the burn of what he'd come to know later as magic. Within a few seconds, a young girl lay on the ground where the wolf had been, clutching a broken arm to her chest, one of her legs twisted at an unnatural angle. Her eyes shone with desperate fear and Sebastian was aghast at what he'd almost done. This was no injured animal. Though he'd never seen one before, he realized the poor child was a *were*wolf.

After calming her fears, they'd struck an accord that night. Sebastian helped the girl get back to her family in exchange for a bit of her blood to keep him going. She was a long way from home and would have died without help, but he was newly turned and needed to feed. Small amounts of her blood fueled him as he carried her back to her pack.

There were tense moments as he returned the youngster, but she was quick to tell them how he'd helped her. After some convincing, her parents were grateful enough to let him live. They gave him a place to sleep for the day, since it had taken the rest of the night to carry her home. Thus was born a lasting friendship between Sebastian and the *were*. It also propelled him to greater power than any vampire of his age. That's why, only three centuries into his immortal life, he was highly ranked among his kind and could hold his own among some rather powerful—and ancient—friends.

He wanted to give that strength to Christina and the only way to do it was with Matt's help. Though the hunger to make love to her grew to nearly unbearable proportions, tonight she would feed freely from the *were*cougar for the last time, and on the morrow she would be able to stand on her own against any man—supernatural or otherwise.

"Come over here, sweetheart." Matt's voice sounded from across the room. She stood between the two men, shifting her weight to one foot, indecision written all over her body.

Sebastian went to her and placed his hands on her shoulders. Kneading her tense muscles, he pulled her back against his chest.

"You need this, my dear, and I need to feed off the energies released when you climax. We both do. Let Matt give you this. Just one more night."

She surprised him by turning in his arms. "Will you...?" She flushed under his scrutiny and in that moment he could deny her nothing.

"I'll be here with you. I promise." He gave in to his own desires and kissed her, allowing his hands to drop to her waist and slip under the hem of the baggy sweatshirt. Her skin was so soft, so warm, as he skimmed a seductive path up her small ribcage, tugging the shirt up and out of the way. He had to break the kiss to pull the sweatshirt over her head, but she went right back to him, kissing him breathless as she pressed her soft, bare breasts against his chest, rubbing all over.

A warm presence came up behind her and Sebastian opened his eyes to find Matt grinning at him across the top of Christina's petite head. With a few tugs, the *were*cougar relieved her of her pants and she was bare between them. She made a delicious whimpering sound against Sebastian's lips as Matt's hand settled between her thighs and began to rub.

It was almost too much for Sebastian. This night was for Christina and Matt. She had to feed from the cougar and fuck him several more times before Sebastian would be satisfied that all the benefits of Matt's blood and lust had been realized in her transformed system.

With a suppressed groan, Sebastian stepped back, ducking out of her hold, though he couldn't free himself of her pleading gaze. Matt turned her in his arms and Sebastian gave a sigh of relief when she could no longer see him. That had been close. Sebastian had almost given in to the desire plaguing him since the moment he first saw her, but it wasn't yet time. He would have her—repeatedly—but not just yet. No, he had to be absolutely certain she was as strong as she could be before he took her and discovered whether or not she was the woman he'd been searching for all these years.

Even if she wasn't his One, he knew he'd keep her as his lover for many years to come. It would take at least a decade to sate the lust riding him for this petite woman. And that was only the tip of the iceberg. He could see himself fucking her happily well into the next century.

But first things first.

He watched with forced detachment as Matt cupped her fleshy buttocks. He backed toward the couch, taking her with him as he kissed her. She was under his spell now, that magical *were* tongue doing its job on her senses, no doubt. Matt sat, pulling her over him, forcing her legs apart to straddle him on the couch. One hand teased a nipple, while the other settled in the folds of her pussy.

She squirmed on his lap, her heart-shaped ass lifting and rolling in a way that made even Sebastian's loose karate pants too tight to bear. He shifted, adjusting himself, but couldn't draw his eyes away from the arousing picture of Christina, naked and spread, on Matt's thighs.

"She's wet and ready for me, Sebastian." Matt insisted on increasing Sebastian's level of discomfort by giving him a play by play. But Sebastian was a strong man. He'd play along.

"Then what are you waiting for?"

Sebastian could see three of Matt's fingers pushing deep inside her body as she rose up on her knees and let out a keening cry. She was more than ready. And so was he, but he had to refrain this night. It was too important not to.

"Good question." Matt removed his fingers, and positioned his cock in their place as he guided her down onto him with one hand on her shoulder. Christina was lost in pleasure, her head thrown back, her mouth open as she panted, her eyes shut tight. She moved down onto Matt's body, biting her lip as the pleasure seemed to overwhelm her.

The alluring sight was nearly his undoing. Sebastian couldn't help himself. He moved closer.

"Ride him, sweet. Take him as far as he can go inside you."

"Sebastian!" Something inside roared when she cried out *his* name as her body tensed around Matt's. When she quieted, Matt lifted her and placed her on her back, positioning himself between her thighs and driving home again. He hadn't come, though she'd certainly felt the first of many completions she'd experience that night. Sebastian moved closer to look down at her beautiful face. Her gaze held his as Matt pushed her to another high, this time going over himself, sending his potent *were* seed deep inside her.

Matt sat back after a few minutes and smiled. "Well, that took the edge off. How are you feeling, sweet thing?" He trailed his large, calloused fingers over her soft, damp skin. That last orgasm had been a strong one and she quite obviously needed a little time to recover. Sebastian realized also that she hadn't fed. That would have to be rectified sooner rather than later. Perhaps now was a good time to teach her to bite without fucking, for she certainly wouldn't want to fuck every mortal she might feed from in the future, if she proved to not be his mate. Even if she was, it was his duty to prepare her for every eventuality, and there was always a possibility that she would have to feed off mortals in certain situations.

Sebastian lifted her shoulders and sat behind her, supporting her as she floated back to earth. He couldn't resist reaching down to tease her pouting nipples. They bloomed under his touch and her eyes opened.

"You didn't feed, little one."

She looked up at him, a charming, embarrassed flush staining her cheeks. He realized she probably perceived his words as criticism and it hit him like a blow to the chest. He hated the look of self-conscious insecurity on her face. Dipping his head, he kissed her open mouth, wiping the fear away with his tongue as he turned her around to face him on the couch.

"That wasn't a complaint about your performance." He

drew back to meet her gaze. "Merely an observation. You need to feed."

A smile broke over her lips and warmed his heart. "So what do you want me to do?"

"Go to Matt." Those three words were harder than any he'd ever spoken, though she'd never know it. He didn't have it in him to push her toward the other man, but she turned nonetheless, following his spoken orders.

Matt tipped his head to the side, guiding her with one hand on the nape of her neck. Matt watched Sebastian, and Sebastian watched them both.

"Feel for the sweet spot with your tongue," Sebastian coached. "Take your time. Reach out and dampen his pain with your mind if you can." Sebastian checked, extending his own power, glad to find she was already exerting her new power to protect Matt. She was a natural when it came to not causing another being pain, but he should have expected it. Her life to this point had been one of self-sacrifice to the point of foolishness. "Have you found it?"

She nodded slightly as she dragged her luscious lips over Matt's neck. Sebastian envied the younger man in that moment, more than he'd ever envied another being in his long life.

"When you're ready, bite him. Do it fast to cause the least trauma."

Sebastian felt the moment of her decision, saw the way her delicate jaw moved, clamping down on Matt's corded throat as she sank her teeth in and sucked. Matt jumped too, but in a movement of pleasure, not pain. Sebastian could clearly see the *were*cougar's cock hardening once more next to Christina's hip.

She fed well this time, letting go just at the point where Sebastian would have told her to leave off.

"Very well done, my dear," Sebastian complimented her as she smiled. Her new fangs were petite, just like her, and sexier than hell.

"You taste good, Matt. Have I thanked you yet for helping me this way?" Her eyes grew serious as she turned to the other man. "I'll never be able to repay you," her voice broke with emotion, "for this gift." She held out her hand, taking Sebastian's, surprising him. "Either of you." She squeezed

Sebastian's fingers. "You gave me a second chance, and you," she looked at Matt, "have given me a strength I'd never otherwise have. Sebastian told me, Matt, and all I can do is say thank you." She shrugged with a soft smile. "It seems inadequate."

Matt regarded her with a serious expression. "Just promise me you'll use this power well. Help others when you can."

She nodded. "I will. I promise."

"That's good enough for me." Matt stood and picked her up, dumping her back on the sectional couch on her hands and knees. "Now for some more fun. Are you game?"

Sebastian fled the couch, afraid if he stayed near her head, he wouldn't be able to resist the idea of feeling her mouth on his cock. That would come soon enough. Tonight was for her. He had to keep reminding himself of that.

By the time he looked back, Matt had mounted her from behind, driving his cock deep as she moaned, her breasts swinging in a rhythmic, arousing display under her as Matt pounded home. He varied the speed and depth of his thrusts, kneeling behind her on the couch, watching her ass with a speculative expression.

"If you were a cougar, and we were fucking in our fur," Matt mused as he stroked his big hands over her rear, "your tail would be right about..." he spread her cheeks and rubbed one big thumb over, then above the tiny hole, "...here." He rubbed again and she moaned. He sped up his thrusts, both nearing another pinnacle. "Fucking as a cat is nice, but nothing beats...the human...experience." He punctuated his words with hard thrusts that lifted her off her knees as she cried out in the grip of another huge orgasm.

Matt followed her over the cliff, but pulled out after a few quick spurts inside her, spending himself in the crack of her ass. Sebastian almost feared what he could predict was coming next.

Matt leaned over her, resting a moment as he used one hand to rub his semen into the crack of her ass, using it as lubrication for his fingers. One dipped inside the tight rosette as she whimpered, but it wasn't in distress. Sebastian watched her every reaction. He'd stop this at the first sign of trouble, regardless of the fact that she needed as much of Matt in her—

in every place possible—to grow as strong as she possibly could from this encounter.

"You like this, sweetheart?" Matt whispered as he bit down on her earlobe. "You like my fingers in your ass?"

She panted as he added another finger, stretching her. "Yes!" she cried and Sebastian's cock hardened to the point of pain at the sexual anguish in her voice. "Yes!"

"Then you'll like this even more, I bet." Matt didn't rush. He pulled his fingers from her, observing her level of readiness before proceeding. He was nothing if not a careful lover, which Sebastian was glad of at this moment. He wouldn't have trusted any other man to initiate Christina this way. Matt rose so he could feed his cock—hard once again—into the tight rosette he'd stretched and made ready.

Sebastian moved closer, lured by the sight. He was entranced by the look on Christina's beautiful face. She was in some far-off place where pleasure mixed with pain. He knew it well. It was the realm of the vampire, the one that fed them and claimed them as they fed. Ecstasy edged with the barest hint of pain was their existence.

Matt, by contrast, was earthy and very mortal, regardless of the fact he would live the length of several human lifetimes, as did most *were*. He was careful with Christina, but he could never understand that realm where the vampire dwelled and flourished. Not completely.

Sebastian wanted so badly to join Christina in that place. He wanted to be inside her, his cock in her pussy, his fangs in her flesh, hers in his as they fed on each other, so close none could tell where one began and the other ended. He wanted all that. With her. Only her.

But not yet. He could wait. He must.

Once more should do it.

Let Matt have her this one last time and then she could rest and recover. Sebastian would bide his time until she became his alone.

Matt seated himself fully in her tight ass as Sebastian watched, his mouth dry, his pulse pounding through his body. Matt shifted and sat back on the couch, bringing Christina with him in an unexpected move that set off another climax in her quivering body. Matt sat, content to have her on his lap, her legs straddling his, his cock buried in her ass.

But Christina wasn't coming down. She was strung taut on the edge of something huge, and clearly in distress. Sebastian moved in front of her, wanting to help. Her eyes opened and the fire in her gaze struck him like a body blow. Her expression pleaded.

"Sebastian!"

Matt's hands moved around and spread her pussy, playing with her clit as Sebastian watched, entranced. "There's room for one more here, old buddy. Want to join us?" The *were*cougar licked her ear and bit down on the fleshy lobe from behind. "I bet she'd like it." Matt seemed unaware of the danger. Sebastian was a man on the edge of control, a beast barely leashed.

"I cannot," Sebastian breathed, knowing he shouldn't, but wanting nothing more than to join with the woman whose eyes pled with him, whose heart tugged at his.

"Sebastian," she panted, in an agony of desire, "I need you. Please! I'm begging you!"

It was the begging note in her voice that pushed him beyond reason. With a growl, Sebastian lost control of the beast within. He tugged down his loose pants and knelt on the couch in front of her, between Matt's legs. With a single, harsh thrust, he joined with her, plunging and fucking like a wild animal.

Teeth bared, he pulled her forward, his cock tight within her pussy while Matt's filled her behind, but Sebastian was too far gone to know or care for possible consequences. He fucked her hard, nuzzling into her neck, panting hot breaths across her skin as she did the same. His mouth sought and found the point of her pulse, the sweet spot of her neck, savoring only a moment before plunging home with his fangs at the same time as his cock.

Dimly, he registered the feel of her petite fangs buried in his flesh and the wonderful feel of her sucking sent him over the edge of all reason. He sucked and fucked, coming to a blinding orgasm in a huge fireball of urgency that swept all three of them up in it together.

He blacked out for a while, but as he came back,

knowledge filled him.

She was in him.

As he was in her.

Her blood, her body, her lovely mind was joined with his, as he was with her. They were true mates. She was his One.

"Christina."

"Sebastian? What is this?"

"The true bond. Can't you feel it? We're joined. Now and forever more."

He lifted away from her and pulled free of her luscious body. In the wonder of finding his mate, he'd forgotten momentarily about the shapeshifter. He'd been part of them as the bond had formed. What consequences could that have? He didn't know.

"Matt? Are you all right?"

The *were*cougar shook his head as if coming out of a stupor. And perhaps he was. "Holy shit. What was that?"

Chapter Five

"You felt it?" Sebastian eyed his old friend.

"I felt..." Matt hesitated, a look of wonder coming over his features. "It was the most beautiful thing I've ever experienced in my life. But...what was it, exactly?"

Sebastian pulled her into his arms and rested against the soft couch. "Christina is my mate. She will be my bride."

"But I'm already married." He heard the objection in his mind, joined as they were. They shared thoughts now, as only true mates could.

"Not for long."

"What does that mean?"

"We'll discuss it later. Right now, we need to deal with Matt."

"I heard that," Matt groused, out of breath still and looking dazed. "You two are buzzing at the back of my mind. Almost, but not quite out of earshot. This is weird. What's going on?"

"I fear some of our bond may have extended to you." Sebastian's mind raced. This was unprecedented. He'd never heard of such a thing happening before, but then, vampire and *were* rarely shared words, much less a lover between them. This was uncharted territory. "I'm sorry, Matt. It's my fault. I wasn't strong enough to resist."

"It's not your fault." Christina stroked his cheek, love shining in her eyes. "I enticed you. I begged you."

"Never be sorry for that, my dear. I should have been stronger. I should have waited until we were alone." He turned to his friend. "Matt, I don't know exactly what ramifications this will have."

"I hear you, buddy. In my ears and in my mind. Is that how your kind joins? You can share thoughts, like telepathy?"

"Not quite telepathy. It's something much deeper. We share minds and souls. Right now, my mind is open to Christina's as hers is open to me. Over time, we will come to know each other as deeply as if we were one person." Sebastian took a moment to seek outside himself, comparing the amazing connection with Christina to the fainter connection formed between them both and Matt. "The good news is, from what I can see, you've received only a backwash of what we have. It's faint, but it's there, Matt, and for that I apologize. I didn't intend to cause you harm."

Matt put a hand to his chest and rubbed over his heart, wonder in his eyes. "This doesn't feel like harm, Sebastian. It's...it's...really beautiful. Like nothing I've ever known before. It's amazing, man. I feel the love between you. I feel the glow of discovery, the connection. It's kind of humbling."

Sebastian felt Christina's heart open up to the other man, but experienced no jealousy. He was in her mind, in her soul, and he knew the kind of affection she held for Matt was quite different from the deep and true feelings that flowed from her heart to his and back again. In that moment they were of one mind. As long as Matt didn't suffer, they would gladly share the echoes of their love with him. It was a joyous thing, meant to be shared with friends, not hidden.

Okay, most friends wouldn't share their new connection on this deep a level, but Matt had always been a special case. He was one of the few *were* whom Sebastian—and now Christina—thought of as family. They were brothers under the skin and had been close for many years. Oh, Matt was still a youngster compared to Sebastian's three centuries, but the kinship they shared went beyond their differences.

Christina learned all this as Sebastian thought it. He reveled in the close bond they shared and marveled at the compassion and friendship she felt for the *were*cougar. Sebastian understood the depth of her gratefulness for the gift Matt had bestowed. Sebastian also saw how she liked the idea Matt would learn what love should be by hearing some of their internal discussion. Sebastian took it one step further and thought of the potential uses such a connection could have.

"Can you hear me, Matt?" Sebastian asked.

"Loud and clear. Well, not real loud, but that time was definitely louder than before. It's like you're speaking to me through a door. Weird."

"This could be useful. I wonder if the connection works both ways. Try thinking something back at me."

"Your woman has the sweetest pussy I've ever tasted."

Christina blushed to the roots of her hair and Sebastian laughed out loud. Leave it to Matt to be as audacious as possible.

"I guess you heard that, huh?" Matt winked at her, a broad, unapologetic grin on his face. Christina lobbed a throw pillow at his head, but he ducked.

"Do us a favor and stick around here today, Matt. Unless you have other business." Sebastian was thinking fast, planning ahead.

"Nothing that can't wait."

"Good. See if you can figure out what Jeff Kinsey has been up to."

"Who's Jeff Kinsey?" Matt wanted to know.

Christina stiffened in Sebastian's arms. "My husband."

"The swine who hurt her. I want to know if he's still in jail. And if he is, I want you to use your contacts on the police force to get someone to notify us the minute he gets out. If he's already out, I want you to call that *were* private eye and get him on surveillance. He'll do it for you, though I suspect if I asked, he wouldn't give me the time of day. I'll pay, of course."

"Hastings owes me a favor. If Kinsey is out, he'll be watched by *were* twenty-four/seven. Count on it. Now," Matt rose and stood in front of them for a moment, unashamed of his nudity, "I'll leave you two lovebirds alone. I'll be outside prowling the grounds." He shimmered with magic and a moment later, the man was replaced by a golden cougar with topaz eyes. He padded out the door with a last look over his shoulder and the wink of one feline eye.

Sebastian took Christy back to his room—*their* room now—

the luxurious master suite, built on the interior of the fortress-like house, with no windows and heavy doors. She knew from the memories he now shared with her that this room was his retreat, but he seldom slept here. No, this room had a well-concealed secret doorway which led downward into the sublevels of the house, below ground.

"Why didn't you take me below ground last night? It's got to be safer for us to be away from the sun altogether."

"Because for most newly turned, it takes some time to get used to the idea of being underground. I didn't want you to feel threatened in any way and showing you my dungeon could have been interpreted as a threat by some people."

"Dungeon?" The word tripped through her mind as he chuckled.

"Just a small part of the underground complex beneath the house. You'll see it all, eventually. But not tonight. Tonight I only plan to show you the bedroom. We still have a few hours before sunrise. The rest of the night is ours."

"I can still hear you, you know," came Matt's voice, more faint than before, through their shared link. *"It's not quite as loud, but you're definitely there, buzzing in the back of my mind. Man, this feels weird."*

"No doubt," Sebastian answered. *"I'm hoping distance will dull the connection so you won't be subject to our internal dialog all the time. Is it lessening at all?"*

"Yes," came the reply, fainter than the last as they moved downward into the earth. *"I can barely hear you now."*

"Good. Rest well today, my friend. We'll see you tomorrow night."

"Goodnight, friends."

That last was the faintest communication yet and Christy knew a moment of relief that Matt wouldn't suffer too much for what had happened. She felt guilty about enticing Sebastian into that threesome, though it had felt wonderful at the time. Still, if anyone was going to be joined with them for all eternity, she supposed Matt was a good choice. He was a steadfast friend, with enormous strength and a good heart. She felt the truth of those thoughts as she saw some of Sebastian's memories of Matt in their shared minds.

They'd been through a lot together, Sebastian and Matt, and had been criticized by each other's races for their close friendship. She saw that Matt had brothers, and two sisters, one now dead at the hands of her mate. Sebastian was friendly with the entire Redstone Clan, which was led by Matt's oldest brother Griffon. They were builders by trade, and Christy remembered seeing the name Redstone Construction and a cougar emblem on the side of more than a few trucks and construction vehicles throughout her travels. Very successful builders, Sebastian's memory soon affirmed.

Apparently *were* strength was put to good use in such occupations and many of the Redstone employees were no doubt *were*creatures of one kind or another. Matt was the youngest of the brothers, but by no means a child. He was a few decades older than Christy herself, though he looked to be in his mid-twenties or early-thirties. Again, those *were* genetics and corresponding long lifespan played a role in her perception. She had to get used to the idea that these people didn't always look like what they actually were. Sebastian, for one example, was more than two centuries older than her, and some of her friends' new husbands were even older than that.

It was a lot to take in.

"Hiro is coming back tomorrow night and we'll continue your training." Sebastian broke into her thoughts as he stopped before a door in the secret passageway. There was no need for lights in the dark tunnel. Her vision adjusted to allow her to see in the dark as clearly as if it were day. Another cool thing to get used to.

"What are you training me for, exactly?"

Before the words were even out of her mouth, she saw the truth in his mind.

Jeff. He wanted her to face Jeff.

"No!" Her mind rebelled, but Sebastian was there, his strong arms around her shoulders, guiding her through the door he'd opened. "I won't do it. I don't ever want to see him again!" She lost control of the fear filling her mind. She thought she'd been doing so well, putting her past behind her, but apparently the terror Jeff had taught her would not be denied. She knew Sebastian felt her uncontrollable response and that made it somehow worse. He saw the full extent of her weakness now. She was a coward.

"No, my love," he crooned, rocking her in his arms. "You're no coward. Jeff is the coward. It's easy to beat up on those weaker than yourself, but not honorable or brave. I'd like to see him try to hurt you now. You'd show him a thing or two. You'd teach him a lesson he'd never forget."

"Is that what you really think? Is that why you had Matt give me his super-blood? Because if that's what you're after, I don't think I can do it, Sebastian." She drew comfort from his embrace, even while her mind objected. "I'm not strong enough."

Sebastian seemed to consider her words. "Physically, you're much stronger now than any human—especially a weakling like Jeff Kinsey. It's the psychological strength we need to work on, my love. And we will. We have lifetimes ahead of us to work on it, but it starts with you facing your fear of this mortal head-on."

She would have objected, but he shushed her with a gentle finger on her lips. "Not tonight, not tomorrow night either, but one night soon, you'll be ready to take the first step on your path to recovery. I'll be beside you every step of the way, my love." Leaning close, he kissed her lips, little butterfly kisses meant to comfort. "I will always be with you now. We are One."

"Sebastian." She breathed his name as he lifted her in his arms and carried her to a soft, wide bed draped with blood red silk sheets. It was an antique no doubt, with heavy velvet curtains in the same dark red and black, and wider than any bed she'd ever seen in her life. He deposited her on the cool sheets, and followed her down into the softness of a mattress stuffed with down.

"I've wanted you since the moment I first saw you, Christina. You'll never know how hard it was for me to let you leave your friend's wedding with Jeff. I knew something was wrong with your relationship, but I didn't know the extent until Jena called Kelly from the hospital. Thank heavens I was at Marc's that night. Otherwise I would have heard too late." His voice cracked with emotion as he drew her close, cuddling her under his chin. "I comfort myself that your friends would have saved your life anyway, but another would have been your maker. I knew the moment I saw you, I wanted that responsibility—that honor—for myself. I wanted to teach you and coach you, and stand back and marvel while you blossomed into the woman you always should have been. The woman you would have been without Jeff in your life."

"I'm glad you were there. I can't imagine sharing this with anybody else." She began undoing his buttons one by one.

"I know I surprised you with Matt. I'm sorry for that, but I had my reasons."

Christy paused, spreading one hand over his warm, hard chest. "I understand, Sebastian. It startled me at first, but last night and earlier tonight were some of the most amazing moments of my life."

"It's just the beginning, my love." He lifted her hand to his lips and kissed her knuckles with teasing nibbles. "Our lives are joined now and things will only get better from here. I promise."

"Sebastian, I want to make love to you." She couldn't control her wayward emotions. She'd wanted this man for a long time but hadn't dared dream he could be hers in any way. Now here she was, with Sebastian in his secret lair, alone at last. She wanted to join her body to his once more as they were now joined in mind. "Just you. Only you."

There wasn't time for words as Sebastian rid them both of their clothing. Within moments they were skin to skin on Sebastian's luxurious bed. The silk of the sheets felt cool and soothing against her overheated skin while Sebastian's masculine fingers trailed down her body with an expert's precision. He knew just how to touch her to stimulate every last nerve ending and erogenous zone.

But if she wanted to change her life, she was going to start now. No longer would she play only a passive role. Jeff hadn't wanted her to take much initiative in the bedroom. She'd been a virgin when they'd married and let him take charge. That had been enough when they were newlyweds, but over the course of their marriage, she'd often felt she wanted more. Jeff wasn't inclined to let a woman take the initiative, but it had taken her years to realize how insecure Jeff really was. She knew Sebastian was quite different though. He wanted her to spread her wings and experiment. She saw that in his mind and in his heart.

Reaching up, she drew his head down so she could kiss

him. When they broke apart after long moments, both of them were breathing hard.

"I love what you do to me, Sebastian."

"You'll not get an argument from me, my love. You're more than I ever could have dreamed of having for myself and I will cherish you the rest of our nights." He clasped both of her hands, kissing her lips, her cheeks, her eyes and then moving downward over her collar bones, pausing at her breasts to nibble and suck while she writhed in ecstasy beneath him.

"Sebastian!" His name was torn from her lips as her fever rose. All Sebastian had to do was look at her a certain way and her body responded with overwhelming passion. "I need you now."

He rose over her and smiled. "I need you always, my Christina."

"Then come to me now, lover. Make me yours alone." Christy felt sexier than she ever had and knew Sebastian was with her. He wanted her. Her! And he felt the same way about her as she did about him.

It was fantastic. In less time than she could have believed, the bonding they'd undergone made them closer than any mortal could understand or hope to achieve. The magic that was Sebastian lived in her heart and soul, never to be displaced.

Sebastian rose over her, gazing down at her with love and longing as he slid between her thighs. With tender motions, he joined them, sliding into the place that welcomed him now, and would for eternity. When he was seated fully, he rested there, holding her gaze.

"I wish I could stay joined to you like this all the time." His sexy, low voice fired her senses, while his masculine scent drove her wild.

"Mmm. Me too. But right now..." she whimpered as he moved by small degrees, setting off shockwaves within her core, "...I really need you to move, Sebastian. I need you to make love to me. I need you to make me come."

Sebastian's eyes glowed as he thrust. His motions were slow and deliberate at first, then increased in urgency as their passion expanded. He moved like a wild man, but she wanted it all. She wanted him, any way he chose to come to her and she knew he felt the same. It was a novel experience, feeling your partner's thoughts, but the more time she spent joined to him, the more natural it felt.

"Come with me now, my love. Come for me."

"Sebastian!" She crested the highest wave yet. She'd never felt such an explosion of pleasure, never known a person could fly so high. "Sebastian!" She shouted as her orgasm rocked her world to its core. She felt him convulsing inside her, joining her in the greatest bliss she'd ever known.

"I love you, Sebastian." Her voice was weak with strain, her mind barely functioning as she drifted down, her body still quaking with aftershocks as he cradled her close. "I love you so much."

He kissed her face with soft touches, stroking her hair with one large hand. "I love you too, my lady, and I want you to be my bride." When she would have objected, he soothed her with gentle motions. "Let's not think of the difficulties right now. It's enough to know that as soon as you're free, you'll consent to join your life to mine in the eyes of man. Will you marry me, Christina?"

A soft smile hovered around her lips as she drifted. "Yes, Sebastian. Nothing would make me happier."

He brushed her lips with his as he shifted them to lie side by side on the large bed. He didn't release her. He held her close, stroking her skin as sleep claimed her, his proposal and her answer foremost in her mind.

She slept with a smile on her face the rest of the night and all the next day, as did Sebastian.

Chapter Six

The next evening Christy awoke wrapped in Sebastian's strong arms, her body and mind humming with the knowledge that they were One. He'd let her sift through some of his memories, as he'd seen into her past. Of course, he'd lived a couple of centuries longer than she had, so the marvelous things he'd seen and done in eighteenth-century England were like something out of a romance novel to her. It also would take some time to sort through all she could now see in his mind.

There was bad and good, mixed with the fond memories of friendship with people like Marc LaTour, but under it all, a deep loneliness that haunted him. When they'd joined the night before, that vacant space in his soul had been filled, just as its mate in her own soul had been forever filled with the new beauty of their union. It was the purest form of magic and it humbled her to think this wonderful man could want and love her as much as she wanted and loved him.

It was all so sudden, but ever so right.

Sebastian leaned down to kiss her, a smile lighting his handsome face.

"Good morrow, my love."

"Mmm, Sebastian." They kissed, communicating on that new pathway between their minds.

"Glad you two are finally awake." The teasing tone of Matt's unmistakable voice sounded through the intimacy of their link, breaking them apart.

"Would it be too much to ask for a little privacy?" Sebastian groused.

"Sorry, friend, but we've got a situation and you need to know about it, like yesterday. So no rest for the wicked. Get your asses out here and let's get to work."

"Where the hell are you? I thought you couldn't hear us last night after we put some distance between us all." Sebastian's tone was suspicious.

"That's true, but I'm waiting outside your door. I knew if I didn't, you'd spend all night holed up in there, making love."

"This better be important then," Sebastian grumbled as he rose and scrambled through some drawers looking for clothing. He tossed one of his shirts to Christy, along with a pair of gym shorts that came down past her knees, but at least she was covered.

"It is. I wouldn't have intruded otherwise."

Sebastian opened the door and waited for Christy to precede him up the dark passageway to the chamber above. Sealing everything behind him, Sebastian paused a moment outside the above-ground bedroom door to kiss her once, with promise, before opening the door. Matt waited outside, leaning against the wall, dressed in worn jeans and a tight-fitting black T-shirt. Christy was struck once again by his movie-star good looks and killer body.

"Stop that." Sebastian ruffled her hair, his expression teasing. He had to know from the way they shared their minds that she was merely admiring a thing of beauty. Her heart was well and truly Sebastian's, but Matt was just too good-looking not to notice. She shrugged and smiled at Sebastian, knowing from his teasing growl that he understood.

"Now, what was so important?"

Matt straightened and pulled a large envelope out from behind his back. With an apologetic look at Christy he shared his news. "Jeff Kinsey's out. Seems the first thing he did when he realized Christy was gone from the hospital was place a call to a man named Benjamin Steel. We have reason to believe he's a highly placed *Altor Custodis* agent. Hastings had a thick dossier on the man and was already tracking him. Hastings got a heads up from one of his contacts on the East Coast when Steel moved out here a few weeks ago."

Sebastian opened the envelope and rifled through the

papers as they moved down the hall toward the more public areas of the house. Arriving at the living room, he stopped short. Christy looked between the two big men to find a third seated on another large leather couch, studying what looked like a batch of eight by ten photos strewn on the coffee table in front of him.

"When Hastings put out a feeler for more information, he turned up." Matt nodded toward the newcomer. "I thought you should probably meet."

"We've already met." Sebastian strode forward as the stranger stood, hand outstretched in greeting and a broad smile on his face. They pounded each other on the back like old friends and Christy took a moment to scan Sebastian's memories for the stranger's identity.

"Cameron." The name slipped from her lips as the men broke apart. Blue eyes twinkled at her, taking her measure.

"And who's this wee lassie? Can it be you've found your One, Sebastian?" The teasing light in his eyes belied the almost awed tone of his lightly accented voice. Curious, Christy moved closer.

Sebastian put one strong arm around her. "I have, Cam. May I introduce my mate, Christina."

"A pleasure to meet you, milady. Though I wish it were under better circumstances."

Christy quickly searched a few of Sebastian's memories of this man and realized he was a long time friend. There was something different about him though—different from the earthy energy of Matt and not quite the raw sexual energy of Sebastian and his vampire friends. This man was something else altogether.

Christy held out her hand and was charmed by the gallant way Cameron raised it to his lips for a gentle, polite salute. Her hand tingled where he touched. Magic. It had to be. But it was different from any of the magic she'd felt before.

She turned puzzled eyes up to Sebastian.

"What is he?"

On the other side of the couch, Matt laughed and she realized he'd heard her as well. Sebastian sent the shifter a stern look while speculation filled the gaze of their new guest.

"We'll discuss it later," Sebastian told her quickly. "Shall we sit?" Sebastian invited his guests to relax as he and Christy claimed the cozy love seat.

A troubled expression crossed the newcomer's face as he ran one hand through his fiery red hair. He had freckles too, but his build was that of a giant and he looked like he had muscles on his muscles, though he seemed a gentle soul, on the surface at least.

"So tell me, why are you here, Cam? I haven't seen you in a hundred years or more."

Christy stifled her gasp at the casual way Sebastian spoke in terms of centuries. She'd have to get used to this immortality stuff.

The other man sighed. "When your shifter friend sent out that information request, red flags went up all over the globe. Of late, there's been some trouble with the *Altor Custodis.*"

Sebastian leaned forward. "What kind of trouble?"

"After consulting with some of the mountain *were*tribes and the *were*folk's High Priestess in Montana," Cam said, "we're drawing a rather ugly picture of infiltration at the highest levels. Sebastian, the *Venifucus* are back. Or perhaps it's more accurate to say, they never completely left."

Both Sebastian and Matt looked as grave as she'd ever seen them, but Christy had no clue what was going on. All she got from Sebastian's memories—what he'd let her see of them—was a frightening account of a society of watchers. The *Altor Custodis* watched all kinds of supernaturals, though they had never been known to interfere in any way.

"But if they don't interfere, why are you so worried? I mean, if they only watch and record..." Christy betrayed her knowledge of Sebastian's thoughts, but nobody seemed surprised.

If possible though, Cameron's face grew even darker. "That's the problem, lass. Recently, they've been interfering in a very big way. Last Samhain, a mage who was definitely a member of the *Altor Custodis* tried to assassinate a young priestess and her *were*wolf mates. He would have succeeded too, if not for the intervention of two of my kin and one of your kind, a fellow named Dante d'Angleterre."

Sebastian whistled through his teeth. "I didn't know old Dante was still around, but that explains where Marc got the information. He warned me that the *Venifucus* might be back, but I was hoping it was some kind of hoax, or maybe a misunderstanding."

"I heard about this too, Sebastian," Matt confirmed. "An alert went out to all Alphas after the attack on our priestess. Dante d'Angleterre was given safe passage among all *were*. It came down from the current Lords themselves."

Sebastian turned back to Cameron. "So the *Altor Custodis* have gone bad?"

Cameron tilted his head. "Not all of them. But some? Certainly. It's my belief they've been infiltrated. I think the *Venifucus* used the *Altor Custodis's* existing hierarchy to rebuild and hide in plain sight all these years."

"For what purpose? What could they hope to gain?" Sebastian wanted to know.

"You're not going to believe this, but multiple reliable witnesses heard it from the *Venifucus* mage himself before he was dispersed. They've got a plan to bring back Eslpeth. They want to return her to power in this mortal realm."

"Good Lord!" Sebastian shot to his feet, while Christy was left to wonder who the heck this Elspeth was. Suddenly, the words came to her from Sebastian's agitated mind. *Elspeth, Destroyer of Worlds.*

"Destroyer of Worlds?" Christy's voice rose with shock. "You mean like the apocalypse or something?"

"The very same, lass." Cameron's blue eyes focused on her. "If Elspeth comes back to this realm she'll finish what she started eons ago. It *will* be the end of this world. That's the honest truth."

"Well then, we've got to stop it." It seemed straight forward to Christy and her stark statement won the attention of all three men.

"We? Good lord, woman!" Sebastian was clearly upset as he stalked over to her. "You're newly turned. You're my mate! I'm not risking your safety for anything in the world."

His arms caged her in the seat and she withdrew, memory shooting her back to the times Jeff had physically threatened her. She knew it was unreasonable, but she couldn't help it. Sebastian was just so much bigger than she was. Even though she knew in her heart he would never hurt her, in that moment, she grew afraid.

She knew Sebastian read the fear in their shared minds as anguish etched his face. He calmed and dropped down beside her on the loveseat, pulling her into his arms and snuggling her close with gentle hands.

"I would never hurt you, my love," he crooned in a low whisper, rocking her as the fight or flight reaction shook her body. "I'm sorry, Christina. I didn't mean to frighten you. Please forgive me."

She became self-conscious, knowing the other men were watching, but when she peeked up at them, they wore expressions of compassion. Pushing against Sebastian's hold, she worked to gather her scattered emotions. She had to pull herself together. This wouldn't do. She refused to be a coward.

She felt Sebastian kiss her head as he let her go. *"You were never a coward, my love,"* he whispered in her mind. *"You're the bravest woman I know."*

"So where does all this leave us?" She tried to breathe deep, and calm her racing pulse. Somehow Jeff was mixed up in all this. Her problem marriage had just become a much bigger problem for them all.

Christy didn't miss the significant look that passed between Cameron and Sebastian before the redhead resumed speaking. They all seemed to realize her predicament.

"It leaves me wondering just where Benjamin Steel's loyalties lie. I've been tracking him for a few months, but he's a wily son of a gun. For the safety of all supernaturals, we need to find out if the *Altor Custodis* organization is aware of its own problems and if so, what they're doing about it. My goal is to locate and talk to Steel. Your difficulties lie in the fact that he might or might not be a damned *Venifucus* agent. Or even if he's still loyal to the *Altor Custodis* traditions, those in his chain of command may not be. If such is the case, they won't like what you've become, Lady Christina. Female supernaturals, most of all, threaten the return of Elspeth, for it was prophesied eons ago that Elspeth would finally fall at the hands of a woman of great power and that lady *were*, vampire, priestess and fey would be there, working together against her at the end. As a result, they target our women when they're young and just coming into their powers. Like you."

"Well, hell." Matt's angry voice cut through the silence as he flopped back in his chair. "He only just finds her and now her life is in danger? That doesn't seem fair."

"That it's not, laddie," Cameron agreed, "but it's the way things are. The question is, what are we going to do about it?"

"We?" Sebastian sat forward, his stance tense.

"Aye." Cameron nodded. "I'll not leave you alone on this, my friend. The fey—well, at least I—will stand with you to protect your lady."

"Fey?" Christy was trying to make sense of his words when his meaning penetrated. "You mean you're a fairy?"

Matt stifled a laugh and Cameron shot him a dirty look before replying. "Not in the modern sense of the word, but aye, I'm of the fey realm, though I prefer the comforts of this one."

"Thank you, Cam." Sebastian's voice was filled with grim gratitude. "I can never repay such kindness." She knew Sebastian felt immense relief at the other man's words, though she didn't quite understand what help a fairy could be in this situation. Sebastian turned his gaze to Matt.

"My friend, you know I would never ask you—"

Matt didn't let him finish. "Hey, man, you didn't expect me to bail on you now? Please." His expression was one of exaggerated disbelief. "You and your lady deserve a shot at happiness and an absurdly long life together. Besides, she had me wrapped around her little finger the moment I heard about her bastard husband." Matt scowled, but managed to wink at her, setting her more at ease in the tense atmosphere. "I'll see what help I can conjure from my clan and maybe a few of the others you've befriended during your time here, Sebastian. I imagine a few extra sets of eyes and ears would be welcome?"

Sebastian nodded. "You've got that right. As long as they can be trusted."

"I'll recruit only those you know, Sebastian. Only those I trust."

"And I suggest you get your own on this, Sebastian," Cameron advised. "This situation may grow a wee bit larger than any of us bargained for."

Sebastian pulled a cell phone from his pocket and started dialing. "Can you stick around for an hour or two, Cam?"

The redhead nodded. "Unless my trackers find Steel."

Sebastian stood as the phone connected with Marc LaTour. Sebastian asked the Master to come by. Christy understood from scanning Sebastian's surface thoughts that he protected Marc by inviting him here rather than moving the meeting to the Master's home. The less people who knew where Marc lived and the layout of the place, the better. She also realized Sebastian regretted he'd made his own home so easy to access by his many supernatural friends now that he had her safety to consider.

"Now, lassie," Cameron claimed her attention with the soft burr of his voice, "would you mind telling us a bit about your husband?"

Matt leaned forward in his chair and took her hand. "You don't have to if you don't want to, but it might help."

She smiled at the *were*cougar while Sebastian was occupied on the phone. "It's okay. What do you want to know?"

She spent the next half hour or so describing small details—from the kind of car her husband drove to his work schedule. She drew a floor plan of their house and even answered questions about where things were stored in the home, if there were any large silver objects, weapons, and the like. Things that never would have occurred to her before she'd been changed. They wanted to know the layout of the windows and furniture and where the alcohol was kept, especially any wine. They also wanted to know about her husband's habits, his character and his typical response to other men, women and even children and animals.

Christy didn't understand the motivations behind half the questions, but she had her suspicions. Sometime during the gentle interrogation, Hiro came into the room, his gaze questioning, but Sebastian settled him into the group with a soft request to hang around. Patient as a stone Buddha, Hiro sat on the floor, his back straight and stance attentive.

Matt made a quick phone call and ten minutes later, a huge bird of prey swooped down onto the patio and hopped into the room to listen in as well. Christy's eyes widened, but she could only assume this was another of Matt's shapeshifter brethren. Shortly after, Sebastian went to the door to greet Marc, Atticus, and the enforcer, Ian Sinclair, all vampires of great age.

Christy felt self-conscious as the growing crowd listened to the details of her life, but Sebastian sat at her side, a reassuring presence. She knew the remnants of the life she'd led to this point would have to be dealt with before they could move on together. This added threat only made it all the more imperative. So she struggled to tell her story and answered the odd questions put to her as best she could.

When she'd finished, everyone in the room sat back with varying expressions of compassion, anger, resolve and calculation on their faces. Sebastian took the opportunity to introduce everyone. Christy was amazed by the respect shown to Marc. Apparently being the Master Vampire really held some weight with other supernaturals, if the way they deferred to him was anything to judge by. Christy knew Atticus as Lissa's husband, but it was clear he was also well respected. She'd met Ian only once before but remembered the handsome man well. She knew now that Ian was an enforcer. As she understood it, his job was to police vampire society to ensure nobody exposed their secret existence. He also dispensed justice to those who broke their laws. Ian was a scary guy, built of solid muscle, his stance rigid in a way that didn't invite familiarity, and he had the look of a killer.

Matt disappeared into one of the hall closets and came back with a pair of sweatpants he threw toward the giant hawk. The bird hopped down behind the couch and a tingle of magic filled the air. Seconds later, a handsome sandy-haired man rose from behind the sofa, tugging at the drawstring of the borrowed pants. He was good-looking in the same rugged way as Matt, but his nose had a pronounced bump, like it had been broken once or twice and his eyes were both cunning and sharp.

"This is Collin Hastings, the private eye." Matt introduced the other shifter.

"I've heard good things about you, Mr. Hastings," Marc said

on behalf of the vampires.

"Thank you for coming," Sebastian added. "Thank you all for coming. I had no idea our situation would turn into a cross species operation, but I thank you for standing with me and my mate in this time of difficulty."

Christy liked the way he included her and appreciated the warm feeling of his hand in hers as he sat close beside her on the loveseat.

Cameron shuffled through the photos on the coffee table, passing a few around the group. "These are surveillance photos of both Jeff Kinsey and Benjamin Steel."

Christy's hand tightened on Sebastian's as the pictures made their way around to her and she saw Jeff's sneering face for the first time since he'd almost killed her. Sebastian put his arm around her shoulders, and she sank into his hold, feeling as if nothing could harm her with him there. And perhaps nothing could. Certainly not Jeff. Sebastian would eat him for breakfast. Well, maybe dinner, after the sun went down, she amended with an inner smile.

"They've met on more than one occasion since Kinsey got out of jail," Hastings spoke as he passed the photos on. "I have reason to believe it was Steel who posted bail for Kinsey, though I've yet to receive final confirmation." Hastings held up another photo and pointed to a man in the background. "I'm also awaiting confirmation of the identity of this man. He's been seen with Steel each time we've been able to track the man. Steel is slipperier than an eel. We've caught him with Kinsey a few times, but when we try to follow, he manages to slip away. That goes double for his associate. We've heard the name Mario, but other than that, we don't know who this one is yet."

"May I?" Ian reached for the photo and Hastings handed it to him. Ian looked at it for a few minutes before passing it to Marc. "I've seen him before."

"Recently?" Cameron asked.

Ian shook his head. "It was some time back. Mexico in the eighteen hundreds. Mario Gonzalez was his name back then. He was a bandito. We crossed paths when he robbed the night stage I was on. He's a mage of some kind. I smelled the magic right off. When he realized what I was, he took what he could and headed for the hills. I tracked him down a few weeks later, but he claimed he'd gone straight. I watched him for a bit, but he seemed okay, so I let him be. Figured he'd have been dead long ago, but maybe his magic is such that it gives him long life." Ian shrugged.

Cameron nodded. "*Venifucus* magic has been said to extend the life of mortals. At the expense of others, usually." His attention turned to Christy. "If it's as we fear, you're in more danger than you know, milady."

"This is definitely not cool." Christy sagged back against Sebastian. "You're telling me some kind of evil human magician has teamed up with one of these *Altor* guys—who are only supposed to watch—and is coming after me because I'm newly turned and therefore weak? Great. Just great."

"Hey, girl, don't sweat it," Matt tried to cajole her with a smile. "You've got a bunch of angry vamps, some equally pissed off *were*, and a fey warrior on your side. Not to mention the tricks you have up your own sleeve, sweet thing. They won't know what hit them if they start messing with you. I can guarantee it."

"What tricks?" Cameron wanted to know.

Sebastian sighed and ran his hands through his hair. "You really want to tell them, Matt?"

The *were*cougar shrugged. "Why not? Besides, I think they need to know."

"What do we need to know, Sebastian?" Marc stepped forward, asserting his authority as Master.

Christy stood, not liking the implied threat to her man. She surprised herself a bit with the instinctive action, but nothing and no one would threaten Sebastian while she was present. Sebastian stood behind her, placing calming hands on her shoulders, while Matt stepped in front of her, using his imposing height to face down the Master Vampire.

Matt shrugged again. "It's no big deal, really. It's just that I was her first meal." Matt seemed to gloat as he spoke the words. "Come to think of it, her second and third as well." A smug smile lit his face while the vampires wore expressions of shock.

"What have you done, Sebastian?" Marc wanted to know.

Sebastian pulled her back against him. "What I had to do,

to keep her safe from the mad dog who was her husband." His words dared the other vampires to object.

Marc backed down, shaking his head. "You know her better than anybody. Can she handle the power and responsibility you've given her?"

Christy didn't like the way they talked about her as if she wasn't there, but she understood this was something the men had to work out between themselves first. After all, they'd known each other longer than she'd even been alive. She was the newcomer here. She was the one who had to prove herself.

"Her heart is pure and almost too self-sacrificing." He kissed the top of her head. "She'll be a strong addition to our people and she'll protect her friends to her last breath."

Atticus stepped forward. "It could be useful to have a woman who can help protect our mates. For one thing, no one would ever expect it of her. For another, Lissa and Kelly already know and trust her. Maybe they'll be able to learn some defensive skills from her, once she's trained."

Marc seemed to think through the possibilities. Sebastian pointed to the silent, half-Asian vampire who sat nearby, observing. "Hiro's already started her training."

"How good is she?" Marc asked the *sensei.*

Hiro smiled for the first time since entering the room. "She's a natural. Light on her feet, with a cat's grace." Hiro nodded in Matt's direction. "She will surprise anyone who challenges her when she's ready. I have no doubt."

Christy enjoyed the warm feeling Hiro's words inspired, but at the same time worried she would never be able to live up to his expectations. Still, she would try. She'd enjoyed their lesson the night before and had looked forward to renewing the experience tonight, until all this happened.

"My intention was to make her strong enough that she never felt threatened by me or any other man ever again," Sebastian said. She leaned into him, needing his warmth, his reassurance. "I wanted her to face her past and conquer it before we could start our new life together. I figured when the divorce was final, we could get married." He squeezed her, a hint of playfulness entering his tone. "Or we could go on living in sin for the rest of eternity." A few chuckles met that statement before Marc brought them back to the matter at hand.

"The question remains," Marc spoke directly to her, "can you handle the power you've been given? I trust Sebastian's judgment, but the real decision rests within your own heart, young one."

Christy swallowed hard before answering. "I won't let you down."

Marc nodded and moved back. Sebastian turned her in his arms, his gaze searching her face. "Then you'll confront Jeff about the divorce?"

He looked so hopeful, she couldn't bear to disappoint him, though the thought of facing Jeff, after what he'd done the last time, still gave her the willies. "If it'll help."

Sebastian kissed her, right there in front of everyone. A wolf whistle finally penetrated the sensual fog that surrounded them, and he lifted his head with a rueful grin. *"I love you."*

"I love you too, Sebastian."

"Knock it off, you two. We've still got work to do." Matt's teasing voice sounded through their connection.

She turned back around, heat staining her cheeks red with embarrassment, but the men seemed to have gone on without them. Sebastian held her around the waist, her back to his chest, his chin resting on top of her head as she tried to follow the conversation.

"When will she be ready?" Atticus was asking Hiro.

Hiro shrugged. "A week, maybe less."

That soon? Christy couldn't believe she'd be ready for anything in so short a time, but she trusted Hiro to know his business better than she did.

"That gives us plenty of time to plan this out." Cameron nodded as he turned to the others. "Will you keep up surveillance on Steel and this Mario character?"

Hastings nodded. "I have agents on it right now, but this pair is hard to track. Now that we know there's a mage involved, I can guess why. Do you have anything we can use to help dispel the mage's influence?"

Cameron thought about that for a moment. "Perhaps," he

finally answered. "I'll work on something tomorrow and stop by your office later in the day, if that's all right. I need to consult with a friend who knows this kind of magic better than I before attempting the spell."

Hastings nodded. "That works for me."

"And you can send the surveillance bills to me," Sebastian said, drawing their attention. "You and your team deserve just compensation for your efforts, and it's our little problem that drew you into this, so it's only fair I pay you for your time."

Hastings seemed to take Sebastian's measure for a moment before replying. "I've heard good things about you from Matt, though I'll be honest, I've never dealt much with your kind. Now that I've met you, and now that I know who and what we're dealing with, I'll do the job for free. Our current Lords have sent down directives about this kind of thing. They've impressed upon us how very real the *Venifucus* threat is. They even warned that we might have to work across species to solve this problem. I wasn't crazy about the idea, but I can see the advantages. I'll work with you on this. No questions. No bill either."

"Very gracious of you, Mr. Hastings. Nevertheless," Marc said, taking the floor, "your company will receive some compensation for the time you put in on this. If not by Sebastian, then by me and my organization. We have the economic resources you do not, but you have the manpower and the ability to track these mortals during the hours of daylight, both of which are very valuable to us. As Master of this region, I thank you for your willingness to assist."

"Now then," Cameron brought them back to the plan, "we have about a week to set this up. When we're ready to go, we'll have Lady Christina well guarded as she confronts her husband. Chances are, nothing will come of the initial meeting, unless we're extremely lucky." Christy's stomach clenched at the idea of facing Jeff, but these amazing beings would back her up, and Sebastian was with her, in her very soul. She'd be okay. She had to do this.

"More than likely," Cameron continued, making notes on a pad as he spoke, "Jeff Kinsey will contact Steel or Mario shortly after Lady Christina leaves his presence."

"Why does he call me that?" she wondered silently.

"Because he first knew me as a British lord and you are my mate. In his mind, you are therefore my lady." Sebastian's calm voice answered her idle thought. His voice felt like a soft caress through her mind.

"Should I be calling you my lord?"

"Only under very special circumstances." The scandalous image he sent to her mind made her heat rise to her cheeks.

"Oh, you are wicked...my lord."

"Would you guys save that for later?" Matt groused. *"Or are you purposely trying to give me a woody I can't explain, in front of all these old dudes?"*

Christy had to camouflage her laughter by faking a cough, but Sebastian was much more in control.

"I'm going with Christina when she confronts Kinsey," Sebastian spoke, his voice rumbling against her back.

"Are you sure that's wise?" Cameron asked. "Your presence will take any doubt out of their minds that she's still mortal."

"I know, but I want to be there. I have to be there."

"But I thought you wanted me to do this on my own?" She turned, breaking free of his light hold.

"I want you to confront your past, but I never said you had to do it all by yourself. I'm your mate now, Christina. Where you go, I go. You'll confront Jeff, but I'll stand beside you every step of the way."

She shook her head. "I love you, but you don't know Jeff. If you come with me, it'll drive him to violence."

A spark entered Sebastian's eyes. "Let him try."

Christy laughed. It was a strange reaction, but she almost felt sorry for Jeff, with this amazing being wanting to tear him apart. Poor Jeff. He didn't have a clue just who—or what—he'd angered.

"Perhaps putting Sebastian out there will work to our advantage," Hastings said from the sidelines. "For one thing, he can help protect his mate if things turn ugly. For another, he'll serve as a focus for the *Venifucus*. If she goes on her own, the mage will keep a sharp eye out, looking for her maker. If he's with her, the mage might relax his guard, not expecting any further threat."

"Good point." Cameron wrote on his pad. "All right, laddie. You'll go with your lady. We'll back you up."

They talked a little more after that, but the majority of the points had been covered. Sebastian sent Christy off with Hiro to begin training while he dealt with the other men. It was a few hours, after a vigorous workout with Hiro, before Christy saw Sebastian again, but he'd been there, in the back of her mind all along. His existence in her mind was comforting, even when he wasn't an active presence. Just knowing they were connected on such an intimate level made her feel more secure than she'd ever felt in her life.

Chapter Seven

Sebastian was careful to shield Christina from the rest of the meeting while he laid down the law to every man present. He would brook no argument when it came to the safety of his mate. They discussed the very real dangers to her, both from her mortal husband and the potential threats from *Altor Custodis* and *Venifucus*.

When everyone else left, Sebastian and Matt headed for the *dojo*. There they spent a few enjoyable hours sparring, practicing and alternately teaching, testing and teasing Christina. The men had spent many evenings training together, but having Christina there made it more special. She brought life and happiness to the entire room. Even Hiro was lighter of spirit for her presence.

Christina left the *dojo* first, excused while the men practiced a few things that were beyond her abilities, and would be for some time. There were some limitations after all, to the acceleration the *were* blood had given her. Not many, but enough to make the moves the men practiced well outside her abilities—at least for a while yet.

By the time they finished, all three men were sweating, but they each wore pleased expressions on their faces. Hiro left first, heading for his home, which wasn't far.

"Are you staying today?" Sebastian asked Matt as he wiped his face with a towel.

Matt nodded, snagging his own towel. "Yeah, I thought I'd stick around, if that's okay."

"You know you're always welcome here, my friend."

"Well, I thought—until we're sure what's going on with Kinsey and Steel—I'd keep an eye out."

"Your vigilance is much appreciated. I'm not comfortable with recent developments."

"I figured as much. I've got that itchy feeling at the scruff of my neck and it's got me worried."

Sebastian's eyes were grim. "Yeah, me too."

The men left the *dojo*, parting at the door to the guest room that Matt used when he stayed over. He'd probably sleep until daylight, then change form and head out to prowl the grounds. Sebastian couldn't thank him enough for helping protect Christina. Matt's willingness to help went beyond friendship. This was the act of a brother—regardless of the fact they were different species.

By the time Sebastian entered the master suite, Christina was out of the shower, dressed in a lovely silk nightgown. Sebastian was glad to see she'd found the things he'd had delivered for her. She looked so lovely, sitting there, brushing her hair at the small vanity he'd brought into the room, just for her. Sebastian stood in the doorway, staring at her. She was so beautiful, it almost hurt. But it was the best kind of hurt in the world, for she was his. All his.

"Are you going to just stand there all night, or are you coming in?" Christina didn't even look at him, sensing his presence through their link. The same way he sensed her at all times.

Sebastian moved behind her. She sat before the vanity, brushing her hair as she watched her progress in the mirror. It was a fable that bloodletters had no reflection. Only those without souls had no reflection and while some indeed, had relinquished their souls over the centuries, Sebastian had never been acquainted with anyone who'd done so.

He leaned down and nuzzled her neck, holding her in front of him. She smelled so clean and good, he realized he needed a shower himself. Badly. Hiro and Matt had given him a hell of a workout.

Rising, he winked at her in the mirror. "Give me ten minutes. I need to get cleaned up."

"It'll take me that long to dry my hair. Take your time."

Sebastian didn't dally in the shower, but did spend a few minutes thinking of all the things he'd do to—and with—his lady love in the hours left before dawn. He grew hard just thinking about it. Luckily, the solution to his problem was waiting for him outside. All he had to do was decide how he would take her.

He wanted to show her something new, something a little bit wild. Perhaps it was time to visit the dungeon.

Minutes later, Sebastian led Christy through a doorway she hadn't noticed the night before inside the secret passageway.

"Where are we going?"

"There are still a few hours before sunrise. I plan to make good use of them." The look on Sebastian's face was downright wicked.

The passageway branched off to the left. Sebastian led her down the dark corridor to another door, well secured against casual invasion.

"There's a whole network of chambers and passageways down here, isn't there?"

"Very astute, my sweet." Sebastian unlocked the door and motioned her through, hitting a switch that brought honest-to-goodness torches flickering to life. "I had this place built a century ago with lots of little secret rooms, clever air vents and many ways out so I could never be caught down here without an escape route. The torches are gas powered. Nice effect, don't you think?" He seemed to consider the flickering flames as she noted for the first time the sparse furnishings of the room. "I haven't been down here in years, but I'm especially glad I had this room put in now that I have you."

"What is this place?" Christy turned in a circle, taking in the strange furniture, eventually coming back to face Sebastian. He had a mischievous glint in his eye as he watched her.

"Why, it's my dungeon, of course."

"Dungeon?" she repeated. It didn't look scary at all. She gazed at the strange furnishings with new eyes, but the padded table in one corner didn't look like a torture device. Nor did the horse-like bench in another nook. There were other things she didn't understand, and then she noticed the wall display filled with whips and paddles of different kinds. Still, none of them looked as if they could cause serious injury.

"I see you're confused. Have you never been spanked or tied up by a lover? Have you never been driven to the edge of madness by a loving, slightly rough touch, then allowed to catapult over only at the command of your man?"

"With Jeff?" She snorted. "Not likely. The only kind of sex we ever had was plain missionary and when he started getting violent, there was nothing sexy about it."

"Did you never have a lover besides him?"

She shook her head. "I was a virgin when I met him. Actually, I stayed a virgin until we were married."

"Ah, an old-fashioned girl. I like that." Sebastian moved closer to her. "It just so happens, I'm an old-fashioned man." He tickled her waist with teasing fingers, lightening the mood. "Did the unimaginative clod never tie you up for pleasure?"

She shook her head, titillated by the idea.

Sebastian grinned like a pirate.

"I think we'll start with that. I know he struck you, my love. I don't ever want you to be afraid of what you and I do together. I've never beaten a woman and I never will. But I have been known to spank, even tease with the lash, but never to hurt. Only to tantalize. Still, I don't think you're ready for that yet. Perhaps you never will be." His gentle expression reassured her. "And that's all right with me. I want only your pleasure."

"You think tying me up will bring me pleasure?"

"Don't tell me you've never thought about it. Before you met your boring husband, perhaps? Didn't you ever wonder what it would be like to be at the mercy of your lover, tied up for his convenience?"

She had to admit, there'd been times she'd wondered about it when she was younger. Sebastian saw the truth in her mind and grinned like the Cheshire cat.

"There is one big difference now though." Sebastian led her to the padded bench in one torch-lit corner. "With your new strength, there's little in this world that can hold you if you do not wish to be held. The bindings are merely decorative. You'll submit to me by choice, not because you're unable to do other than what I ask. You have free will in this, my love, and you always will." He helped her sit on the high table and kept his hands at her waist as they gazed into each other's eyes. "Will you submit to me? Will you at least try?"

Licking her lips, she gathered her courage. "I want to try, Sebastian. I want to do whatever you want. If I can."

He leaned in and kissed her. "That's all I can ask of you, my love." He settled her so she lay flat against the soft padding. Tugging the gown off her shoulders and down her arms, he pushed it downward until it was off her body, leaving her bare to his gaze. The soft silk slid over her skin, tantalizing each and every nerve ending on its way down.

He grasped her wrists and raised her arms above her head, positioning them at the corners of the table. Padded, mechanical restraints popped up from the edges of the table to encircle her wrists when he hit a lever with his foot. He checked the fit by slipping one large finger between her skin and the padded cuff. She had room to move without chafing her skin and he seemed satisfied. Skimming his big hands down her bare body, he repeated the process with her ankles, binding her to the devilish table, smiling all the while.

"Comfy?" he asked. She nodded, then gasped as the lower part of the table began to separate, drawing her legs apart. When they were spread wide, Sebastian stood between her legs. "Now the fun begins." He moved his foot on the levers near the floor. A motor activated, lifting the table until her hips canted toward Sebastian, her legs bent and spread as wide as they'd go.

It was decadent. It was heady. It was incredibly erotic to be displayed before him in such a way.

She was confident enough in her new strength and abilities to know she could easily escape the slender cuffs and table contraption if she wanted. She also knew Sebastian would let her up the moment she asked. But she wanted to stay. She wanted to see where his little game would lead, where his passion would take them. She trusted him and she wanted to please him, and in so doing, please herself.

Spread before him, her pussy grew damp. It was an amazing feeling to have the circulating air of the dungeon wafting against her most sensitive folds. She also felt the impact of Sebastian's gaze like a soft caress. His fingers stroked over her folds and into her core, testing her, measuring her readiness for what he planned next.

"You know," he spoke almost conversationally as he explored her most private place at his leisure, "back in my day, some medical men made a specialty of bringing women to orgasm. I've heard some of them employed special machines to excite the woman in question, or some of them would use their fingers." He leaned closer and she felt his hot breath whisper over her exposed folds. "We could pretend you're a society wife with a feeble husband who can't see to your needs. They often called these doctors in for nervous disorders. Tell me, my lady, are you of a nervous disposition?"

Christy gasped as he filled her with two fingers, stroking deep.

"What was that, my lady? I didn't quite hear you?" Sebastian chuckled as he pumped into her. "I asked if you were of a nervous disposition. Given to swoons and jitters, are you?" Christy nodded, unable to speak as she neared a peak of pleasure. "Ah, well, I have a solution for that, my lady. My, how much moisture you have here. That's a very good sign." He winked at her as she writhed on the table, his fingers pulsing in her core. Sebastian brought his other hand up to tease her clit and she went over the edge without once looking back.

"That's it, my dear. You come beautifully for me." His hands rode her throughout the climax, pulling out only when she'd quieted, to pet her damp curls. He placed a soft kiss on the top of her mound and moved away while she recovered, her eyes closed in pleasure.

Drifting in bliss, Christy felt a teasing sensation on her arm. Her eyes flew open to find Sebastian smiling down at her, a large, fluffy ostrich feather in one hand, a strip of black cloth in the other. It was the feather that had brushed her arm, she realized, raising gooseflesh with its tingling touch.

"Ready for more, my lady?" he asked, moving closer. He laid the feather aside, using both hands to show her the strip of cloth. "I'm going to blindfold you, sweetheart. Is that all right?"

Her pulse leapt at the idea. Moisture flooded her pussy. She couldn't believe how quickly Sebastian had her ready for more. All with just a few words.

"Yes, Sebastian." She raised up a little so he could put the blindfold in place. "Whatever you like."

"Oh, I like the sound of that." He kissed her, just once, as he lowered her back to the padded table. She felt movement at her side and knew he'd picked up the feather once more. A shiver coursed down her spine just thinking about the soft brush of that feather down her body, but Sebastian made her wait.

"You know," even his tone teased her, "anticipation can be something of an aphrodisiac. For example, here you lie, ready and waiting for me to touch you, anticipating where I will stroke first. Will my touch be light or hard? Firm or soft? Feather or fingers...or something else entirely?" She was aware of him moving around to her side, but still he didn't touch her. "Tell me, do you want my touch, my love?"

"Yes!" Her voice was whisper soft, but she knew he heard. She could feel the satisfaction in his mind as he teased her. Knowing that he drew pleasure from her excitement only made the yearning rise higher.

"Where do you wish me to touch you? Here?" He didn't wait for an answer, stroking the feather over her waist, down one side and up to her arm. "Or do you prefer here?" He drew the feather down the outside of her arm, raising gooseflesh in the path of the soft tormentor. "Do you like that?"

"Yes, Sebastian. Yes."

"Or how about here?" Suddenly the feather was at her ankle, rising up the inside of one thigh, sliding upward and leaving a wave of longing in its wake. He stopped just shy of the apex.

"Sebastian." She panted as her stomach clenched. The feather followed the ripples of her abdominal muscles as the need rose and thrummed through her being. "Please, Sebastian." The whispered plea moved him, she could tell from a hitch in his breathing. She felt the eager satisfaction race through his mind a moment before he stepped between her thighs and used the mechanism to lower the table, positioning her legs to his satisfaction.

A moment later, his cock filled her. He took her by storm, shoving home in one swift move. Then he stilled.

"Is that what you wanted, my lady?"

"Oh, yes." She moaned as he filled her. He was hot and hard, long and perfectly formed. She loved the feel of him inside her, but she needed more. She needed him to move. "Sebastian, please!"

He withdrew and rocked home again. She could feel how close he was to losing all control. It would take very little to drive him over the edge. She needed to drive him to that point, but she was blindfolded and restrained, unable to move. Still, there was one set of muscles sure to drive him insane.

She clenched around him, pleased when he groaned deep in his throat. She released, then did it again, with even better results.

"Christina! Lord, what you do to me!" Sebastian exclaimed as he started to move faster and she knew he was ready to burst. So was she. All it would take would be a few hard thrusts and she'd be over the moon. Tightening on him as he thrust deep, she matched his rhythm somewhat, unable to concentrate as sensation swamped her.

She cried out as the wave hit her, sweeping Sebastian along for the ride as he climaxed within her. He gripped her hips in his large hands, riding her deep and hard, pulsing hot in her depths as he came in spurts of creamy satisfaction.

Both of them were breathing hard as they crested the peak and started the lazy spiral back to earth. Sebastian stood over her, the wicked table cradling her still. Only then did she realize he hadn't fed.

In the aftermath, she thought through some of the things she'd seen in his mind. The knowledge he shared was plentiful, but she could only process a bit at a time and he had the ability to close off certain areas of this thoughts, which she considered a good thing. She followed his example and walled off the memories of violence at Jeff's hands.

She suspected Sebastian limited her access to things that he'd prefer to keep private. Past lovers, indiscretions, moments of violence, and the like. She didn't mind at all. She knew the measure of this man and she wouldn't change her mind about him no matter what he'd done in the distant past. She loved him for who he was now.

But the idea of other lovers still rolled through her mind.

"Sebastian," she asked as they both came back to earth, "will you still need to feed from other people now that we're...um...together?"

Sebastian pulled free from her body and began to undo the restraints on her feet. "Not anymore. From what I understand, the passion and blood we share between us will be enough to sustain us both."

"So I won't have to bite anyone but you?"

"Not if you don't want to. Now that we know for certain that we're mates, our love and the mingling of our blood will be enough to feed our souls and our bodies for the rest of our lives, barring some unforeseen circumstance." He removed the bindings from her wrists, hitting the controls to move her into a more comfortable position on the naughty table. "The only time I can foresee a need, possibly, to feed from another would be in case of emergency." He removed the blindfold and smiled down at her, leaning in for a languid kiss. The satisfaction in his eyes melted her heart.

The relief she felt at his words calmed her fears. She didn't want him biting other women any more than she suspected he wanted her to bite other men. What she'd learned of vampire feeding was both physical and psychic. At the moment of orgasm, energy flooded her system, renewing her life force with amazing power. The blood did the same, but in a different, more earthy way. With the psycho-sexual energy they generated between them—and Sebastian's reassuring words—Christy believed they could sustain each other for all eternity.

He led her from the dungeon room back to their bedroom and they made love again, and fed from each other, just before the sun rose. They slept the day away locked in each other's arms.

Chapter Eight

The days went by all too fast. Each night, the men gathered to discuss plans while Christy spent time with Hiro, learning the basics of self-defense with her new agility and strength. Sometimes Sebastian would join them, sometimes Matt, but each night after the training session and after the planners left, Christy would spend time with Sebastian. They'd sit and talk, or take a walk over the grounds and he'd teach her things she needed to know about being a vampire.

On one such night a few days after that first strategy session, they walked through the woods surrounding Sebastian's home. It was an estate, really, up in a secluded area of the hills. The place was a mansion, but not ostentatious at all. On the contrary, from the outside, the appearance of the house was very low-key, blending in nicely with the surrounding woodlands. Inside, of course, the house was a home. Comfy and lived in, she felt at ease there once she learned the layout of the many rooms in the vast space.

This night, Christy knew Matt prowled the woods. He'd stayed nearby more often since the news broke about just who might be gunning for them. Matt took the *Venifucus* threat very seriously and more *were* became involved in the case—at least those who would work with bloodletters. That was a term she'd heard them call Sebastian from time to time. It didn't sound very nice, but Sebastian seemed to prefer it to the word vampire. She didn't much care what word was used. Though "vampire" brought to mind Bela Lugosi and late night horror flicks, it was the word that sounded most modern to her.

Something the men had said the night before caught at her memory. She turned to Sebastian, gazing up at him in the dappled moonlight. He really was the most handsome man she'd ever seen.

"I'm glad you think so." He'd undoubtedly read the thought in her mind before she had a chance to speak.

"I know we're sharing a brain and all, but would you at least let me get a word out from time to time?" She shook her head in mock indignation as he tucked his arm around her shoulder, drawing her close as they walked along.

"I'm sorry, my love. I'll endeavor to do better from now on."

"You're not sorry at all. This mind reading thing goes both ways, you know."

Sebastian stopped and pulled her into his arms for a quick kiss. "You can read my mind anytime."

"Honestly." She sighed. "What I was going to ask, was if you knew how to shapeshift."

Sebastian let go of her arms and faced her. "It's something most of our kind take centuries to master. I became proficient early on, but only truly mastered the technique in the last century or so. Atticus and the others are older than me though, and have been shifting form for a long time."

"Really?" She grew excited by the idea. She'd seen Matt shift a few times and each time, she wondered what it would be like to walk on four paws instead of two feet. "What form can you take?"

Sebastian leaned against a tree, watching her with amusement clear on his handsome face. "I prefer the form of a wolf, but I can shift into almost anything. I can even be fog."

"Fog? Really?" The very thought of it amazed her. "I didn't know anyone could do that. So, it took you a while to learn, huh?"

"Actually, it wasn't the learning that took time, so much as the building of power. It takes a great deal of a certain kind of magic to be able to shift form. The *were* are born with it, but our kind must earn it and learn it over the centuries. Each new form takes a while to learn."

"Do you think I'll ever be able to do it?" She hated to get her hopes up, but it was something she'd thought about more and more since her conversion.

Sebastian straightened and put his hands on her shoulders, his expression quite serious. "I think you could probably do it right now, my love. It's one of the reasons I asked Matt to feed you in those first days. I was able to shift much sooner than most newly turned because my own first meal was from a wolf shifter. I knew feeding from Matt would give you the same advantage."

"Is that why you prefer the wolf form? Because your first meal was from a *were*wolf?"

"You know, I never quite thought of it that way, but perhaps you're right. I like the speed, agility and cunning of the wolf, not to mention the strength and deadly acuity. But my first blood might've had something to do with that preference, now you mention it."

"How do you do it? How do you shift?"

"You want to try?"

Her heart leapt with excitement. "Oh, yes. But what will I turn into?"

"It's very important to have a clear idea of what you'll become. You must hold the image of your new form in your mind's eye while you release the magic to change shape. Since you've seen Matt change and have a taste of his magic, why don't you try for a cat this first time?"

"All right." She closed her eyes picturing the form as clearly as she could in her mind.

Sebastian talked her through the process, coaching her to keep the image of the cat foremost in her mind as she gathered and released the energy that would cause the change.

He felt her focusing her will and was awed by the strength she already had for one so young. She shimmered and her form shifted, a moment later he was looking at a small, fluffy, white cat, no bigger than the common house cat.

Sebastian burst out laughing.

"What is it?"

"Oh, my love," he couldn't contain the laughter, *"I was expecting a cougar and you give me a kitten. Only you."*

She stumbled on her uncoordinated paws. Sebastian

chuckled as he bent to pick her up and stroked her soft fur.

"Of course," he mused aloud as she scratched her head along his sleeve, "it is rather *a propos*. You being a pussy cat, I mean." He chuckled as he walked back to the house, greeting the cougar that waited for them like a carved statue on the steps to the small stone terrace.

"Who's your little friend?" Matt asked in the back of their minds.

"Meet your creation." He dumped the fluffy white kitty onto the stone patio. She teetered to one side, unused to having four legs under her as the cougar bent down to sniff at her. "I give you, Lady Christina, the pussy cat."

"You've got to be kidding." Matt's reply was both shocked and amused. *"She's not much more than a mouthful, is she?"*

"Back off, big guy." Christy groused as she tried to steady herself on dainty paws.

Matt sat back, just looking at her. *"You're a vampire, sweetheart. You can take almost any form you want, and you choose this?"* The cougar shook his head from side to side, making a coughing noise that sounded a bit like rough laughter.

"He said to try for a cat. I'm a cat, aren't I?" She jerked her furry little head in Sebastian's direction. He couldn't help his amusement at her feline indignation.

"Well, you're cute, I'll give you that." Matt bent his head and touched her with one massive paw. *"But not very functional, are you? And not well camouflaged for night work either."*

"He's got a point. Can you change color, my love?" Sebastian thought it would be a good exercise of her new powers to try.

"How?" A plaintive meow accompanied her question.

"You must've had the image of this white puss in your mind when you shifted, right? Now imagine a black cat instead. Same cat, just color her black in your mind. It should only take a touch of magic this time. Not as much as you needed to shift fully, just a little zap to change color. Can you manage it?" He bent to stroke her soft fur, offering comfort as he monitored the struggle to control this intricate little detail in her mind.

As his hand brushed down her flank, the soft fur beneath

his palm turned from snow white to purest black. Her glistening green eyes stared up at him with triumph. *"Did it work? It feels like it did."*

Sebastian scooped her into his arms. "It worked, my love. My talented little mate. You're a natural." He held her close in his embrace, petting her silky coat.

"That is so cool." Matt sounded impressed. *"Wish I could do that."*

"You can't?" The black cat held out a little paw toward the cougar, her tail swishing lazily back and forth.

"No, sweetheart. That takes a different kind of magic than what I've got. What you see is what you get."

The black cat yawned, showing off her tiny, sharp teeth. Sebastian petted her, enjoying the slight purr of satisfaction under his fingers.

"I know you're tired. Shifting can be draining when you're new to it. What say you shift back and we'll rest up a bit?"

"Only a few hours to dawn, my friends," Matt observed as he stood and loped down the steps leading to the woods beyond the terrace. *"My advice to you...make the most of it."*

"Oh, we plan to." Sebastian didn't bother watching the big cat go, already heading indoors with the purring black pussy cat in his arms.

"If she needs any help shifting back, call me. I coached my little sister through it her first time."

"Thanks, Matt." Christy spoke in all their minds. *"You're a good friend."*

"I'll call if we need any help," Sebastian added with a chuckle, heading for their private getaway beneath the house.

Seeing the world through cat's eyes was a new and disorienting experience for Christy, but even stranger was the sensation of walking on four paws. She loved the way Sebastian's big hands could wrap completely around her furry body and each stroke of his fingers down her length sent shivers of delight through her from head to toe.

Having a tail was different too, and Christy knew she'd need to practice a bit in this form if she wanted to be able to walk straight. It made her think about other forms she could take. She honestly hadn't thought of herself as a cougar, but realized now it probably would have been a better alternative. Still, when Sebastian had talked about imagining a cat, she hadn't thought of Matt's beautiful, fierce and very masculine cougar. No, she'd thought of her neighbor's housecat. Silly her.

She'd always wanted a cat, but Jeff had been against it. He didn't want pets or children for that matter. At least not until *he* was ready.

Christy would have loved a baby, but was willing to wait to start a family. They'd married right out of college, so it made sense back then. Later, when Jeff started getting unpredictable, she realized it might be dangerous to bring a child into a home with his increasingly violent nature. Still, she'd dreamed about a baby, but that dream had been denied her. Hell, the selfish bastard she'd married wouldn't even agree to a pet.

"It's all behind you now, my love." Sebastian kissed the top of her feline head as he cradled her close. She knew he was sharing her thoughts. She wasn't used to that yet, but it was getting easier. It was comforting in a way, to know she was never alone, and she learned incredible things from looking into his memories. Still, she figured it could take a lifetime—maybe several—before she knew everything about the new man in her life.

And just having a new man in her life was a huge adjustment. The idea was intensely liberating. She almost didn't believe it, but for the new freedoms living with Sebastian brought her. Not to mention the magic.

Sebastian was the purest form of magic to her. He was love. He was hope. He represented everything she'd dreamed of but never had before...and so much more she couldn't even have begun to imagine.

"Are you about ready to try changing back?" He placed her in the center of the large bed, stroking her fur as he lay down next to her.

Her tail moved of its own accord, a sensuous sway behind her body. *"I'll try."*

Using images in their shared minds as well as coaxing, coaching words, he talked her through the energy build-up and the change that came with dispersal of the magic. When she blinked, she was looking at his beloved face once again through her own eyes.

And she was naked.

"What happened to my clothes?"

"Who cares?" Sebastian laughed and drew her into his arms. She slapped at his arm to get his attention and he drew back, sighing. "You have to think them back with you when you change back. That's another thing *were* can't do, but we can. It takes practice, my sweet, but you'll get there. For now though..." he swooped down and nibbled on her neck, "...I like you just the way you are."

"Mmm. Me too."

℘

About a week after their first encounter with Cameron, Christy was asked to forego training with Hiro one night and sit with Sebastian and his guests. That was new. She'd been sent to the *dojo* with Hiro to train every night while the men gathered to plot and plan. She'd used her time well with the vampire *sensei*, and had skills now she never would have dreamed of before.

But then, everything had changed for her in a short span of time. Jeff's complete loss of control had wrought repercussions he would never fully realize. Christy was still learning about her new life and her new abilities, though she was good enough now with her new skills, she didn't fear Jeff's physical strength anymore. She was way stronger than he'd ever be and intellectually she knew he wouldn't be able to raise a hand against her ever again, but emotionally it was still hard for her. She couldn't completely control her fear when the Master Vampire proposed they move on with the next step in the plan.

She had to confront Jeff for them—and even more importantly—for herself. She had to move forward with the divorce, and get her stuff. There were things in the house she wanted. Family photos and mementos from her childhood and college days. Jeff would relinquish them, she vowed, or he would regret it.

"Are you all right?" Sebastian stood behind her as she paused at the entry to the living room where the men were gathered. "I admire your determination, but you know, you aren't in this alone, my love. I'll be with you. If Jeff so much as looks at you funny, he won't know what hit him."

She turned and hugged him. Sebastian was her anchor, her safe haven, but more importantly, he gave her confidence she'd never had before. He complimented her shy nature and brought out the backbone Jeff had done his best to grind into the dirt. Sebastian was good for her.

"I love you, you know."

He kissed the top of her head. "I do. Almost as much as I love you."

"You guys about done with the mushy stuff?" Matt's voice came to them from the living room archway, making them laugh. He had been a good friend to them both in this crisis. Christy was a little shocked at how comfortable Matt was in their lives—especially after the way he'd been introduced to her. Christy wasn't in the habit of confronting former lovers every time she turned around, but then, she'd only had sex with three men in her entire life. Jeff, the bastard. Matt. And Sebastian.

Two out of three wasn't bad. *No*, she smiled as she walked into the room on Sebastian's arm, *not bad at all.*

Matt walked beside her, giving her a little tap on the butt that made her squeak. She sat on the couch between the two men. Matt hadn't been intimate with her since the night Sebastian and she had joined fully, but he'd been around the house. She knew he was guarding her—guarding them both actually. Matt obviously cared a great deal for Sebastian. She'd sifted through some of the memories of their friendship in Sebastian's mind and knew Matt was a very special man who'd faced his own demons. His willingness to put himself in harm's way for his friend spoke a lot about his character.

"Hiro says you've made good progress." Marc spoke as the meeting came to order. Hiro was seated in an overstuffed chair near the windows leading to the veranda. He nodded as the focus shifted to him, and Christy felt the weight of his approval. It gave her a warm sensation to know this patient, skilled man thought she'd done well under his tutelage.

"I feel good," she agreed. "I know you want me to go see Jeff and I think I'm ready. He's got some things of mine in the house I want." She twined her hand with Sebastian's at her side, drawing strength from his solid presence.

"That's good, and it fits well with our plans," Marc said, motioning to a man walking in from the patio. "Ah, Mr. Hastings, what do you have for us this evening?"

The *were* detective was bare-chested, but had on a pair of jeans he must've had stashed in the yard.

"We've got taps on the phone lines and a satellite trace on Kinsey's cell phone. If he makes the call, we'll have a decent shot at locating the other party." Hastings took a seat and Christy could see the lines of fatigue around his eyes. "We've got a positive I.D. on the second man in that photo. He's still going by the name Mario Gonzalez, but like Steel, he's hard to trace. Looks like he hooked up with Steel after the action in Montana, though. We were able to find no connection prior to last Yule, but after that, they show up fairly regularly together and in each sighting, there was something a little more sinister afoot."

"Such as?" Atticus prompted the man.

Hastings sighed and sat forward, bracing his elbows on his knees. His expression was not reassuring.

"Late last December they hooked up in New Mexico. During the last week in December, a newly mated *were*wolf couple were found shot to death, execution style, with silver bullets, in their own home. A hefty bounty is still out for the murderer, but there was no trace of entry or exit and the pack scented strong, foreign magic at the crime scene."

"That's not good." Matt's face was grim.

"It gets worse. The next time I can confirm a sighting of the two men together is late March in Tampa. A week later, a family of *were*panthers were found hanging from a tree in the Everglades. Mother, father, and six cubs of varying ages. Poisoned with silver and strung up to die."

"That's horrible!" Christy couldn't help the shudder of horror that passed down her spine. "Who would do such a thing?"

"*Venifucus* are ruthless, ma'am," Hastings answered, grim resignation in his eyes. "I hadn't seen it before in my lifetime, but these murders match up to descriptions of things done in the distant past. These aren't the only incidents. *Were* clans and tribes from around the world have reported an increase of murderous deaths in the past year when I sent out the request for information. Normally we don't have all that much interaction, but now that the red flag's been raised, the current Lords are going to do something about it. They're calling a Gathering."

"That's going to be dangerous." Matt looked truly upset.

Hastings nodded. "Which is why I'd like to have this matter cleared up before the leaders come together. If we can eliminate at least this one threat, perhaps we can make the Gathering that much safer."

"When are they meeting?" Marc asked quickly, then held up a hand. "I know you won't give me specifics, but we need a round estimate so we know what our parameters are here. And I want one of you to carry a message back to your Lords." Marc's stern gaze passed from Matt to Hastings and back again. "I want a meeting. *Venifucus* threaten both our people. I'd like to work with the *were* to counter that threat." Marc laughed at the shocked looks on both *were* faces. "It's not unprecedented. Read your histories, boys. Elspeth was banished before only when all supernatural races worked in concert against her. I, for one, won't wait until I'm looking into her damned eyes to form an alliance. You tell your Lords, I'm looking to broker a deal between us for mutual cooperation and protection. The sooner we get comfortable working together, the better we'll be able to face the coming threat."

Sebastian nodded in agreement. "Marc's right. This situation is a case in point. Working together, we'll be more of a match for whatever's coming than if we each try to work separately. I think it's a good idea."

"All right," Hastings said, his expression wary, "I'll try to set up a conference call."

"Thank you." Marc looked relieved, if Christy was any judge. He leaned back in his chair, more at ease. "Now, what other terrible things have followed Steel and his buddy, Mario, around?"

Hastings shook himself, getting back to his report and Christy feared what he had to say by the look in his eyes. "Outside of Boston, May of this year. A week after Steel and

Gonzalez were confirmed in the area, a den of vampires were staked out in the sun. Twelve in all, mostly women and two young."

"Good Lord!" Sebastian's hand squeezed hers as the news hit him hard.

"And in July, after the last confirmed sighting, a very strong magical attack was made against one of your kin, Cameron." Hastings nodded toward the back of the room where Cameron had snuck in at some point without her realizing it.

"Who?" he demanded.

"Duncan," Hastings sighed, "but his vamp buddy, Dante d'Angleterre, was there to help and he escaped mostly unharmed. Just a bit singed from what I heard. Turns out, since the action up North with the *Were*Lords and their Lady, Dante and Duncan have been hanging around together. Good thing for your kin, in this case."

"I last saw Dante decades ago," Atticus mused. "I had no idea he'd hooked up with a fey."

"Half-fey," Cameron corrected. "Last I heard, Duncan was banished to the Isle of Nevermore for pissing off Queen Mab. Had to be some pretty powerful magic to get him into this realm."

Hastings nodded. "The new priestess brought him here. She's formidable, from all accounts."

"So are you, my love." Sebastian's voice sounded through her mind as his fingers squeezed hers in reassurance.

"All right. This is good to know. We need to take this threat as seriously as possible and we all might just live through it." Marc took charge of the meeting once more. "We need to catch these two. We need to know if Steel is the *Venifucus* or if Gonzalez is the infiltrator."

"Or both," Atticus put in dryly from the side of the room.

"Or both," Marc agreed. "But we need to find them first. That's where you come in, Christy. If you're sure you're up to it."

Swallowing hard, Christy sat up a little straighter. "I'm up to it. I need to face Jeff and set the wheels in motion. I want a divorce and I want my stuff. It's as simple as that."

Sebastian folded her hand into his and held it against his chest. "Then it's a good thing I asked my lawyer to come here tonight. She's already started the paperwork and I want you to sit down with her and go over the particulars." Christy was surprised, but she read the real shock on Matt's face when Sebastian turned and spoke to him. "Would you be so kind as to let her in, Matt? I believe she's coming through the forest as we speak. Show her to the gold guest room. She sent her things ahead."

"She's a shifter?" Matt's expression screamed curiosity, as did the expressions of some of the other men in the room. "You been holding out on me, old friend?"

"She's a long-time associate who's been hiding out, more or less, for the past several years. I respected her right to inform the *were* community of her presence when she was ready. It appears, that time is now." Sebastian sighed. "She's been my lawyer for the past five years, but I didn't want her connected to me publicly, for her sake. So far she's managed to live under everyone's radar."

Christy was curious about the woman she could now see in her lover's mind. He felt a fondness for the girl, but it was more like fatherly interest than that of a man for a woman. She looked a bit deeper and realized Sebastian had played a large role in this woman's life, rescuing her when her family was killed and supporting her while she finished high school, then college and eventually law school, all from behind the scenes.

She saw more about the woman in her mate's mind and a smile spread slowly over her features. Matt was going to be in for a shock.

Matt's head lifted and he sniffed the air, zeroing in on the big patio doors. Quickly he stood and opened the nearest one.

Head and tail held high, a sleek Florida panther padded daintily into the room, surprising everyone but Sebastian and Christy. The cat stood on the threshold, seeming a little skittish when faced with so many people. Matt crouched down and held out one hand towards her.

"Where've you been hiding, little lady?" Christy saw Matt wink, his charm coming to the rescue. "I'm Matt. If you'll follow me, I'll take you to your things."

With a regal nod of her feline head, the cat assented and

followed silently after the big man. Sebastian smiled indulgently, waving once to the cat, before turning back to Christy.

"Give her about five minutes, then go save her from Matt's curiosity, will you?" A smile played about his handsome face. "You two should discuss the legal aspects of your divorce in private." *"Plus,"* he added in her mind, *"as you can probably guess, she's shy around other supernaturals, especially shifters. I'd rather not everyone here see her human face so she can retain at least a little anonymity in this."*

"I understand." Christy leaned in to place a soft kiss on Sebastian's cheek. *"You're a good man, Sebastian. Morgan is lucky to have you for a champion."*

"Morgan?" Matt's triumphant tone sounded through their minds. *"So that's this little panther's name? Sebastian, you realize she could be under cougar clan protection, right? She's a related species. A cousin, more or less."*

"That's up to her, Matt." Sebastian's voice was firm. *"She's been through a lot and doesn't have much trust for anyone. Not even her fellow shifters."*

"That's a shame, Sebastian. Truly." Matt sounded genuinely upset at the idea. *"But I'll have to tell my brother Grif. He could at least keep an eye out for her from a distance, if nothing else."*

"Why do you think I asked you to escort her, Matt? She needs her own kind, even if she doesn't quite realize it yet. Take it slow, my friend. Tonight you've met. Next time, perhaps you can take it a bit farther. Believe me, it was hard enough to get her to agree to outing herself even this much. She would rather have stayed hidden for the rest of her days, but that's no way to live. Not when there are other were *like her nearby, willing to accept her for who she is. Just tread lightly. That's all I'm asking."*

"Heard and understood, my friend."

Christy checked her watch and realized enough time had passed. She stood gracefully and gave Sebastian a peck on the cheek before excusing herself from the room full of men. Following Matt's scent, she found him pacing outside a door in one of the far hallways.

"She's changing," he said quietly, a hurt and troubled

expression on his face. "Ordered me right out of the room with an imperious tail wag. This little kitty isn't used to being around other shifters."

Christy went up to him and hugged him. It was the comfort she would offer any friend. Regardless of how they'd met, and the intimacies they'd shared, she knew they would always be friends. He'd given her a part of himself and she would be forever grateful to him for his generosity of spirit, loyalty, and incredible strength of character.

With a reassuring smile, she stepped back and knocked on the door. "Morgan? It's Christy. Matt's here too. May we come in?"

The door opened and a gorgeous young woman stood there, looking a bit nervous as her topaz eyes darted from Christy to Matt and back again. When they made no move forward, she relaxed a bit and seemed to get a hold of herself. She stepped back for them to enter.

Christy went in first, but stopped Matt just inside the door. "Matt's not staying, but Sebastian thought you should meet."

The woman nodded, swallowing hard. "So he said on the phone. I'm Morgan Chase."

Matt towered over both women, though Morgan was quite a bit taller than Christy. He held out one hand to the woman and gave her his best roguish grin. "Matt Redstone." They shook hands and Morgan seemed to ratchet down her nerves another notch. "I want to extend a little invitation to you, Ms. Chase. My oldest brother is Alpha of the cougar clan in these parts. Your breed is like a cousin to ours and you'd be welcome in the clan. If you ever need anything, please don't hesitate to call." Matt reached into his pocket and fished out a business card, handing it to Morgan. "You can reach me or any of my brothers through Redstone Construction at any time. All of the office staff are *were*, so you can talk freely to anyone who answers the phone."

Morgan examined the card then tucked it away in her pocket, her expression thoughtful. "That's very kind of you, Mr. Redstone. I can't say for certain whether I'll take you up on the offer, but I'll definitely think about it."

Matt nodded, not entirely happy with the answer, Christy could tell from the tightening of his mouth, but willing to move in slow steps, as Sebastian had requested. He backed toward the door, leaving the women to their business.

"I'll be here all night either talking with the guys or prowling the perimeter. Perhaps I'll see you on your way out?"

Morgan nodded, seeming not entirely pleased by the idea. "Perhaps. It was nice meeting you, Mr. Redstone."

"And you, Ms. Chase." Matt winked at Christy then headed back down the corridor toward the living room. Christy closed the door and leaned against it.

"I understand you're Sebastian's lawyer." Christy opened the conversation with an innocuous observation, hoping to get the tense woman to relax a bit.

Morgan nodded as she moved toward the small sitting area that had a low table and several chairs. "Sebastian saved my life when I was a teen. He put me through college and law school."

"I know." Christy moved nearer the other woman and took a seat, satisfied with the surprise on Morgan's face. "Sebastian and I are joined. It's very new to me, but I can read his memories, and I've seen you in them. He's very fond of you, you know."

Morgan seemed troubled as she sat opposite Christy and pulled out a large brown folder, setting it on the table between them. "It's nothing romantic. He's like an older brother or father figure to me."

Christy decided to cut Morgan some slack. "Oh, I know that. Don't worry. I can access his feelings too. I know he loves you like a kid sister. It's very different from the love he and I share. I just wanted you to know where we all stand. This vampire business...and the *were*...it's all very new to me. I didn't know a thing about any of this supernatural stuff until a few days ago."

"When your husband beat you to death."

It wasn't a question and Christy realized this woman didn't pull her punches. Her momentary good mood shattered, Christy nodded.

Morgan opened the big envelope and started sorting through papers. "Well, the good news is, we have a good case for divorce. Even with the altered medical reports, there's still enough evidence to prove he mistreated you, and your testimony will clinch it, if he wants to fight you in court. Any lawyer worth his salt will tell your husband to give you what you want because you could easily pursue criminal charges against him, not only for the assault and battery, but also for raiding your bank accounts. Did you know he's made you a pauper?"

"What?" Dismay filled her. She knew Jeff was a rat, but she wouldn't have thought he'd be bold enough to rob her blind.

Morgan nodded. "I've followed the paper trail and it's pretty clear he's been setting this up for a while. He's been siphoning money off the trust your parents left to you for the past year or so, but now he's come out in the open and started making huge withdrawals. If you were a corporation, I'd call Jeff Kinsey an embezzler. But since you're still married, the law is tricky."

Christy sat back in her chair and puffed out air, trying to control her anger and dismay. She was angry at Jeff and even angrier at herself for being so stupid.

A perfunctory knock sounded before Sebastian opened the door and entered. He moved straight to the small loveseat Christy sat on and pulled her into his arms, kissing her temple and drawing her close. A knowing look passed between the lawyer and Sebastian. He'd known what Morgan had discovered already.

"It'll be all right, my love. We'll fix this. Don't worry."

"But all my money—"

Sebastian shushed her with soothing strokes of his hands down her arms. "I have all the money we'll ever need, Christina, but Morgan will see to it that Jeff makes restitution. Won't you, my dear?"

Morgan nodded, a cunning feline smile lighting her tawny eyes. "With pleasure. Sebastian's right, Mrs. Kinsey. Your husband wasn't very smart about the way he took your money. I have more than enough evidence to get him to do pretty much anything we want."

"Don't call me that. Call me Christy, okay? I don't ever want to be called by his name again."

Morgan smiled, an understanding light in her tawny eyes. "All right, Christy. Shall I start the paperwork to change everything back to your maiden name then?"

"No," Sebastian objected. "She'll be taking my name. As soon as possible, we're getting married."

Congratulations were offered by the young attorney and Christy basked in the fond feelings Sebastian directed her way. She also reveled in the idea this would be no quickie wedding like the one she'd had with Jeff in Las Vegas. No, this time would be for keeps. Forever. With their friends gathered to witness their happiness.

Sebastian left a few minutes later and the women got down to the nitty gritty of the divorce papers. There were certain provisions Christy wanted to insist upon and others that didn't really matter. The house for example. She didn't want anything to do with that house. Jeff had chosen and bought it without her input and it held nothing but bad memories for her.

They talked over the specifics for about an hour. Christy liked Morgan's quick mind and dry humor. She was efficient, witty and a little ruthless, which was a good quality in a lawyer, and Christy thought perhaps, she'd made a new friend in the young *were* woman.

Chapter Nine

The next evening, right after sunset, Sebastian and Christy headed to her old house by very conventional means, taking one of Sebastian's cars—a midnight blue Lamborghini—and driving the forty-five minutes from Sebastian's estate to her old neighborhood. Christy had lived in a very nice upper middle class section, but it was nothing like the exclusive area Sebastian called home. Seeing his estate from the outside, she was once again amazed by the simple majesty of his home. Just driving down the winding driveway that led from the seven-bay garage building to the front gate was impressive.

After seeing the way Sebastian lived, it was a little embarrassing to worry so much over the money Jeff had stolen from her. Though a huge amount to her, it was probably pocket change to Sebastian. Still, it was her money and she'd also paid for the house Jeff had bought after the wedding. Standing on principle, Christy wanted what was hers back. She deserved at least that after putting up with Jeff.

Christy clutched the papers Morgan had drawn up and left with her the night before. All she had to do now was work up the nerve to give them to Jeff. He'd heard about the divorce, which was what had set him off, but he'd yet to be served the papers. Sure, they could've hired someone to give him the papers, but it was important to their plan that Christy see Jeff in person. It was also important, on a personal level, that she confront him.

After his last blowup, Christy feared Jeff's reaction, but another part of her—the brave part that gained strength every day from Sebastian's loving care—was looking forward to seeing how she'd do against Jeff now. She almost relished the idea of giving him a little back of what he'd dealt.

While not a violent woman, Christy had been pushed beyond her limits and she figured it was healthy to fantasize about planting her fist in Jeff's face. Not that she'd ever do it. Well, not unless he swung first. She felt a surge of excitement and fear mixed together. If he tried to hurt her, she wondered if she'd freeze or if she'd have the wherewithal to defend herself this time. Now that she knew how to do so and had the power to back it up.

Sebastian reached over the center console and placed one warm hand over hers. She was gripping the envelope with the divorce papers so tightly, her knuckles were white.

"I'll be with you, Christina. Kinsey will never be able to harm you again."

"Is it bad of me to want to punch his face in?" Christy turned in her seat to watch Sebastian's strong profile as he drove with confidence down the streets of her old neighborhood.

He laughed. "Not at all. And if you don't, perhaps I will." Sebastian lifted her hand to his lips and kissed her knuckles before releasing her to downshift.

Within moments, they pulled up in front of her old house. It had never really been a home to her, though she'd tried her best. It was a beautiful place, but she wouldn't miss it.

"Are you ready?" Sebastian shut off the engine and turned to her.

Christy took a deep breath, trying to steady her nerves. "As I'll ever be, I guess."

Sebastian got out and came around to open her door, ushering her from the low-slung sports car. His manners were impeccable and Christy smiled up at him as she stood, though inside, she quaked with nervous excitement. The coming minutes would set events in motion, both in her personal life, and in the plan the men had devised to deal with the magical threat.

Christy had been taken to the hospital with little more than her bathrobe, so she had to dig up the spare key from the side of the house to enter. She considered ringing the bell, but dammit, it was still her house. She could enter it if she wanted to. And she could bring a friend inside as well.

Christy opened the door and stepped inside. Sebastian waited outside until she turned. "Please come in, Sebastian."

Sighing, he stepped over the threshold. *"Glad you said that."*

"So those old myths about having to invite a vampire in are true?"

"It's tradition, love." He tugged at his collar and looked a tad uncomfortable. *"We are creatures of habit and after living so long, sometimes tradition is all we have left."*

"Well, consider yourself permanently invited into this house. It's still mine and I can damn well invite whoever I want inside."

Sebastian placed one warm hand on her shoulder, squeezing with gentle pressure. *"Well said, my love. Feeling independent, are we?"*

"I'm preparing to do battle."

Sebastian chuckled as they moved down the hall toward the back of the house. *"Good for you, Christina. Remember, I'm here for you if you need me."*

She stopped to look up into his eyes. *"I'll always need you, Sebastian."*

"Well, look who's decided to come crawling back." Jeff stood in the light from the kitchen, a beer in one hand.

Christy spun to face him, her heart in her throat. Sebastian's warm presence behind her gave her courage.

"Jeff."

"Is that all you can say? Where the hell have you been for the past week?" His voice rose. "Who is this guy? One of your friends' wacko husbands? Is that who you've been with? One of your weirdo college friends?"

"Jeff, you nearly killed me." Christy's voice was pitched low, but the words cut across the dim hall.

"You don't look hurt to me," he sneered.

"But I was," she whispered.

"Courage, my love." Sebastian's voice in her mind steadied her.

She moved forward, and incredibly, Jeff fell back, moving into the kitchen. He put the island in the center of the room between them, placing his half-finished beer on the counter. Christy and Sebastian stayed on the other side of the large kitchen, but the lighting was better in here. Jeff's eyes followed them with rage and suspicion. Christy remembered that look, but this time, she didn't have the same level of fear. In fact, the more time she spent in Jeff's presence with Sebastian beside her, the more she saw how pathetic Jeff really was. All the fear he'd taught her in recent months dropped away to be replaced by contempt.

"You've abused me for the last time, Jeff. I came here get my stuff and give you these." She slapped the papers on the table between them but he made no move to retrieve them.

"What's that?" Jeff eyed the folded stack of papers, anger causing color to rise in his face.

"Divorce papers."

Jeff swore, but didn't touch the papers, eyeing them, and her, with building rage. "You little bitch!"

He stormed around the table and raised his hand, but the blow never landed. Christy was long gone and Jeff's balled fist struck empty air, throwing him off balance.

Everything happened in slow motion. Christy saw Jeff's fist coming at her face, frame by frame, as she moved lightning fast out of the way. She went low, as Hiro had taught her and used a sweeping motion of her leg to drop Jeff to the floor, easy as pie. Jeff hit the table leg on the way down and lay on the ground, a look of surprise on his face as he clutched his side.

"What the hell was that?" Fury shone in his eyes. Fury...and fear.

"That was me not taking any of your crap anymore, Jeff. I came to get my things. I expect you to stay out of my way while I do it." She smoothed her shirt as she spoke, trying to control the trembling of her hands. She'd just stood up to Jeff's anger and it felt good. Damn good.

"In fact," Sebastian spoke for the first time, "you should probably go have those ribs looked at. That was a nasty fall. How clumsy of you." Sebastian's chastising tone increased Jeff's anger, but she wasn't afraid anymore.

"Who the fuck are you to tell me what to do in my own home?" Jeff rose to his feet, clutching his side, his breath hissing out in fury and pain.

Sebastian towered over Jeff, using his greater size to intimidate. Christy could also feel a bit of Sebastian's mind magic in the air. She'd bet he was adding some psychic persuasion to his words and it appeared to be working. Jeff's face went a little slack and a fraction of the anger drained away from his features.

"I'm the man who will rip your heart out if you ever raise a hand to this woman again." The growling promise in Sebastian's voice sent a shiver down her spine. Jeff staggered back, using the kitchen counter for support.

He looked from Sebastian, to her, and back again. Rage showed in every stiff line of his body, as he edged toward the back door that led to the garage.

"This isn't over, bitch. You and your freaky boyfriend had better be gone when I get back. I don't know what he did to you, but you're not the woman I married."

Christy faced him as he drew the door open. "No, I'm not, Jeff, and I never will be again. I should have found the courage to shoot you the first time you slapped me. It would have been worth the prison time just to get away from you!" She screamed at him, but Jeff was already out the door and heading for his ego car—a late model Lexus he'd bought with her money. "You bastard!"

Tears formed in her eyes and her body shook with turbulent emotion. It felt good to fight back, to say some of the things she'd bottled up inside. It was cathartic to see Jeff scurrying away like a mangy cur with his tail between his legs.

It was about time.

Sebastian came up behind her as Jeff roared out of the drive. Warm hands settled on her shoulders, rubbing in comfort as he moved his body into alignment with hers. She relaxed back against him.

"You're sexy when you're angry."

Sebastian's rumbling words tickled her ear and startled her into laughter. That felt good too as his arms lowered to her waist, embracing her.

"You're good for me, Sebastian. Without you, I never would have found the courage to stand up to that bastard."

"You always had it within you, my love. You just didn't have the means or opportunity to let the real woman out. Now you do, and I, for one, am proud of you." Sebastian turned her in his arms and held her close, kissing the top of her head.

"Oh, Sebastian." She raised her lips to his, seeking his kiss. Whenever he kissed her, all was right with the world and nothing else existed.

But he pulled back much too soon. With an apologetic smile, he reached for the cell phone at his waist.

"I have Matt on standby. He's got a pickup truck, so anything you want, we can take with us now."

"What would I do without you? You've thought of everything, haven't you?" She marveled at the effort he'd put in on her behalf.

"I try." He punched a speed dial button, said a few words, and a moment later shut the phone. "He's around the corner. He'll be here in a few minutes. Why don't we go through and see what you want to take with you?"

She reached up to cup his cheek, looking deep into his eyes. "I love you."

He turned and kissed her palm. "And I you."

While they were lost in each other, Matt arrived and rang the doorbell, breaking them apart. Christy felt flushed as she headed down the hall to open the door. Matt winked, greeting her with a kiss on the cheek as he entered.

"You okay, sweet thing?"

"As good as can be expected, I guess." She tilted her head, considering. "Actually, better than that. Thanks for coming over, Matt. Once again, you're saving my life."

He shrugged. "What are friends for?"

Over the next twenty minutes, the three of them went through the house room by room and cleared out the few items Christy wanted. Most were heirlooms from her family of little monetary value, but precious to her for the memories they held.

℘

As Jeff drove himself to the emergency room for X-rays he placed a call on his cell phone. Damned if that weirdo Ben Steel hadn't been right. The woman who'd just decked him was most definitely *not* the same mousey girl he'd married after college. Christy was different now. She had a strange look in her eye and a backbone she'd never possessed before.

The man with her gave him the creeps as well. Eyes of a stone killer, Jeff hadn't liked anything about the sinister character and it killed him to think his wife was most likely fucking the bastard.

Well, Jeff would find a way to put a cramp in the asshole's style. Steel didn't say much, but his friend Mario had told Jeff a few things. He claimed Christy's old college friends had gotten mixed up with a bunch of vampires. Vampires! For cripes sake.

Jeff had laughed at the little man when he'd said it, but after looking into those cold eyes, he wasn't so sure. And what else could give his wife her sudden Supergirl complex? Christy had always been a klutz, but tonight she'd gone all *Crouching Tiger* on him. It wasn't normal. Not in a week. Not after a lifetime of ineptitude.

And she was strong too. He'd felt the power behind her leg sweep. She had new skills that couldn't be learned in a week. Not even if she'd been a top athlete before she'd disappeared from the hospital without a trace. That was weird too. Oh, he figured her friend, Jena, was hiding her at first, but he'd kept an eye on Jena and knew Christy hadn't been with her do-gooder doctor friend.

So where had she been for the past week? And how could she have healed so quickly? He knew damned well he'd hurt her bad. He'd been a little out of control, and had probably gone too far, but the bitch pissed him off. She truly did. All she had to do was breathe and he started to feel the need to slap her. Over the years he'd lost it a time or two, but nothing like that last encounter. The devil had been riding his shoulder that last time and he'd damned well intended to kill her.

In retrospect, he was glad she'd lived because otherwise he'd still be in jail. So the bitch was good for something, besides her money.

Jeff placed the call to Steel, as requested, surprised when Steel seemed to take for granted Christy's new superpowers.

The man was just like his name—steel. Nothing affected him, and nothing caused a reaction. Jeff wondered what it would take to get a rise out of the guy, but didn't care to push him too far. Steel had eyes like that guy with Christy. Cold, calculating, and their icy blueness chilled Jeff to the bone.

Steel ended the call and sat silent, thinking over the possibilities. Christina Kinsey was, almost without a doubt, a vampire now. Otherwise, she never would have been able to stand up to her bully of a husband. Steel had a good idea of what had happened last week. Christy ended up in the hospital, and her friends were notified. Then suddenly she was gone. Poof. No record of the specifics of her injury or prognosis, and memories all over that floor of the hospital were suddenly fuzzy.

Steel had seen it before. He passed no judgment on the bloodletters, but for the woman he felt compassion of a sort. No female deserved to be beat up by the man who'd promised to love, honor and protect her before God and man.

Kinsey was a bastard, but he was also Steel's best source for information at this point. Of course, Mario Gonzalez seemed to have an inside track too, but Steel hesitated before placing the call to his associate. More and more, he felt something about Mario was off, but he didn't know quite what. Mario's information was good and he seemed nice enough on the surface, but there was something...

Steel sighed, letting go of his reservations. He needed backup and like it or not, Gonzalez was it. Flipping open his cell phone, he dialed the number. A few minutes later, it was done.

He went out to get lunch and a thermos full of coffee before he sat down to work on his report. A good meal would go a long way toward making the necessary paperwork easier to bear. Spotting a likely deli down the block from his hotel, he got a sandwich and sat down at one of the casual tables out front to eat. It was a nice day out, but the quiet made him too introspective.

Steel had laid down his weapons, for the most part, several years ago. He'd resigned after a mission turned hideously bad.

In a war-torn rain forest, he'd learned the real truth about the world. He'd learned the hard way about shifters and other kinds of supernaturals.

And he would never be the same.

He'd been contacted by a representative of the *Altor Custodis* not long after. How they'd gotten his name, he still didn't know, but this band of watchers had even more resources than Interpol or the CIA. He ought to know. He'd worked with both during his long career in black ops.

All in all, this new gig wasn't bad. Steel traveled the country at his own pace, doing investigations and sending back reports. His expenses were taken care of and he got a nice, hefty bounty for each report he sent in. The money was going straight into his retirement fund—an overseas account he'd set up with an eye toward disappearing and reinventing himself once he was too old to work and still young enough to enjoy life a little. But the AC job wasn't that difficult. At least his life wasn't in constant jeopardy, as it had been elsewhere.

Sure, he had to be covert. A lot of the supernaturals he investigated would take exception to being watched and documented, so there was still enough of an element of danger to amuse him and keep him on his toes. But it wasn't nearly as bad as the old days. Steel was too good now to be tracked, seen or caught.

Or so he thought.

He'd just taken a bite of his sandwich when the hairs on the back of his neck prickled in alarm. He was being watched. No, more than that. He was being *stalked*.

Steel set aside his lunch and took a casual look around. Three marks—southwest, northwest and due east. That left him little choice for escape, but he spotted a few small alleys and driveways between the buildings that could prove useful. The three all had the look of *were*. Well, wasn't *that* interesting?

They'd crept up on him, though how they'd managed to do it, he didn't understand. Sure, they were *were*, but Steel prided himself on his instincts. He'd have thought no supernatural could take him unaware after the training he'd received from the AC. Perhaps today was the day he'd be proven wrong, but he wouldn't go quietly.

Aware of his odds, he had to make a quick decision. Flee, fight or surrender. It wasn't in his nature to surrender right off the bat, and he wasn't in the mood for a fight. For one thing, he had no beef with these people. He had a few principles left and one of his cardinal rules was never to kill someone who didn't deserve it.

He didn't recognize any of these shifters, but could tell right off they were supernaturals. They didn't try to hide it. In fact, they let the distinctive shift show in their eyes—about the equivalent of a muscle man flexing. It was a silent signal that said, "Don't fuck with me." He saw the eyes flare on the woman heading straight for him and didn't stick around to find out why a bunch of *were* had tracked him down. So he took the third option. He fled.

But he didn't get far. They'd double teamed him, which meant they wanted him bad. The second string was waiting as he fled down an alley, and this time he recognized the leader of the group, a *were*hawk named Collin Hastings. Steel knew the man's reputation as an elite private detective and had even seen his service record.

Hastings had served in the U.S. Army Rangers. Seemed he was a natural parachutist. If only his superiors had known the man gliding so effortlessly on the wind currents was as at home in the sky as he was on land. But the army didn't know everything about Hastings. They'd signed him up, trained him, and let him go when his last stint was over.

To be fair, Hastings had spent more than his share of time in the army. He'd re-upped a few times, rising through the ranks to retire as a captain. Privately Steel thought the *were*hawk would still be in, had his lack of appropriate aging not been so visible. Even the army would eventually look twice at a man who didn't seem to age at all.

Steel stopped running when he saw the second team closing in. He was in an alley and *were* blocked both ends. They'd trapped him good and well. Even with all his training and experience, he knew he didn't stand a chance against six *were*creatures, at least one of whom he knew could claim the high ground in the form of a raptor. He cursed as he raised his hands in surrender. No sense getting the snot beaten out of himself by seeming to resist. These folks wanted to talk to him and they'd gone through a hell of a lot of trouble to do it. The least he could do was hear what they had to say.

"All right, you got me." He spoke loud enough to be heard by sharp *were* senses. "Now will someone tell me what the fuck is going on here?"

Hastings strode forward, his people closing in around Steel. "We mean you no harm, Mr. Steel. As long as you're not *Venifucus*."

Venifucus? Steel started at the word. He'd been briefed about the ancient evil society, but his handlers in the *Altor Custodis* claimed the *Venifucus* were long gone. His interest was piqued. Why would these people think he was one of those long-gone bad guys? Unless...

"I heard they were wiped out a few centuries ago. You've got the wrong guy."

He stared down the leader of the group, impressed with the way Hastings carried himself. Here was a man who knew the score, and how to operate in the real world. Steel respected that. He thought they might've even been friends had they met under different circumstances.

"Haven't you heard? They've been making a comeback. Whether or not you're one of them remains to be seen, Mr. Steel, but you'll understand we have to make certain."

"I'm listening."

Hastings' head tilted, his ears cocked. Steel knew that look. The *were* had exceptional hearing and could pick up stuff most humans would never hear.

"Not here," Hastings said shortly. "Please come with us, Mr. Steel. We have quite a bit to discuss and I can assure your safety as long as you're not on the wrong team."

Shrugging, he decided to play along. They had him. Six *were* against one mortal were bad odds, even for him. They walked in formation, Steel in the center of the group, to a parking area a short distance from the mouth of the alley. Two black SUVs waited there. Hastings and two of his operatives escorted him into the first vehicle, the rest of the team taking the second. They piled in and headed out on a circuitous route. They wasted little time getting out of the downtown area, but after that, they took quite a few twists and turns to foul their trail.

As soon as they were on open road, Hastings seemed to relax a bit. "I regret the abduction, Mr. Steel, but as I said, the *Venifucus* are back and we need some answers."

"So why me? I'm nobody."

The *were*hawk leveled a cold stare at him. "Evil has followed in your tracks for the past year, Mr. Steel. Either you're a very skilled liar or someone near you is killing off supernaturals as they find them. Through you. Just on gut instinct, after meeting you, I'll admit my money's on Gonzalez."

"What did you say?" His mind spun as he realized the watchers were also being watched. This guy knew his contact's name and claimed to have information about his movements for the past year. A chill ran down his spine though he didn't let his apprehension show.

"Mario Gonzalez. Don't play coy, Mr. Steel. I have another team picking him up as we speak. One of you has left a trail of bodies in your wake. Right now, I'm willing to entertain the idea that it wasn't you, though knowing your history and training, I would've bet money on you as the perp before today."

"That's comforting." Steel's sarcasm was obvious.

"Come now, Mr. Steel, one old soldier to another, wouldn't you like to hear what Mario's been doing behind your back for the past year? I can't believe the *Altor Custodis* advocates stringing up entire families of *were*, children included, and murdering them in cold blood. Or staking out a quiet den of bloodletters to die agonizing deaths in the blistering sun. And if you haven't heard about it, that can only mean a cover up on the highest levels of your organization."

Steel's mouth set in a grim line. "Who? Who died?" His blood ran cold at the idea he might've been the cause of innocent deaths. All the supernaturals he'd been assigned to ferret out and report on in the past year were more or less innocuous folks who were just living their lives, quietly existing. None were killers or had done anything to earn the ultimate sanction, and several of his reports had included small children and babies. "I want proof of your claims."

Hastings eyed him for a moment before nodding. "I've got files in the house." He nodded out the window as the SUVs pulled up in front of a small house in the woods on the outskirts of town.

As they rolled to a stop, Steel opened the car door and was out before any of the others, but he wasn't making a break for it. No, he was heading for the house. If innocent people had been murdered because of him and his work for the *Altor Custodis*, he needed to know.

An hour later Steel sat defeated, with his head down, resting in his hands. He'd seen the horrors of war and police actions, even terrorist hits, but never had he seen evil in its purest form. The photos of the dead ate at his soul. He knew each and every face, from the oldest to the youngest baby. He'd watched them and reported on their doings to the *Altor Custodis*, believing what he was doing was the right thing. Only it wasn't.

Now innocent people had been killed in grisly ways because he'd outed them. Maybe they weren't human, but they weren't hurting anyone that he could see. There'd been no reason to kill them. Especially not the little ones.

He would live with this on his conscience for the rest of his life.

But there was something he could do in the meantime, to at least try to put an end to such butchery. Steel's life changed in that moment. He'd had a few of these kinds of moments in his life in recent years, but none this profound. When he'd gone from mercenary killer to watcher and guardian after being approached by the *Altor Custodis*, he thought he'd put away his guns for the last time.

He'd been wrong.

Sighing heavily, he realized he'd have to use those skills he'd perfected over the years to clean house. Somehow, the organization that had been set up centuries ago to watch supernaturals and ostensibly protect humanity had been infiltrated. They weren't only watching and recording anymore. They were killing. And they had to be stopped.

Benjamin Steel was just the man for the job.

Sitting back in his chair, he eyed the man sitting across the room. Hastings had given him the files and left him alone. He respected that. He also respected the detailed accounts these files contained, compiled by a professional. Steel trusted his gut. Hastings was on the level.

"I'm sorry."

Steel didn't apologize often, but these people had died because of him and he felt true remorse. Hastings nodded once, slowly, acknowledging his words.

"You've got a fox in your henhouse, Mr. Steel. The question is, what are you prepared to do about it?"

He stood, flexing his muscles as his entire body prepared for war.

"I guess I'm going on a fox hunt."

Hastings stood and grinned. "Then might I suggest you could use a pack of hounds to help out?"

Steel was taken aback, but he guessed he shouldn't have been. Why would the *were* go to all this trouble to alert him of this mess, then leave him on his own to clean it up? If there was anything he knew about *were*creatures, it was that they were very hands on. Wherever the action was, they were in the thick of it.

"The AC doesn't take supernaturals."

Hastings laughed. "They may not take you anymore after what you've got planned. Did you think of that?"

"The thought did cross my mind, but this has got to be done. The killing needs to stop."

"No argument there."

"What do you propose?"

Hastings snapped his fingers and a group of people entered the room. Some, Steel recognized from the take-down squads that had abducted him earlier, and some he'd never seen before.

One man in particular caught his attention. He was young, but built on the large side, even more muscular than most *were*creatures were naturally. Steel knew why. This man worked construction with his brothers and they were part of the reason he'd been sent to this area to do surveillance. Thank goodness he hadn't sent in his report yet or this man and his family might very well be dead. It looked like somebody in the hierarchy of the AC was a *Venifucus* mole and was ordering hits as soon Steel's reports confirmed the identities of the supernaturals he'd been sent to investigate.

The young man walked right up to him and held out one hand. "I'm Matt Redstone."

Steel shook his hand, liking his forthright manner. "I know."

Matt's eyes went cold, then brightened as he turned to the room at large. "That, my friends, was the sound of the stakes being raised yet again." He turned back to Steel with a questioning smile. "So you know about me?"

Steel nodded. "And your brothers."

"Damn." Matt shook his head. "Should we worry?"

"No, thank God. I didn't send the report yet and after what I just saw, I never will."

Matt ran one hand through his shaggy hair in relief. "Well thank the Lady for small favors." He moved over to a chair and straddled it. "I'm here to offer you some help. From what we've been able to discover, the one who's killing our folk is a pretty powerful magic user. He's killed both *were* and vampire. Even we don't like to tangle with bloodletters, though most forms of magic bounce right off us. As a non-magical mortal, you wouldn't stand a chance against that kind of firepower without some help. My brothers and I are willing to extend that help."

"Cougars, right?" Steel sat again, interested in what the other man was proposing.

Matt nodded. "My oldest brother is Alpha of the cougar clan. He's away right now, but I'm authorized to gather the clan in case of emergency and I'd say this qualifies. I can get some volunteers to help out with surveillance, to supplement the people Hastings already has on the case. We're going to need a small army to take down the man who did that." He nodded with his chin to the files still spread on the low table. "If we do this though, I have to insist on one detail."

Steel sat back, waiting for the other shoe to drop. "What?"

"No reports. No photos. No record of any kind. I don't want my people to be immortalized in some *Altor Custodis* file somewhere. Not when there's the potential it could be used later to hunt them."

"I agree." That was a no-brainer as far as Steel was concerned. The minute he discovered his tasks for the AC had turned deadly, he'd broken from their path of watching and recording, but never interfering. The time had come to act and he'd damn well do it, regardless of what the rest of the brotherhood had done for centuries. The game was different now. The playbook had to change accordingly.

"I'm glad to hear you say that," Matt went on. "This is bigger than you might imagine. So big, in fact, we've formed an alliance with a few others you'll need to meet if you're going to be of help to us."

Intrigued, Steel waited to hear what more the *were*cougar would reveal, but the PI's cell phone rang and all eyes went to Hastings. The call was short and terse. He could tell something was wrong from the man's body language and clipped questions about how bad more than one person was hurt. Hastings shut the phone with a snap.

"Gonzalez escaped. He's our mage. No doubt about it. He toasted Kevin's and Sarah's asses, but they'll be all right with time. The bastard also broke Melissa's arm."

"Man, she's gonna be pissed about not being able to fly until it heals," Matt observed. Everyone in the room felt the seriousness of the moment. "You got anywhere you have to be tonight?" Matt asked Steel.

"What do you have in mind?"

Matt stood. "I think it's time for you to meet our allies. They'll be rising when the sun sets."

"No way." Steel found it hard to believe what the *were*cougar implied. From what he'd seen, *were*folk didn't mix with vampires and vice versa.

"Way." Matt checked his watch as he headed for the door. He spared a moment to look back at Hastings. "It's your house, so it's your call. Do we go to them or do I invite them here?"

The PI sighed as he sank back in his chair. "Much as I hate to give up this location, I think it's time we show a little good faith. Sebastian's trusted us with his home. No sense we can't show the same courtesy with a mere safe house."

Chapter Ten

"Where are we going?" Christy asked as they drove down the road. Sebastian was at the wheel of one of his larger cars, a luxury SUV with dark tinted windows and lots of room in back.

"First I'm going to drop you off at the vineyard so you can visit with Lissa for a bit. Then Atticus, Marc and I are heading out to a place Collin Hastings set up as a safe house. He's got someone for us to meet."

"A new ally?" She pulled the thought from his mind, but otherwise her thoughts were still preoccupied by what had happened the night before. The confrontation with Jeff ran through her mind pretty much non-stop and each time she thought of what she'd done, she felt better. She'd stood up to the bully who'd ruled her life for so long and come out the victor. All thanks to the man sitting beside her.

"It remains to be seen if he'll prove trustworthy, but Matt said the signs are good." Sebastian reached over and captured her hand, drawing it to his lips for a soft kiss. "He could be of great use in tracking the killer."

"I didn't realize you were so involved in vampire politics." She could see the survival of his people mattered a great deal to him.

"I'm afraid when it comes to injustice, I still have a bit of chivalry in my soul. It wouldn't be right to sit by while a killer roams loose. Besides which, he could be coming for one of us. I'd rather we take him out first, while we have help from our allies among the *were*."

"Is it really such a big deal?"

"That Matt and I are friends?" Sebastian shrugged as he pulled up to a heavy gate that opened automatically for him. "Actually yes. But it's an even bigger deal that others of his kind are willing to work with us on this. Cross-species cooperation is the stuff of legends."

The vineyard where Atticus and Lissa lived was gorgeous. The house was set in the midst of it all and was built on a grand scale. Lissa answered the door with a big smile and the women hugged each other in greeting. Shortly after their reunion, the men left, headed for their meeting while Christy and Lissa sat together in the spacious dining room, talking. The room opened onto a stone patio, the French doors open to let in the evening breeze.

"I wanted to visit you before now, but Atticus said you needed time. Are you okay? I mean," Lissa hesitated, "with all this?" Her hands made circles in the air, gesturing.

"With waking up as a vampire?" Christy laughed. "It's not so bad, actually. I confronted Jeff yesterday and personally served the divorce papers."

"You didn't!" Lissa beamed. "Oh, Chris, that's great." Lissa's eyes were wistful as she gazed at Christy. She hadn't quite realized how much her friends cared and how much she'd missed them. "How did he react?"

"He took a swing at me." Christy shrugged, a gleeful smile bursting forth as she remembered again what had happened next. "I knocked his feet out from under him and he fell to the floor."

"No way!"

She smiled at Lissa's reaction. "*Sensei* Hiro's been teaching me some moves and with my new abilities, I'm actually pretty good."

"Oh, sweetie." Lissa's eyes were moist, though a smile lit her face. "I'm so happy for you."

"And best of all—" Christy lowered her voice, "—there's Sebastian. Lissa, I've had the hots for that man since I danced with him at your wedding. I never dreamed I'd have a chance with a guy like that, but now...well, it's like a fairytale."

Lissa's eyes glowed. "I know how you feel. It was that way

when Atticus found me."

"I still can't believe you didn't tell me. How did you manage to hide something like that?"

"Well, Jeff hardly let you out of his sight the past few months, so it wasn't all that difficult, actually. Kelly found out, but then Atticus offered her a job here at the winery, so it was okay. I mean, they don't like people to know, so Kelly working here was a good step. Otherwise she probably would have been watched, like Jena."

"Damn, is she the only one of us who's *not* a vampire now?" Christy shook her head at the odd twists of fate that had visited the small group of college friends.

"Don't forget Sally," Lissa said with a quick grin, "but yeah, you, me, Kelly, and Carly are all living on the dark side now." She giggled and Christy laughed with her.

§∩

An hour after sunset, cars started arriving. The *were*folk had shared a large dinner with Steel and he was amazed by how much food those people could consume in one sitting. They'd cleaned up and resumed their places in the living room when the first of their guests arrived.

The doorbell rang and Hastings and Matt went to answer, inviting the visitors inside. The process was repeated for each of the newcomers and Steel realized the vampires needed to be formally invited into the house. He heard them chatting in the hall before they entered the living room as a group.

They were introduced to each of the *were* and made their way over to Steel last. He was glad of the opportunity to study them for a few minutes before being introduced. Even so, he was unprepared for the power of them, or the impact they collectively had on his senses. He'd seen vamps before, since going to work for the AC, but never this close. Now he began to understand a bit more of their power.

In a word, they were mesmerizing. They had some kind of hypnotic mojo that made it hard to concentrate. He was pretty sure most normal folks wouldn't even notice, but he'd always been a little different. Even as a child, he'd been sensitive to currents in the air—the crackle of electricity, the scent of magic. Since being recruited by the AC, he'd received training to enhance his natural abilities. They called him a Sensitive, which meant he was able to sense the use of magic around him.

Why then, hadn't he suspected Mario? If Mario was a strong magic user, and responsible for the heinous crimes depicted in that file Steel had been shown, how could he have missed it? He was better than that. Something was seriously wrong here.

He recognized Marc LaTour even before he was introduced, from the file he'd been given by his superiors in the AC. Steel shook his hand with reserve. He'd never been this close to a vampire before, and he'd never even seen one this old.

The other men with him were introduced as Cameron, Atticus and Sebastian. Cameron had a strong feeling of magic about him that Steel had never encountered, but the other two had the same magical feel as Marc LaTour. They were definitely vampires and both had very slight accents when they spoke. He couldn't quite place Atticus's slightly Slavic tones, but he'd peg Sebastian for upper class English, if he had to guess.

Matt surprised Steel by sitting next to Sebastian on the couch. He looked comfortable with the vampire, though Steel well knew these two races of supernaturals rarely, if ever, mixed.

"Sebastian's the reason we were able to track you down, in a roundabout way," Matt said as he sipped a cup of coffee. "He recently took in a battered woman named Christina Kinsey."

"Battered?" That was news to Steel, though he hadn't liked the woman's husband at all. Still, he hadn't had any contact with either husband or wife in a week or two. He'd been busy tracking down other leads in the area and would've gotten back to the Kinsey file eventually. Now he regretted he hadn't looked more closely at the man before this.

Sebastian spoke with quiet authority. "Jeff Kinsey beat her to death. Luckily for him, she lived."

A chill went down Steel's spine at the menace in the man's tone. "I had some contact with Kinsey. I was investigating his wife because of her connection to Kelly LaTour." Steel noted Marc LaTour's frown but he refused to be intimidated. "The AC knew about you, Mister LaTour, or should I say *Master*? When you married, they wanted to know more about your wife as well. I was sent to look into it and laid groundwork by checking out her circle of friends. Frankly, I didn't expect anything to come of it."

"I won't see her put in danger." Marc's voice was cold but his agitation was clear as he stood and started to pace like a tiger on the prowl. "Don't even think of making reports on her or her friends."

Steel eased back in his chair, taking the man's measure. This vamp loved his wife. That much was obvious. And Steel hadn't been able to turn up anything negative in his recent history. He was a good businessman, respected by the community and seemed to be on the up and up. He also seemed to keep the other bloodletters in line, which was a key position and not something he wanted to mess with. There was no reason to threaten the man, or his wife, and every reason not to piss him off at the moment, while Steel was essentially at their mercy.

"I haven't finished my investigation, so the report hasn't been sent. If all of this is on the level, it never will be."

"I assure you," Hastings spoke from his chair at the side of the room, "we're on the level. You won't have any reason to make further reports."

"That remains to be seen." Steel leaned forward. "What I don't understand is how Mario Gonzalez could be a magic user. I should tell you, I'm what they call a Sensitive. Always have been. And the AC honed that natural ability with training. I don't see how I could've missed it. Every time I've seen him, I've never felt a thing."

"A truly powerful magic user can hide his light even from one as sensitive as you, laddie." Cameron spoke for the first time as he stood. "Watch carefully now."

He snapped his fingers and his magical energies winked out as if they'd never been. Where before, Steel's senses had been bombarded by the most potent magical energy he'd ever felt in one being, suddenly it was all gone. As if it had never been.

"How'd you do that?"

Cameron leaned in and winked, a devilish light in his

twinkling blue eyes. "Magic." There were a few chuckles as the man straightened and reversed whatever spell he'd wrought. As before, in the blink of an eye, the magic was back.

"What are you?" Steel couldn't help but ask.

Cameron smiled in a cunning way. "Fey."

"No way."

"Don't you know it's never wise to contradict the fey?" Atticus teased drolly as Cameron sat back down.

The presence of this most magical of all the supernatural races changed things a bit. Fey didn't enter into the affairs of mortals, vampires and *were* lightly. If this man was part of the operation, it was serious indeed.

"So you're telling me Mario Gonzalez is able to hide his magical energies from me?" Nods all around were his answer. "You think he actually has enough power and skill to do that? I mean, he's definitely a mortal, and certainly not fey."

"Mortal he may be, but he's been tapping into the magic of other realms otherwise he wouldna live so long." Cameron chimed in.

Ian spoke for the first time. "I met him briefly about a hundred years ago. He was a thief then and it looks like his crimes have only escalated. Judging by the caliber of his current offenses, he's learned quite a bit in the intervening years. If he can take down that many supernaturals single handedly, it'd be nothing to hide his magical energies from you, Mr. Steel."

Steel digested that, sitting back in his chair. It felt right, but he was chilled to think he'd been duped for so long. He marveled at his own blindness.

"You can drop the 'mister'. Just call me Steel if we're going to be working together."

And just like that, a new alliance was born.

ℰℭ

Lissa and Christy sat out on the stone patio enjoying the night air. It was crisp, but not too cold. A great night for stargazing. And sharing secrets.

Lissa had brought out a bottle of one of the vineyard's award-winning vintages. Christy was glad she could still enjoy wine in her new life. She hadn't felt the need for food and frankly didn't miss it unless she thought about it, but she'd always enjoyed the flavor, bouquet and sheer romance of a good bottle of wine.

Now however, the experience was something more. There was something almost magical about the fruit of the vine and the healing liquid it produced. Christy could feel the wine effervesce in the most delicious way as it hit her bloodstream, making her tingle with warmth. It also tasted a thousand percent better than it ever had. The crisp vintage settled on her tongue like air, tart and dry in a way she had never fully experienced before. It was as if her taste buds had only just been awakened.

The women talked about their men and the way their lives had changed as they sat under the stars, drinking their wine. It was an idyllic moment for Christy, who hadn't known such camaraderie since her college days, or such peace since her childhood spent in the mountains of Oregon.

"Are you happy, Lis?" Christy gazed at the stars until she realized how rude her question might've been. She looked at her friend, seated at her side. "I mean, you seem happier than I've ever known you to be, but do you have any regrets?"

Lissa smiled. "My only regret is that I didn't meet Atticus sooner. That man makes my life complete in a way I never expected and even though I'll never have a tan again," she chuckled, "all the magic makes up for it. I mean, Atticus can do things..." Her eyes went misty as she trailed off.

"Yeah," Christy agreed softly. "Sebastian is pretty amazing too. I never knew a man could care so much about my feelings, or my safety. He's..."

"Hard to put into words, isn't it?" Lissa smiled.

"I never expected to feel this way after the hell I went through with Jeff."

"Oh, honey." Lissa reached out to Christy. "I suspected something wasn't right with your marriage, but you hid it so well. If I'd known what was really going on I'd have tried to do something."

"I know." Christy patted Lissa's hand. "I didn't want any of you to know what a fool I'd been."

"You were never a fool, sweetie. Jeff was the fool, to squander the happiness you could have had. He's an ass, Chris, and if Atticus hadn't already made me promise not to track him down and give him a piece of my mind, I'd have had a posse over at your old house while you were still recovering. As it is, I'm still tempted, but this connection with Atticus can be problematic when I want to do something behind his back. I mean, he *knows* every thought in my head." She made an exaggerated face. "I can't get away with anything anymore."

Christy laughed, nodding. "It certainly takes some getting used to." They compared notes on how to cope with their new mates for the next few minutes, enjoying the night and the companionship.

The men had been gone for two hours when out of the night a fiery ball of energy shattered the stillness, streaking through the air to land between the two women seated on the patio. Christy saw it coming and shoved Lissa out of the chair and onto the flagstones as she dove the other way. A split second later, a smoking crater was all that was left where the patio furniture had been.

"Get inside, Lis!" Christy yelled as she jumped behind the low stone wall of the patio. Lissa was nearer the door. Christy felt relief when Lissa ducked inside.

But whoever was lobbing fireballs at them was still out there. Allowing her senses to expand, Christy searched the night with her enhanced vision, hearing and olfactory senses. A movement behind the third pine tree on the right. She knew the magic user was there, but she wasn't sure what she could do to distract him until the cavalry arrived. She knew without question that Sebastian was already on his way. He would've felt her terror, even over the miles that separated them, but neither wanted to distract the other with the effort of speech at the moment.

When no further fireballs were forthcoming, Christy gambled on engaging the stranger in conversation. It might help her keep track of him and perhaps she could learn something useful while she stalled for time.

"Who are you? What do you want?" she called into the woods.

Silence met her query.

"What's with the fireballs? And who the hell are you?"

A man stepped from behind the third tree, as she'd suspected. He had a dark complexion in the murky light, but she could see him clearly with her enhanced vision. He wore a smug look on his face, his dark eyes eager.

"Don't hide, little witch. I promise to make it painless if you give yourself up now. Don't make me come after you."

"Sebastian, I hope you're close. This guy means business."

Atticus and Sebastian knew the instant their mates came under attack. Miles away, they shot to their feet, and headed outdoors.

"What's wrong?" Hastings asked behind them, but neither of the vamps wasted any time on explanations. Matt knew what was going on. He explained to the rest.

"The women are under attack at Atticus's place. I think our mage, Mario, just showed himself."

"How do you know?" Marc demanded.

Matt shrugged, speaking quickly. "I'm connected—a little—to Sebastian and Christy. I heard her scream. I'm hearing what she's telling Sebastian. A man came out of the trees and started lobbing fireballs at her and Lissa while they sat on the back patio at Atticus's house."

Marc nodded grimly and headed out the door, after his friends.

The vampires were nowhere in sight. They'd transformed and flown away at top speed for the vineyard. Behind him, Matt heard the rest of the group moving uneasily in their seats. He spared a moment to look back at them.

"I don't know about you, but I'm going over there. We need to stop this asshole before he kills again." Matt shed his clothes, shifted, and then bounded out the door after the vampires.

Cameron stood and rubbed his hands together. "I'm

heading over there too. *Were*folk, I suggest you aid your brethren. My senses tell me we'll be too late to capture Mario this night, but your skills might yet be needed."

Steel was fascinated to see all the shifters take off at high speed. There were a few raptors that simply flew out the door and a large number of wolves and big cats that loped off after Matt. Steel wasn't sure what to do. He had no way of keeping up with the animals or vampires, but he wasn't out of the fight. He caught Hastings' eye before the man shifted.

"Tell me where. I'll take a truck."

"Go right out of the drive, then about ten miles to Mill Road. Go left and up the side of the mountain about halfway. You'll see the vines. The house is set back in the middle of the fields. Take the gravel road on the left. It's marked Private."

"Got it. I'll be there as soon as possible."

Hastings nodded then shifted and flew out the door after his brethren.

A large hand settled on Steel's shoulder. Turning swiftly, he saw it was Cameron. "Mr. Steel, will you accompany me? I prefer not to travel magically unless I have no other choice. It attracts too much attention."

Unsure exactly what the fey warrior meant, he nodded anyway. "I'll drive."

Energy sizzled along the edges of Christy's vision. She rolled away as a ball of fire swept where she'd been not a moment before. Her arm was singed, but she couldn't think about that now. If this man had his way, she'd be a lot more than just singed.

Rolling faster than a mortal could, she gambled and moved closer to the man. She had to jam him up. Running away would only give him a clearer shot at her. If she moved in close where he had no room to maneuver, perhaps she could save this situation after all. Or at least buy some time until Sebastian showed up.

She knew he was coming. She could feel him in her mind, silently advising and reassuring her even as he worried. He was flying but he nixed her idea about shifting shape to escape even before it had fully formed in her mind. She was too new to shapeshifting to depend on it in such a situation.

She rolled once more, a blast of fire making a crater where she'd just been. She used her forward momentum to rise not a foot away from the man. He gasped, shock and a bit of panic showing on his face as he tried to back away. But there were trees at his back. Big ones. Directly behind him.

"Now, what is your problem?" she demanded, angry now that this man would try to hurt her and Lissa. She'd had enough of men hurting her. She was done with that. Forever.

He tried to throw a punch at her, but she threw up a block with her forearm, the way Hiro had taught her. She was a little shocked when she heard the bone of his arm snap. His magical energy flew up into the trees, burning a path through the leaves, but it was otherwise harmless. The man screamed and cradled his arm. It was hanging at an awkward angle that made Christy's stomach turn.

But she couldn't let it distract her.

"Tell your maker. I'll be back, witch. I'll stake you all out for the sun."

"I'd like to see you try, you bastard. I'm through taking this shit from anybody! I refuse to be anyone's punching bag ever again!" Anger rose once more. She was shaking with it. All the recent turmoil in her life had finally come to a head. The incident with Jeff the night before had started something inside her. She wouldn't be a victim again. Ever.

She moved forward, ready to trap the man, but he raised his good hand palm outward and she was just too distracted to duck. A pulse of power hit her, impacting against her whole body and sending her flying back. The side of the house stopped her cold. And very hard.

As she slid down the side of the house and onto the stone patio she saw the man turn and run into the woods, making his getaway. Christy thought about going after him, but she hurt too much to even get up. It was enough he'd left.

"Christina! Are you all right?" Sebastian's voice sounded through her mind.

"I think I'm okay. He only knocked the wind out of me."

"Get into the house if you can."

"I don't think I can move right now, but I'll grant you, it's a

good idea."

"Oh, love, I'll be there in a minute. Hang on."

"It's okay, Sebastian. He's gone. I broke his arm." She still felt a little sick at the thought, but perversely it also felt pretty good to know she'd been able to defend herself and inflict a little damage on someone hell bent on killing her.

"You did well, my love. I'm so proud of you, but this is all my fault. I should never have left you alone."

"Sebastian, don't blame yourself. How could you have known this maniac would be able to attack us at Lissa's place? I mean, this vineyard is practically a fortress."

"Still..." Sebastian sounded agitated, *"...when it comes to your safety, I should never have taken the chance. You are too important to me, my love. Without you..."*

"I know." She lowered the feel of her voice, stroking him with her thoughts. *"I feel the same way."*

A streak of fog shimmered in through the trees. Part of it went straight into the house through the open patio doors and another part congealed before her. A moment later, the mist became a man—her man. Sebastian knelt and lifted her into his arms. He wasted little time taking her into the house.

He laid her on the couch in a room with no windows at the center of the house. Atticus and Lissa were there, but Christy couldn't look away from Sebastian. His beloved face was wreathed in worry as he ran his hands over her limbs as if to reassure himself she was truly all right.

"Are you feeling any better?"

Christy nodded. "I'm okay. Give me a few minutes and I'll be good as new." Unfortunately, she had experience with pain, though this time, her hurts felt like they were healing themselves as she sat there. Instead of the usual days it would have taken her to heal before, she could feel her body repairing itself at lightning speed. This "being a vampire" stuff did seem to have its benefits. She cupped Sebastian's cheek, looking into his eyes. "Really. I'm okay."

He took her hand in his and raised it to his lips.

"Christy," Lissa came over to the side of the couch, "you were amazing! I watched the whole thing. I can't believe the way you took on that man. Where'd you learn all that kung fu stuff?"

Christy smiled at Sebastian, squeezing his hand before looking over at her friend. "I told you, Lis, I've been studying with *Sensei* Hiro. And Sebastian taught me too. He's a man of many talents."

Lissa's look was speculative. "I bet."

Atticus came up behind his wife and drew her back into his arms. He placed a tender kiss on the top of her head.

"Thank you, Christy. Your brave actions saved both your lives this night. I am forever in your debt."

Christy was taken aback. The ancient vampire meant every word. She could hear the ring of residual fear for his mate in his voice and feel the truth of his tone. The very idea floored her.

"Lissa is one of my best friends," she said simply, unsure how to respond.

Atticus nodded, seemingly satisfied with her words, and drew back.

Just then, Marc showed his face in the door, a wolf howled in the distance and a hawk screamed overhead. Atticus patted his wife's hand and headed outside to speak with Marc and meet the *were*.

Christy was feeling well enough to sit up. Sebastian made room, though he didn't relinquish hold of her hand. They both needed the contact after the scare they'd just had.

"I've never been so frightened," Lissa said, perching on the overstuffed arm of the couch. "Nothing like that's ever happened to me before. I mean, there we were enjoying the evening air and suddenly some lunatic starts lobbing fireballs at us. I can't believe how you stood up to that man, Chris. How did you know what to say? What to do?"

Christy grimaced. "I've faced a maniac before. I've been thinking a lot about how I should have stood up to Jeff, but I never did. Not until—"

"Not until now, my love." Sebastian squeezed her hand, encouraging her.

An uncomfortable silence reigned for a moment before Lissa spoke again. "I'm so sorry, Chris. You can't know how glad I am you're away from that jerk. I never liked Jeff."

Christy smiled at her friend. "You were always a better judge of character than I was, Lis. I should have listened to you before I married him."

Atticus came back in, clearly agitated. "Marc and some of the *were* are trying to track your attacker, but are having a hard time of it. He knew enough to foul his scent and he's got some kind of magic that interferes with their senses. Or so I'm told."

"What about Cameron?" Sebastian asked.

"He's not here yet. He's driving over with Steel."

Sure enough, they all heard a truck pull up the drive and skid to a stop out front.

Chapter Eleven

Steel was impressed with the vineyard and cozy mansion Atticus called home. Never in his life would he have dreamed he'd be invited into a vampire's lair, but here he was. In the company of a fey, no less. Atticus met them at the door and ushered them inside. He sent Steel into the living room and took Cameron out back.

Steel saw the woman first. Luminous eyes haunted her beautiful face. He tried to shield himself as best he could from the influence of the vampiress, but it was no good. The men seemed to understand and reined in their natural magnetism, but this lady...she was different.

He stared at her, unable to look away. Sebastian tugged at her hand and drew her back into his arms. It was a clear, protective stance.

"My love," Sebastian said in a gentle voice to the woman in his arms, "tamp down your energies if you can. You're having an effect on our mortal friend here."

"I am?" Wide eyes turned to him. The beautiful woman's expression was truly innocent and Steel knew she wasn't doing it on purpose. That look alone made him relax. She blushed in an altogether appealing way. Then again, everything about her was appealing with the vampire magic drawing him in. "I'm sorry," the goddess said. "You must be Mr. Steel. I apologize. It's just...I'm very new to all this. Up 'til last week I was as human as you."

"Mortal, you mean." Sebastian supplied the word they preferred, correcting the woman who looked very comfortable in his embrace.

Steel refocused on the man. "You changed her?"

"It was either that or let her die."

Steel nodded. He didn't know the entire story, but he could fill in the blanks. For now, he was glad to feel the new female vampire rein in her seductive mojo. Her power drew back and he was able to breathe a bit easier.

He noticed the other woman for the first time, smiling at him from her perch on the arm of the couch. Damned if he didn't feel the heat of embarrassment in his cheeks. Hopefully they wouldn't notice, but then he kicked himself. These were vampires. They'd notice.

"I'm Lissa, Atticus's wife." She held out a gracious hand. He shook it and tried to smile.

"Ma'am."

She laughed and the sound shot down his spine. "Please, call me Lissa. Like my friend Christy here, I haven't been in the supernatural game too long myself."

Atticus returned to the living room with Matt in tow, his face grim. "Cam's not having much luck either, though he's still trying a few things."

"It looks like the son of a bitch got away." Disgust was thick in Matt's voice.

"All right." Sebastian sat back. "Let's take this from the beginning. First, are we certain the attacker was Mario Gonzalez?"

"Good point," Steel agreed. "Ladies, can either of you describe the man?"

"Oh yeah," Lissa said with relish. "I saw the whole thing from the window. He's about five foot ten, maybe a hundred and ninety pounds. Black hair. Curly. Cut neat, but not clean cut. A little shaggy. I assume brown eyes, but Christy got right up in his face. She saw his features better than I did."

"His eyes were green. A kind of creepy aqua green." Christy took up the description. "And it looked like his nose had been broken a few times."

"That sounds like Mario," Steel admitted. The eyes were distinctive.

"And he had a tattoo. Sort of a swirly pattern over his left eyebrow. It..."

"Go on, sweetheart." Matt encouraged her.

"It glowed." She looked at Sebastian and then over at Lissa, but the other woman was shaking her head.

"I didn't see anything like that," Lissa said in a soft voice, as if afraid to contradict her friend.

"Gonzalez doesn't have any facial tattoos," Steel confirmed, struck by the thoughtful look on Sebastian's face.

"What are you thinking, my friend?" Atticus asked Sebastian.

Sebastian stood. "We'll need Cam's help to prove my theory. I'll go see if he's done spinning his wheels in the backyard. Don't go anywhere."

"Please have a seat, Mr. Steel," Lissa invited.

Steel shrugged. The woman was soft spoken and gracious, even after the upset of being attacked and having her patio turned into a series of craters. He took a seat, observing everything. He was on new footing here and wasn't sure of exactly how he fit into this little unit. He'd be cautious until he knew best how he could contribute.

When Sebastian went outside it hit him just how serious the encounter had been. He'd been so focused on Christina he hadn't really taken in the wreckage left behind by the fireballs. Five-foot craters pocked the grounds in and around the patio area. Bricks and plants were strewn all around and loose dirt covered everything.

He found Cam cursing a few yards into the copse of woods surrounding the vineyard's main house. The fey warrior didn't look pleased. In fact, he looked downright pissed off. He was talking to Marc, and the Master Vampire looked as grim as the fey.

"This is strong magic, my friend." Cameron nodded as Sebastian walked up to him. "It has an evil taint that goes deeper than a mere mortal mage should be able to reach."

Hastings joined them. "We've had warnings from the Lords about some damn fool *Venifucus* plan to bring back The Destroyer of Worlds. I was told the bastard who tried to kill the newest priestess used some kind of dark fey magic connected to Elspeth. Think this is more of the same?"

"Aye, it could very well be." Cameron shook his head, breaking a small twig he held in his fingers. A puff of foul-smelling smoke rose from the ground not three feet away. "This one at least, is using something akin to an Elspian ring." He threw the remnants away and turned back toward the house.

"All the more reason to consult with your Lords, Mr. Hastings." Marc's reminder of the meeting Hastings had promised to set up was met with a tightening of the shapeshifter's lips.

Cameron stepped between the two men, facing Sebastian in an obvious ploy to alleviate some of the tension in the air. "What was on your mind, Sebastian? You came out here for something."

"I want to know if you can devise a test for Christina. She says Mario had a glowing, swirling design tattooed above his left eyebrow, but Lissa and Steel never saw any mark on the man."

"So you think your lady sees what cannot be seen?"

"I think it's a distinct possibility."

"It is a rare gift, as you may know." Cameron stroked his chin thoughtfully. "But if any newly turned was to be so blessed, it would be your lassie. With all that *were* blood in her, it's a wonder she doesn't howl at the moon."

Hastings laughed, but Sebastian was too worried to find humor in anything at the moment. Marc stepped away from the group. "I'm heading home. I want to make sure my lady is secure. I think you have this well in hand for now. Mr. Hastings, I assume you'll be in touch when your Lords get in contact with you?"

Hastings bristled a little, but nodded. "I'll call."

"Very well. Sebastian, keep me informed of any developments."

Sebastian nodded as Marc turned and walked deeper into the wooded area behind the house. He'd probably shift form away from prying eyes so none could follow him to his lair.

"I'll gather up the troops and post a thick perimeter while you decide what to do next," Hastings volunteered.

Sebastian stopped the man as he moved to leave them. "You have my thanks. I owe you and your people a debt of gratitude for coming to my lady's aid."

Hastings held his gaze for a moment, nodded once and moved off into the night, calling softly for his *were* friends. The man was a skilled professional and Sebastian was glad to have him around.

"For a hawk, he's a sly one, that Hastings," Cameron observed as they walked toward the house. "For all that, I like the man. He's sharp as they come."

Sebastian nodded, allowing Cameron to precede him through the door. "I agree. Even though he doesn't trust me yet, I think I can trust him to be on the right side of things. He has a pure spirit."

"Sometimes I forget you're only a youngster in the grand scheme of things, Sebastian." Cameron raised his eyebrow. "You have an old soul. As, I think, does your lady. It's a good thing, too, for you both carry more burdens than your years should merit—and more power too."

The men shared a sober look as they paused near the entrance to the living room. Cameron clapped Sebastian on the back and together they walked through the archway to the large room. Christina was sitting up, her color better. She smiled when she saw him and Sebastian's heart lightened. She could do that to him—make him happy with just a smile. She was a wonder to him.

"As you are to me, Sebastian." Her voice sounded intimately in his mind.

Cameron sat before her, unceremoniously plopping down on the coffee table. Good thing the heavy wood was sturdy enough to hold the big man.

"Now, lassie, you say our boy Mario had a tattoo?" She nodded. "And it glowed?"

"Yes. Lissa didn't see it, but I was face to face with him. It was right here—" she gestured to the area above her own left eye, "—in a sort of wiggly pattern. It looked almost Celtic. Like a knotwork design or something, but slightly different."

Cameron sat back and lifted the sleeve of his shirt, baring his forearm. "Something like this?"

Sebastian looked over the other man's shoulder. What he could see of Cameron's muscular forearm was unblemished by any sort of marking. Well, maybe a freckle or two, but apparently Christina saw something, judging by her gasp.

"Yes, very like that, but much darker. More sinister. What is it?"

"It's my mating mark. Part of the reason I stay here in the mortal realm and don't return to the land of the fey is this mark and the woman it represents. You see, I loved a mortal lass. I marked her as I marked myself, transferring some of my magic to her in an effort to extend her life. It worked...for a time. But as all mortal things, eventually she passed on to realms where I cannot follow." Cameron's voice was wistful, his tone sad. Christina, compassionate little thing that she was, reached out to take Cameron's hand, offering comfort.

Cameron smiled at her, but it was a sad smile. He shook his head, making a visible effort to dispel the mood. "Did Mario's mark look like this? Can you remember any details?"

"It was sort of triangular, starting with his eyebrow as the base and working to a point, not circular like yours. And his was red, not golden."

Cameron's face grew troubled as he lowered his sleeve. "Red means it's tainted. And a triangular shape could have several connotations, but at least now we know why this mortal has been around for a few centuries. He's probably being powered from somewhere in the fey realm." Cameron's expression was hard as he sat back. "This is a bigger problem than you know, my friends. I'm not surprised this man has proven hard to pin down, but we must find a way."

"In the meantime, might I suggest we all go to my house?" Sebastian looked around at those assembled. Atticus and his wife would need a place to stay since it was clear their home was no longer safe. Sebastian only hoped his own place would prove more secure. "Atticus and Lissa, you're welcome to stay with us as long as you'd like. I have a spare room you might like and I think Matt and some of his *were* friends will aid us during the day. They like to roam the woodlands around the house and the wall surrounding the property keeps all but the most determined trespassers out."

Atticus nodded. "Thanks, Sebastian. We'll take you up on

151

that."

An hour later, everyone was settled in Sebastian's rambling home. Atticus and Lissa were given a basement room that was part of a different wing of the house than Sebastian's. He'd built the house with multiple secret chambers, some separated completely from the others, and some with small secret passageways connecting them. He'd made it as secure as he knew how and it looked like all his planning was coming in handy now.

Dawn approached, but Sebastian stayed in the upper rooms as long as he could, making certain of their protection for the day. Matt and some of his *were*cougar clan patrolled the perimeter and would for the remainder of this crisis.

Steel was paired off with Cameron for the time being, since Cameron could use his fey magic, if need be, to instantaneously transport them both in an emergency, though he seemed loath to do so.

Hastings and his investigators were working with Steel and Cameron, back at their offices for the day. They'd suffered a bit of a setback when Mario got away, but they'd also learned a great deal.

Christy was still shaken, even after returning to Sebastian's house. She'd been in violent situations before, but being able to defend herself was still quite new.

At least with Jeff, she'd labored under the misconception that he wouldn't kill her. She'd always believed he wouldn't want to go to jail, but that last blow-up had proven her wrong. He'd killed her. Only Sebastian's intervention allowed her to continue drawing air.

Only Sebastian. Her savior.

"Fear not, my love." He came to her in their underground chamber. She'd bathed the stink of fear and the clods of dirt from her skin while he'd dealt with the people above. But he'd been connected to her all the while, in her mind, calming her when fear threatened to take over.

Sebastian threw off his jacket and tugged her into his arms. She reached up to unbutton his shirt collar. She continued down the line of buttons until they were all undone, and pulled the shirt's tails out from his waistband so she could push the sides apart and snuggle into his warm chest.

"I was so scared."

"I know." He soothed her, running his palms over her shoulders and down her back, covered now only in a thin, white silk nightgown. "But you were brave. You stood your ground and used your wits. I'm incredibly proud of you."

"I knew you'd come for me. I think that's why I was able to be brave. I knew all I had to do was hold on until you could get there."

"Sweet stars above, I almost lost you tonight, my love." Anguish filled Sebastian's whispered words.

Christy soothed him, stroking her fingers over his skin as she helped him out of his clothes. "I was frightened at the time, but I had faith in you, Sebastian."

He captured her hand and brought it to his lips for a tender kiss. "You had more faith in me than I had in myself, Christina. Please, don't ever scare me like that again."

She smiled. "Not by choice, lover. I didn't enjoy having fireballs lobbed at me anymore than you enjoyed seeing it happen."

Sebastian covered her on the large bed, his body blanketing her in warmth. "I love you with all that I am, Christina. If anything ever happened to you—" He choked on the words.

Leaning up, she kissed his lips, then drew back to look deep into his eyes. "Nothing happened tonight. The care you took in turning me paid off in ways you never expected. My *were*cougar superpowers kicked into high gear when that jerk came at me. I acted on instinct that certainly didn't come from me, but the cat knew what to do. Sebastian, your foresight is what saved us tonight. Your generosity in giving me what I didn't know I needed. Matt's gift to us both."

Sebastian's eyes darkened with emotion a moment before his lips claimed hers in a devastating kiss. It held all his worry, his torment, fear, love and the triumph he'd felt when she'd proven stronger and more clever than her adversary. She felt all of it again now, sharing his mind and heart as she did, and she gave him back all the confidence, pride in him, gratitude and love she had. Everything she had—everything she was—was for him. He'd given her enormous gifts, first by changing her, then by asking Matt to give her even more potent instincts than most vampires could claim. That alone had saved them tonight.

She owed it to Sebastian's generous spirit and to Matt as well, of course. Without Matt's friendship and willingness to participate in giving a newly turned vampire the benefit of his *were* blood, she would never have survived the encounter with Mario Gonzalez, and both she and Lissa would be dead.

Sebastian broke the kiss as tears formed in her eyes.

"Don't think like that, Christina. You saved both your lives this night, plus mine and Atticus's as well. Without you, I would not want to live. I'd hunt down those responsible and kill them in gruesome ways first, but then I'd join you in death, seeking your soul in the realms beyond. I couldn't go on without you and I'm pretty sure Atticus feels the same about your friend, Lissa."

She leaned up and kissed his jaw. "Make love to me, Sebastian. Make me forget the fear. Make me yours."

He pressed against her. "You are always mine, my love. From now until forever." He kissed her again and this time there was no room for thought, no room for distraction. His kiss was her world, his warm body, her life.

Their loving was soft and gentle at first, then harsh and needy. Both reveled in the glory of each other and seemed to want to make up for the close call in a very physical way.

☙

Cameron stuck to Steel's side like glue the rest of the night and into the next day. Around dawn, he let Steel go back to his hotel for a change of clothes.

"You guys may not need much sleep, but I need to recharge." He yawned as he opened the door to his hotel room. He'd had about enough of his new babysitter.

"You can sleep. I'll just be making sure you don't leave or communicate with anyone while you're in this room."

"You can do that?"

Cameron winked as he lifted one hand. "I can do much more than that, boyo. Now, personally, I feel like you can be trusted, but there's more than me to consider. So get yourself into the center of this room and be still for a moment while I do this."

Cameron crowded Steel inside the room. He didn't like being ordered around, but he also didn't want to mess with the immense power he could feel building. This creature was downright scary.

The amount of magical energy he felt coming off Cameron was like nothing he'd ever experienced before. It also had a weird flavor, not quite of this world. The rise in power peaked and then suddenly...nothing.

Steel felt his skin crawl. After the intensity of the moments before, the room was now devoid of magic, but yet...

There was a small hum at the back of his mind. It was comforting, in a way.

"What *is* that?"

Cameron smiled. "A shield. In essence, you're in a magical bubble. This room, and the attached bath, are contained. No signals—magical or mundane—in or out until I release the shield. It's for your protection and ours. While you're in this room, you can't contact anyone by phone, computer, or even magically. Nor can anyone contact you. Or enter, without me knowing about it. Only someone with magic that rivals mine could hope to breach this shield and by the time they did, I'd be here."

"Wait. What if Mario knocks on the door? He doesn't know I'm on to him. Maybe I could learn something."

"Not a problem. You can still talk to people face to face, but keep him out in the hall. He should have no awareness of the shield unless he tries to cross the threshold. That's to protect you in case things go wrong. In that case, step back from the door and wait for me. Nothing he can throw at you should be able to penetrate my shield before I can get here."

"How comforting." Steel made a face, but the man only laughed. "Cameron, if you don't mind my asking, what the hell *are* you? No creature I ever saw has as much magical energy as I just felt."

"I'm fey, lad, but more than that, I'm a *Chevalier de Lumière*. And that's something even my supernatural friends don't know." He winked with a sly grin.

Steel was shocked. "A Knight of the Light. Well, that explains a lot. Damn." He looked at the older man with new respect. "But why tell me?"

"Despite all you've seen today, I sense you still need some convincing you're on the right side in this. Being what I am," Cameron started to glow with magical energy that even Steel could see with mortal eyes—a sure indicator of his true power and affiliation with the Order, "I can see through to the heart of you, Benjamin. I know where you've been and can glimpse where you're going. You're at a turning point. Where you decide to go next will be crucial to the rest of your existence, and to that of many supernaturals in this realm. I reveal myself to you so you'll know you're on the right path. This is too important to leave to chance. For eons, *Venifucus* have used trickery to lead soldiers of the Light into darkness. You've come very close, but you still have a shot at redemption. Don't waste it."

With his final words, the light began to fade and Cameron didn't seem quite so imposing. Steel guessed he'd only seen a small portion of Cam's true power, but it was enough. The AC's lessons had included information on the Order. They were even more secretive than the *Venifucus*, and had been fighting evil far longer than the *Venifucus* had been in existence. Even the AC was afraid of them, not even trying to ferret out who might be part of their ranks.

"Thanks, Cam. You're right. I did have questions, despite what I've seen so far."

"That's understandable, lad. It's a lot to take in—especially for a mortal. Sensitive or not."

Steel felt the magic die down and then disappear completely. Cameron had some amazing power there. "I won't say anything to the others about you."

Cameron chuckled as he headed for the door. "I knew that already. You're the kind of man who knows how to keep a secret. I'll trust to your discretion. Now get some rest. I'll be back this afternoon to take down the shield and escort your sorry arse back to Sebastian's. I think you should consider moving in there until this is over. He's got the room and I believe a contingent of *were* are planning to prowl the grounds to help keep the bloodletters safe until we're ready to face your Mario again. Something tells me you need to make more friends among their numbers if you're going to be of help to us in the coming battle."

"You mean against Mario?" Steel asked as the fey knight turned the doorknob.

Cameron's eyes narrowed. "Aye, in this fight, and the rest of what's coming. I don't see much beyond the next battle, except that there will be more."

"You have the sight? What am I saying? You're fey. Can't all your people see the future? Or is that a myth?"

Cameron paused. "Most of us can see a bit, but it's not entirely reliable, you understand. And I've made my home in this realm, so I don't always interpret what I see clearly. All I can say for certain is that once we take care of Mario, there are more out there that need dealing with, but I didn't need the sight to tell me that. Your *Altor Custodis* has been corrupted, lad. A housecleaning is in order and I think you're just the man to do it."

True to his word, Cameron picked Steel up several hours later. He felt good after a hot shower and some much needed sleep. Mario hadn't come by, but Steel wasn't really surprised. They'd had little contact except when Steel called on Mario for backup, which wasn't all that often.

He still couldn't quite believe he was traveling around town with a fey knight. He'd had minimal instruction on the fey realm when he'd joined the AC because the fey were said to be rarer than rare here in the mortal realm.

Of course, the AC had also taught him that *weres* and vamps didn't work together either, but he now knew that was false. At least in this instance. But then, these were extraordinary circumstances.

Steel took his duffle bag with him when they went down to the truck, but didn't bother checking out. For one thing, the room was on the AC's tab. For another, Mario might come looking for him and it would look strange if he'd checked out without telling his backup. He also wasn't certain of his welcome at the vampire's home, though Cameron seemed pretty sure of it.

It was late in the afternoon when they drove through the gates of an impressive estate in the hills outside town. Steel noted the tingle of magic as they went through and the creatures who paused to look at the truck as they drove up the long drive. Two hawks, an owl, a wolf or two, and some big cats that were most definitely *were*creatures paused to allow themselves to be seen. He knew it was for his benefit. These special creatures would never have been spotted by a mortal in the thick forest unless they allowed it.

"Nice house," Steel commented as the big mansion came into view. Surprisingly, he meant it. Most fancy places like this annoyed him, but there was something about Sebastian's home that seemed welcoming.

"It is, isn't it? Sebastian modeled it after his ancestral estate, but on a smaller scale. He's young enough to miss the comforts of his mortal life. From what I understand, he still pays for the upkeep of the old place in England through a blind trust or some such. After his mortality was forfeited, he gave up his claim to the lands and title, but he's kept it safe for his brother's heirs all these years."

"So he was part of the aristocracy? What was he? A duke or something?" Steel chuckled at the idea.

"An earl, actually." Cameron's tone was dry as he parked the truck by the side of the house. Nearby, a giant garage stood open to showcase one hell of a collection of high-priced automobiles. The Lamborghini especially, caught Steel's eye. "But he left England penniless, three centuries ago. All you see here, he earned himself."

Steel caught the hint of pride in Cameron's voice. "You like the son of a bitch, don't you?"

Cameron laughed. "Aye, that I do. He's a special lad, for all that he's English."

"He's got a lot of power for a vamp on the young side, doesn't he?"

Cameron nodded as they headed for the big house. "His conversion wasn't a pleasant one. His maker found him near death, turned him to save his life, and abandoned him deep in the woods, all in one night. Not many would survive that ordeal, but the lad not only survived, he saved the life of a hurt little *were*wolf girl in the process. He brought the girl home to her parents, though he was weak as a cub himself, and forged a friendship the likes of which hadn't been seen in this realm for centuries. It's my belief he was put there, in those woods three hundred years ago, for just that purpose. He's a proven friend to the *were*. He's never played a single one of them false and they trust him. The trust he forged over three centuries will be key in the troubled times ahead. Mark my words."

Steel was startled by the idea, but if anyone could predict the future, he knew it would be a creature like Cameron. Steel stood beside him as he rang the bell at the front entrance.

Matt pulled open the heavy door a few moments later. They exchanged greetings and entered the spacious foyer.

"Hastings has set up an office of sorts in the media room. Sebastian already had these giant monitors, so we hooked up the computer to one so we could all look at the images and data together." Matt strode down the wide hall, ushering Steel and Cameron to a large room near one end of the big house. "We've also got the kitchen working, so if you're hungry, food's available." Steel's stomach growled at the mention of food and he knew he'd partake of dinner once he saw what the setup was.

Chapter Twelve

Matt didn't quite know what to make of Benjamin Steel, but so far, his quiet ways were endearing rather than annoying. The man was almost as still as the night. He had that creepy Special Forces way about him—like Hastings, and Matt's older brothers. It was odd to encounter in a person who wasn't supernatural at all.

Not that Matt didn't like human folk. From time to time, Redstone Construction employed some of his brothers' former comrades-in-arms. They were invariably good workers with strong ethics. The few who were close enough to his brothers to get a job with the company knew about the *were*, and their integrity was unquestioned. They wouldn't go blabbing to anyone about *were*creatures anytime soon, though *were*, in general, weren't as obsessive about secrecy as vamps. For one thing, there were a lot of highly placed *were* in positions where they could be helpful in covering up any indiscretions. For another, *were* could pass for human with few exceptions. Unless blood tests were involved—and those could be gotten around in many ways—folks who claimed their neighbors were *were*wolves ranked right up there on the credibility scale with alien abductees and UFO nuts.

Matt knew Steel hadn't learned the truth about the supernatural world until his final mission for the navy into the rainforests of South America. Hastings had a file on Steel he'd let Matt read. It seemed Steel's SEAL team had run into a rogue band of *were*panthers in the rainforest and Steel was the only one who'd made it out alive. He'd been a changed man after that. Not too much later, according to his file, he'd been recruited by the *Altor Custodis*.

"Make yourself at home," Matt said as they entered the media room. It was buzzing now with Hastings' agents, all busy filtering through various feeds of information. Matt perched on a table as Cameron greeted Hastings and his men with hearty handshakes all around. The fey had manners, Matt would give him that. Meanwhile, Steel held back, observing.

He stood near enough that Matt didn't have to raise his voice to be heard by the human. "Cam's a special one, don't you think?"

Steel glanced at him, an eyebrow raised. "I've never even seen a fey before."

"I figured he'd told you. The guy likes you for some reason." Matt snorted with good-natured humor. "But he's not *just* fey. There are rumors he's some kind of elite fey warrior. From what I've heard, he can fight on magical and material levels simultaneously. Not many in our realm can boast that skill."

Steel looked both knowing and curious. "Not even the vamps? They've got a lot of power—physically and magically—at least from what I've seen."

"Good point, but no. Many of them don't have enough time in to know how to do both simultaneously at peak efficiency. At least that's what Ian told me. And he's got a few centuries on the others. He was a knight in the Crusades."

Steel turned to face him, giving him all his attention. "I'm curious how a *were*cougar became so tight with a whole nest of vampires. I was told you guys didn't mix." He gestured to the bustling room. "I mean, Cam told me about how Sebastian helped a *were*wolf way back when, but what about the others? LaTour doesn't seem like the warm and fuzzy type to me, and that Ian guy is a stone killer if I ever saw one."

Matt barked out a laugh before he could stop himself. "Man. Sorry. You're so quiet, you caught me by surprise with that one. Yeah, Ian's intense and so is Marc, but you haven't exactly seen them at their best. Right now, the shit has well and truly hit the fan and they're in battle mode."

Steel seemed to consider. "Okay. I'll give you that. But still, what gives with you and the vamps?"

"Well, it started with Sebastian. We've been friends for a while. My family was suspicious at first and some of the clan still doesn't exactly welcome him with open arms, but they know he's a good guy. When my sister was killed by her mate, he..." Matt felt a lump rise in his throat at the thought of his lost sister. He'd loved her and missed her still. "He helped us track the rogue and helped me, personally, put the grief away long enough to get the job done. He was there for me and I'll always value his friendship." Matt shifted on his uncomfortable perch. "So when he asked for my help with Christy, I couldn't say no. I'd do a lot for that man. And helping a woman who nearly died at the hands of her husband felt right. I could help Christy where I failed my sister."

"I'm sorry for your loss." Steel's voice conveyed his sincerity. Matt nodded, saying no more as Cameron came back to them.

They went through the information gathered that day, but when Matt asked if anyone was up for some dinner, Steel and Cam both nodded eagerly. They dined in the giant, state of the art kitchen that saw little normal use. Now though, it'd been taken over by a contingent of *were* who were turning out some tasty meals for those gathered in the house and prowling the grounds.

When the sun went down, Matt felt Sebastian and Christy stir in his mind. He balled up his paper napkin and threw it in the trash with deadly accuracy from across the room, then rose and rinsed his plate before putting it in the dishwasher.

"We'd better get back." The others had finished eating long before Matt, but had stayed to savor coffee and a slice of pie. "They're awake."

Cameron slapped Matt on the back as they headed back toward the media room. "I can only imagine how you ended up bonded with a vampire couple. I had no idea our Sebastian was that kinky."

"It was sort of an accident." Despite his usual candor about all things sexual, Matt felt some embarrassment on this one issue.

Cameron chuckled. "Oh, I'll bet. I don't believe any vampire, thinking sanely, would engage in a threesome with his One and a *were* friend—or anyone for that matter—before they'd actually bonded. There must've been higher powers at work, my friend. Of that, have no doubt."

"You think?" The idea made Matt feel better...and worse. Better that fate had played a hand, and worse, wondering why fate would have interfered in such a way. What dreaded future role would their bonding play?

"Aye, laddie. Don't worry. The Lady works in mysterious ways. Value Her gifts, even if you don't understand them yet. She has plans none of us can fathom, but we all play our roles."

As they headed down the hall from the kitchen, which was located on the other side of the spacious house, they ran into Lissa and Atticus first, then Christy and Sebastian. After exchanging greetings, they all proceeded together to the media room where the troops were gathering.

Hastings greeted them when they entered. "I've set up a conference call for later this evening with the Lords and left messages for LaTour and Sinclair at the numbers they gave me."

"Excellent. They'll be here soon, then." Atticus escorted his wife to a seat on one of the large couches, then turned to check over the data displays the *weres* had been working on all day.

Christy was content to sit and talk with Lissa while the men conferred. She could easily pull the details of what had been learned while they were asleep all day from Sebastian's mind. The longer they were together, the more comfortable she became with the ability, though at times his stray thoughts still startled her. It was odd to be privy to someone else's innermost thoughts.

"Sebastian says *Sensei* Hiro is coming over tonight, Lis. If you want to learn some self-defense moves, you couldn't have a finer teacher."

Lissa shifted on the couch. "I've never been very athletic, but I'd like to try. Only you can't laugh if I make a fool of myself, okay?"

Christy smiled. "It's a deal."

A short while later, Marc and Ian arrived with an unexpected, but very welcome addition—Kelly. Christy hadn't seen her friend since that night in the hospital. They exchanged greetings and the men congregated around the computers while the women relaxed together.

"Christy, you're looking good. I've never seen such a sparkle in your eyes. Not since senior year." Kelly smiled and Christy could feel her friend's very real happiness for her. "I had suspicions about Sebastian from the way he reacted when I got the call from the hospital. He was working at the house with Marc that night and he got really scary when he heard what had happened to you. I didn't think much of it at the time, but later I realized he'd insisted pretty strongly on coming with us to the hospital. Now of course, I realize why. Congratulations, sweetie. You've got a good man there."

"I know. He's the best." Christy watched him move across the room, working with the other men. To her, he was the most handsome, the most amazing, of them all. "I still can't believe he's in my life. It all seems like a dream."

Lissa snorted delicately and shook her head. "Well, last night was more like a nightmare."

Kelly's face clouded. "Marc told me. I was so worried about you guys. And Marc's concerned for my safety now too. It's part of the reason I'm here tonight." She looked around at all the men in the room, most of whom were quite lethal with or without weapons. "With so many of us and the *were* here, Marc figured we'd be safe enough. Plus, I put my foot down. I wanted to see you guys and I'm sick of being under virtual house arrest. Marc is too overprotective!"

They all laughed when the man in question looked up and blew a comical kiss across the room at his wife. His wink was pure deviltry and Christy began to understand a little of the Master Vampire's charm.

On the other side of the big room, another large video display flickered to life. The colored bars were soon replaced with a new signal and a rather startling image of two identical men staring back at them. These, then, were the Lords of the *Were.* Christy pulled the information from Sebastian's mind as he faced the small camera pickup that would send his image to the twin men on the other end of the connection. Seems the supernaturals were down with technology. This was an honest to goodness videoconference.

Marc moved to the front of the group.

"Thank you for taking the call."

The twin on the right nodded. "Hastings said you had a

situation we might be able to help with."

"Did he send you the information he's gathered so far?" Marc looked over at the private eye, who nodded.

"We got it. Sounds like you've got a serious problem."

"You could say that." Marc smiled for the first time and the men on the other end of the line seemed to relax marginally.

The twin on the left sighed and shook his head. "Hell, if you've got *Venifucus* on the loose, we know how you feel. We've been there. Done that. Got the scars to prove it." He sat back in his chair, relaxing even more. "I'm Rafe. That's Tim." He pointed with his pen at his twin.

"Pleased to finally meet you. I'm Marc, this is Sebastian, Atticus, Ian and Cameron." He gestured to the men ranged around him in turn. "Do you know Matt Redstone? He's one of yours."

"We know his brother Grif. How is he? Still up in the mountains?"

Matt nodded. "Yes, Alpha. He's got some soul searching to do, but he's in touch. If he's needed, he'll come home."

The twins nodded. "No need for that quite yet. He needs this time and you've proven yourself well able to handle things so far."

A commotion on that end of the call momentarily halted discussion until two females came into view on the camera. One was older, and incredibly feminine. She walked right up to the camera and stared hard, her beautiful eyes squinting.

"Is that you, Cam? Darnit! I knew you were into mischief."

Cameron stepped forward with an easy smile on his face. "Guilty as charged, Bette. How've you been? Long time, no see."

"Well you can remedy that anytime, Cam. You know where I am." The petite woman moved back from the camera and took a seat. The other woman who'd come into the room with her was seated between the men. Christy wasn't surprised when the information came to her from Sebastian that the younger woman was married to both men. "Now, I'm sorry to burst in on all this male bonding, but there are important matters to discuss. Where is your mate, milord?"

Christy jumped as she realized the woman was talking to

Sebastian. He looked a little nonplussed as well, but recovered nicely, motioning for Christy to join him by the video setup. When she walked into the picture, the older woman's face softened.

"It's good to see you, child. Your image has haunted my dreams for many weeks now. I'm Betina. What's your name?"

"Christy. It's nice to meet you." She didn't know quite what to make of the woman, but then she moved and her sleeve fell away to reveal a glowing, swirling pattern. Christy gasped.

Betina's smile was cunning. "Ah, so it's true. You see what cannot be seen?"

Cameron stepped forward. "That she does. Tested her myself."

"Listen well." The older woman's demeanor changed and Christy perked up. "This skill and others will be key in the confrontation to come. It will take all of you, working together, to defeat this evil."

"You always did have strong sight, Bette," Cameron commented, breaking the somber mood.

"And you always were a loudmouth, Cam." Betina smiled and her entire face lit up. She winked, softening her words and Cameron obliged by bowing his head as he smiled.

"Guilty as charged, milady."

"So how are you all getting along down there?" Tim, the more serious of the twins asked. "Any cross-species problems we can help clear up?"

"Because," the other twin spoke up, "we're all going to have to learn to work together to get this job done. It's not *were* or vamp anymore, it's good versus evil. Plain and simple. We're either working together or we're all sunk."

"I couldn't have said it better myself, Alpha." Marc endorsed the *were*wolf's words. "As for my region, I've sent out the word to those under my dominion. As far as I'm concerned, we have an alliance against the *Venifucus*. As long as you're in agreement?"

Both men nodded. Rafe spoke first. "We've sent out the word to all our Alphas. Our governing structure is a little different than yours, but few will contradict us in this, I think, and those who do will be given a chance to reconsider before more serious action is taken. This fight is too important."

"The cougar clan is the largest in your area and you've got the Redstones on board, so you shouldn't have too much trouble with any of the other tribes, packs or clans." Tim spoke with calm certainty. "Hastings, I assume the raptors are in line with this?"

"Yes, Alpha." Raised eyebrows met Hastings' reply since none of the vampires had known the man was that high up the *were* food chain to be able to speak for the entire group of birds of prey.

"Let us know if you run into any problems. We'll do what we can," Tim said.

"Thank you, Alpha," Marc said, "we appreciate the endorsement and I want to assure you, for my part, my brotherhood is fully aware of our understanding. If any of mine cause problems, they will be dealt with. They have been warned."

The men talked a bit more about logistics and passed along some rather innocuous-sounding information about Mario's habits and phone records while Christy listened. She was fascinated by the women on the other end of the videoconference. Both shone with a slight glow of energy, but it was more pronounced around the older one. They were alike, yet different somehow.

"When this is all over," the younger one spoke as the men began to draw the meeting to a close, "I'd like to meet you in person, Christy. Maybe you and your mate could come visit us?"

"Yes." The older woman nodded. "You two are sisters under the skin. More alike than you know—a vampire with *were* blood and a priestess with *were* genetics. Both of you have your feet in two worlds. You have much in common."

Christy nodded politely. "I'd like that. Thank you for the invitation."

"Some time in the country might be just the ticket, Christy, after what you're embarking on." The younger woman's smile was friendly, almost teasing, as if she knew more than she was saying. And perhaps she did. These women were strange...and powerful. Christy could see that, even over a video screen.

They ended the call after a few more minutes and the men settled around a large table to go over reports and data. Hiro came into the room sometime later and offered to take the ladies to the *dojo* for a little self-defense class.

Christy hadn't had so much fun in ages. She'd almost forgotten what it was like to laugh, hang out and have fun with her old college friends. Hiro was good-natured about all their fumbles and even joined in some of the jokes himself. Christy hadn't known about his mischievous side, but she was charmed by his wit and earthy humor.

He even talked her into doing an advanced *kata* with him in front of her friends. Normally not one to seek the spotlight, Christy thrilled to the approval in her friends' eyes when she finished the form with a flourish.

"Where in the world did you learn how to do that?" Kelly seemed astonished as she walked over and took Christy's hand. "Chris, that was amazing!"

"*Sensei* Hiro has been a big help." Christy blushed a little while Hiro stood back, taking no credit.

"I bet all that *were* blood didn't hurt either," Lissa said with a knowing grin. "Atticus told me what *were* blood can do to our kind."

"Christy!" Kelly looked shocked. "You've been biting *weres*? And they let you? Or rather, Sebastian let you?" She chuckled at her own words.

"Just one *were*, actually." Christy moved toward the bench against the wall, wanting to escape the good-natured interrogation. This was embarrassing. "And it was before Sebastian and I..."

"Sebastian was your maker." Kelly appeared to be thinking through the sequence of events. "So you mean to tell me, he brought in a *were* for you to bite before he even claimed you? From the way you can jump, it'd have to be a *were*cat. Holy crap! You've been biting Matt Redstone?"

Christy gulped, caught. "Now how did you arrive at that conclusion?"

"Well, he's a cougar, and he's one of Sebastian's closest friends." Kelly dropped down onto the bench next to her. "Marc always seemed a little perplexed about the friendship. He likes

Matt. Respects him." Kelly turned to her with a wicked gleam in her eyes. "And *I* think Matt's totally hot!" She pressed forward a bit. "So tell me, have you done it with him? I mean, before you joined with Sebastian. I don't see Sebastian sharing." Christy's blush deepened as she squirmed. "Holy crap! You did them both? At the same time? Details! Girl, I want details!"

"Kel, you're embarrassing her." Lissa sat on Christy's other side, offering support. She'd always been the mother of the group. "Of course, I want to know too, but she can tell us later...in private." Lissa's eyes gestured comically to where Hiro stood across the room, trying hard not to laugh. Lissa's eyes turned speculative. "But it would explain what Atticus said, about you two being joined to Matt. Seems Matt was the only one who took time to explain to everyone else what was going on at our house last night when my husband and Sebastian took off. Handy, that."

Hiro came over and crouched down in front of Christy, commanding the attention of all three women. "Matt and Sebastian gave you a gift, Christy. You need never feel embarrassed or shamed by it. Your life is different now. Our customs are different. That's something I had to learn when I was first changed. In time, you'll come to understand it too, but it takes a while. So—" he looked pointedly at Kelly and Lissa, gentle humor in his dark eyes, "—give her a break, ladies. Okay?"

"Taking a break?" Sebastian asked from the doorway. Atticus and Marc were visible over his broad shoulders.

Christy stood, jumping nimbly around Hiro as she went to Sebastian, glad for the distraction. He pulled her into his arms and just held her, cuddling her head under his chin.

Hiro stood. "I think that concludes the lesson for today. You did very well, ladies."

The other women thanked Hiro, as did the men, but Christy and Sebastian were lost in their own little moment of time. It felt so good to be in his arms. So safe. So warm. It was like a slice of heaven on earth.

"I think we'll leave you two lovebirds alone." Atticus's tone was teasing as Christy looked up at him. He had Lissa tucked under one of his muscular arms as he headed for the hallway.

Marc took his leave as well and Christy waved to Kelly as

she headed out with her husband. Christy knew they'd be going to their own home for the day. Hiro cleared out a moment later with a nod in their direction.

"Did their teasing really bother you?" Sebastian looked down into her eyes.

Christy felt the heat rise to her cheeks as she remembered. "I was never one to kiss and tell, Sebastian, even in college. Those guys always enjoyed torturing me the day after a date, so this is nothing new." She shook her head, smiling. "I *should* be used to it, but darnit, I'm just not, and they know it."

"But you know they love you." Sebastian's voice was soft, almost wistful. "Which is why they're not going to like the plan we've come up with."

Christy pulled back to look up at him. "What are you guys up to now?"

"You don't know how rare it is for one of my kind to find his One. After so many years, I'd almost given up hope." He stroked her hair back, with loving attention. "Atticus had. I know that for a fact. He told me his life was empty before he met Lissa. He was ready to die. He welcomed it. But finding her changed that. Just like Kelly did for Marc. I convinced them to take their mates far away, where they'll be safe until all this is over."

Christy thought about that for a moment. "I can't imagine those men are too pleased to stand down from a fight."

Sebastian nodded, smiling. "You've got that right, but for their ladies, they'll do anything. I'm more concerned that Lissa and Kelly will balk at leaving you, but they're only fledglings and have no real control over their abilities yet."

She chuckled. "Yeah, they won't like it at all. But I'm glad they'll be safe." She rested her head against his shoulder, snuggling close again. "I don't want to see any of them hurt. We've got a lot of help between the *were* and the others, right? I'd hate to see our newlywed friends torn apart by any of this. They deserve a little happiness."

Sebastian stroked his big hands over her back. "You are a miracle of understanding, my love, and you're braver than any person I have ever known."

Chapter Thirteen

Marc and Kelly left for safety the next night. Atticus and Lissa went with them after taking their leave of Christy and Sebastian. One of Hastings' kin had been attacked and all evidence led to Mario as the perp. He'd left the youngster alive— just barely. He would recover, but it would take a very long time, and he'd never be quite the same again. A bird shifter, the *Venifucus* operative had seemed to take pleasure in maiming him so he would never fly again.

The attack was a message. Mario knew something was going on, and he knew Hastings was part of the team surrounding Sebastian and his mate. The attack upped the ante in a terrible way, driving home the necessity for the mated couples to go to safety. None of them liked it, but they saw the sense in taking precautions.

After Lissa and Atticus left Sebastian's house, Christy seemed more alone. Sebastian held her and offered reassurance, but there was little he could do. Christy wasn't alone, but they were in a very bad situation that was likely to get worse before it got any better. If it got better at all.

So it was a somber couple that entered the media room that night to greet their *were* guardians and friends. Matt waited for them, seeming to know without being told, that Christy's spirits were low. He slipped a brotherly arm around her shoulders and hugged her close while he and Sebastian shared a concerned look. The three seemed to communicate on an unspoken level that didn't go unnoticed by the others in the room. Such communion between *were* and vampire was abnormal, to say the least, but each person who saw them felt a tug at their emotions. These three were closer than mere friends. They were family.

Seeing their intense feelings for one another made this operation more personal, somehow. Even Steel felt a sort of kinship with these supernaturals. They felt sorrow and fear, happiness and pain, just like everyone else, he realized in those moments. For too long he'd been in awe of the abilities of these creatures. He'd missed the realization that almost every vampire he tracked had once been human, and every *were*creature had family and friends, living and mixing within human society. Sure, they were different, but they weren't entirely alien.

He remembered that when they sat down to discuss the events of the day, while their hosts had been asleep. Mario Gonzalez had raised the stakes and they would answer.

"We can't wait any longer," Sebastian said decisively. The entire team was gathered around. Steel and Cameron sat together. Matt sat between Christina and Hastings. "With Marc and Atticus safely away, this is up to us now. Gonzalez has to be stopped here. By us. Before he goes after anyone else."

"I agree," Cameron said easily. "By hurting the boy today, he was sending us a message. He knows more than we gave him credit for, I'll wager. At least about us." Cameron's crafty eyes shifted to the mortal at his side. "But I don't think he has a clue about you, Steel. You might be our ace in the hole—if you're willing."

The former SEAL shifted in his chair. "I hope you're right. And of course, I'll help in whatever way I can."

"All right then." Sebastian took control once more. "Let's do this simply. Steel, I want you to call Mario. Get him to meet you at a warehouse I own downtown. Tell him you've got a lead on Christina. There's a caretaker's cottage attached to the guard house on the property of the warehouse. You can say she's been hiding out there since the run-in with her husband."

"Sounds plausible." Steel nodded.

"We'll be lying in wait, though Christina will have to be exposed more than I like to get him to take the bait." Sebastian reached out to cover her hand with his. "I'll be with her. When Mario comes, he'll find us together. Cam, at this point, I hope you'll be nearby."

"Wild horses couldn't keep me away," the fey warrior confirmed.

Sebastian turned sad eyes to the *were*hawk. "Your people have already taken enough casualties in this battle, but we need backup, in case Mario doesn't do as we expect."

"This is personal now," Hastings said. "He's hurt my people. We'll be there. I'll have operatives at every perimeter point. Gonzalez won't escape, no matter what happens inside the warehouse compound."

"Good." Sebastian nodded. "So that leaves Steel outside near the target, with Christina, myself, and Cameron inside the warehouse."

"And me." Matt spoke for the first time, his voice strong and clear, as if he expected an argument.

"No, Matt." Sebastian didn't make him wait. "You can watch our backs well enough from the perimeter."

"I beg to differ." Matt's voice was firm. "Look, you, Steel and Christy have got to be out in the open. Gonzalez is expecting you, but Cam will be hidden, biding his time for the right moment to spring the trap. I propose to do the same. If Gonzalez zigs when Cam expects him to zag, I want to be close enough to redirect the bastard. We can't wait for him to hit the perimeter. We need at least one other person hidden on the inside of the compound to help steer the man in the right direction for Cam to do his thing."

"The lad has a point." Cameron scratched his chin thoughtfully.

"I don't like it." Sebastian bit out the words.

"There is also the fact that I'm connected to you two." Matt clinched the deal. "If something goes wrong, you can communicate with me without anyone—and I mean *anyone*—being the wiser."

The plan worked like a charm. Up to a point.

Mario Gonzalez seemed normal on the phone. Steel called him in for backup, as he had many times before. Mario responded as always with cold efficiency. No hesitation. No questions. Just as it had always been.

Why then, Steel asked himself as they waited within the empty warehouse compound in a desolate part of town, did the hairs on the back of his neck stand on end. Something wasn't quite right, though he couldn't place his finger on exactly what it was.

"He's coming." Steel flipped his phone shut and looked at the assembled players. Sebastian and Christy stood arm in arm, Matt hovering nearby. Cameron watched all with a discerning eye and Hastings, as always, looked ready to move. He was finalizing his team on the perimeter and would join them shortly.

"What's wrong?" Cameron asked quietly.

Steel shook his head. "Maybe nothing, but I've got this spooky feeling."

"You think Gonzalez knows something?"

"At this point, I wouldn't put anything past the man," Steel said grimly. "I can't believe he fooled me for so long and frankly, I don't trust my own judgment when it comes to him."

"A wise course when dealing with *Venifucus*." Cam's eyes darkened. "It's good to listen to your inner voice. What is yours telling you now, Benjamin?"

Steel was silent for a moment. "Trouble," he finally said. "There's something bad on the way and my hunch says Mario knows more than we want him to."

"There's no way to stop the wheels we've put into motion now," Cameron said with a sigh. "Best we make the most of this opportunity. It will not come again."

"I'll hit the perimeter now." Hastings began moving away. "Unless there's trouble, I'll keep my team out of sight until you signal."

Sebastian nodded. "The rest of you had better go too. Get in position and wait for all hell to break loose."

"I'll be outside the gate." Steel turned to go, walking to his agreed-upon position outside, looking in, as if he'd been conducting surveillance. He had a view of them all as he left.

Cameron took off for the concealment of a stack of crates on the other side of the yard. Matt hugged both Christy and Sebastian before trotting off after Cameron. Steel watched them go as he took his position outside, moving around a bit to make it look as if he'd been in the area for a while.

Steel had his senses fully extended, hoping to catch some glimmer from Gonzalez, but when the man appeared at his side about twenty minutes later, he didn't feel even the faintest hint of magic around him. It was unsettling. For the briefest moment, doubt crossed his mind, but then he thought of the people he'd gotten to know over the past few days. He knew them now. He'd witnessed the very real love between the mated pairs and the decency of the other folk. No way could all of them be deceiving him. He'd been able to sense the magic in the air around them. They had nothing to hide.

Unlike Mario Gonzalez.

"What's up?" the man asked, eyeing the warehouse compound through the fence.

"Christina Kinsey. This is where she went to ground. I checked around and this land is owned by a shell corporation. Ultimately, the owner is a vamp. He's in there with her now."

"Convenient," was Mario's reply. It set the hackles on the back of Steel's neck to tingling.

Current *Altor Custodis* policy was to have two eyewitness accounts to any supernatural surveillance, hence the need for a backup man in the vicinity when Steel was actively investigating. Mario was here to document Steel's observations, and then, if all went as it should, they'd both leave and move on to the next case.

He'd been sent to check out Kelly LaTour's friends, of which Christina Kinsey was one. This lead had panned out and now they knew she was, at the very least, under the protection of a vampire and the facts would be filed with the AC hierarchy. That was supposed to be the extent of his work. Others would be sent to keep tabs on the couple from time to time, now that they'd been identified.

But in the case of the others he'd tagged with Mario as witness, normal procedure flew out the window shortly after Steel left the scene. Mario—if all the evidence was to be believed—had left a bloody trail in Steel's wake from one end of the country to the other.

It would stop here. Tonight.

They watched for a few minutes until Sebastian came out

of the small cottage with Christy following behind. He went to his car, removed a few shopping bags and stopped to give Christy a quick kiss before they both headed back inside.

"Looks like they're a couple now. This guy moves fast. Good collar, my friend." Mario lowered his binoculars. "What do you sense from them?"

"Vamp," Steel said shortly. "Not too old. The guy...maybe a few centuries. The girl is new though. A lot of unfocused energy around that one."

Mario gave him a sharp look, but didn't say a word. They went through the motions of signing the paperwork Steel had prepared. If he sent it in to his superiors at the AC, it would net him a hefty bounty, but this particular file would never see the light of day. It would be destroyed tonight, before anyone else was killed because of his work for the AC.

"So, you want to grab a beer?" Steel asked, as he usually did after they'd finished a job. Mario always refused and this time was no different.

This was it then. Steel had done his part, but he couldn't leave the others to face Mario on their own. Plus, there was still a small part of him that needed to see the proof of Mario's treachery with his own eyes. Steel took his leave of the other man, but didn't go far. He would wait in the wings, just in case.

"Soon now." Cameron spoke in a low voice to Matt. They'd used Matt's ability to communicate with Christy and Sebastian to good advantage already. Cameron sensed the slight stir of energy when Mario showed up and was able to stage the scene, alerting Sebastian and Christy. They'd done their part, traipsing out to the car and back, letting Gonzalez get a good look at them. "Tell them to prepare. Steel just left, but he didn't go far."

The things Cam could sense amazed Matt while he played go-between for the fey and the couple inside the small cottage. This was tough on Christy, Matt knew. He could feel the echoes of her fear in his mind. The poor woman had been through a lot and though she'd stood strong through it all, at some point, Matt was afraid she was going to break. No one suffered through years of abuse without residual effects of some kind.

"Cam says Steel just took off, but he didn't go far," Matt

relayed the message. *"Gonzalez is still hanging around. Cam thinks it won't be long before he makes his move."*

"I hope Steel knows what he's doing." Christy's worried tones came back to Matt.

"Don't worry about him, Chris. He's a SEAL, and not the shifter kind either. Those boys know how to take care of themselves. My brother has some spec ops friends who work for us from time to time and to a man, they're every bit as resourceful as the were, even though they lack our native abilities. For mortals, they're damn ingenious."

"Watch now, the sorcerer is making his move. Tell them to be on guard." Cam's voice came to Matt's sensitive ears in the merest whisper. "Our boy just jumped the fence in a single bound. Nice trick, that, for a mortal mage." Cameron sounded suspicious, but continued to give Matt the other man's track.

"He's coming," Matt passed on the details as Cam relayed them.

There was a yard in front of the cottage, between it and the larger warehouse. It was an open space, with only a few strategically placed shipping containers and metal crates they'd positioned ahead of time. Cam and Matt hid behind one of these, waiting for Mario to get into a spot where they could ambush him.

But this wasn't your typical ambush. It was more magical than physical, though both aspects would have to be watched. They'd agreed beforehand that Matt would stay in human form. For one thing, he was an effective fighter in both his forms, but as a human he wouldn't have the extra telltale magical energy around him that might tip off Mario to the trap. Of course, changing to cougar was always a possibility if things went not quite as planned.

"He's not going for the cottage. Something's wrong. Our boy isn't playing by the rules. Warn them." Cameron moved to get a better view and Matt was chilled by the dangerous glint in his eyes. The lighthearted fey he'd seen to this point was suddenly all warrior and as deadly as they came.

The cottage was a decoy. Sure, the couple had gone into the small building, but they'd quickly gone out again through a secret, underground passage that led to the edge of the warehouse and then into the far end of a large, empty shipping container positioned right outside the warehouse's large doors.

Vampires had a habit of outfitting their properties with secret passages in order to keep them out of the sun. Perhaps Mario had guessed that, though there was no reason for him to single out the particular shipping container where the couple was hidden. The warehouse would have been the obvious choice if he didn't fall for the cottage and the trap they'd laid within its sturdy little walls. They'd prepared accordingly though, leaving Hiro, Ian and several others inside the warehouse to keep the mage busy while Cameron did his work, but Mario moved as if he knew exactly where the couple was, and that didn't fit with their plans at all.

"He's heading your way," Matt warned them. *"He's not making for the cottage or the warehouse. He's heading right for you. I wouldn't recommend getting caught in that tin can."*

The shipping container was large, but not big enough to maneuver in, should the fight come to them. Sebastian had considered this when they devised the plan and thought it worth the risk. He also had two clear exits from the container, and an ace in the hole—Matt on the outside, able to relay just where the mage was headed.

"He's coming in from the south," Matt said.

"Let me know when he's at the door. We'll go out the north end and circle around him, but I don't want to move too soon, in case he has some way of tracking us." Sebastian reasoned that for the mage to home in on them so quickly, there had to be something about them that he sensed and was able to follow. Timing was critical. Move too soon and the mage would adjust his course to intercept. Move too late and be caught in the box.

"He's almost there. Any second now."

Sebastian kept one hand on Christina's back, ready to push her out the door, should it become necessary. He didn't like the way this was playing out, but they'd make the best of it.

"Cam says something's happening. Get out of there now! Now!"

Matt's warning came a second too late as Sebastian felt his world turn upside down. He had time enough only to shove Christina out the door before the shipping container became a rolling maelstrom of death and destruction.

"Holy shit!"

It took a lot to take down a vampire of Sebastian's skills, but a crashing, rolling, ton of steel with wildly flying doors could do it. Matt saw one of the swinging metal doors clip Sebastian in the temple as the shipping container thundered away, rolling like a giant, steel tumbleweed. When the thing came to a rocking halt after a revolution and a half, it was yards away, creaking ominously. Sebastian was nowhere to be seen and Matt couldn't feel the vamp's presence in his mind. Sebastian was either dead or out cold.

Christy sat alone, her small face white with terror as Mario walked calmly toward her. Matt willed himself to change, but found he was frozen in place by some kind of magic that not only restrained his shift to cat form, but also glued him to the spot. He could move his jaw just enough to whisper to Cameron. The fey's face was grim, his concentration total as he cursed under his breath.

"I can't move."

"I know, lad. I'm working on it. Can you still communicate with the lass?"

"Yes, but Sebastian's gone."

Cameron's face grew darker, but he seemed able to move his hands. He made small gestures that Matt couldn't follow, but knew they had something to do with his way of spellcasting.

"Talk to the lass. Ask her about the mage. Blast! This angle is all wrong. I can't work from behind him. I need to see his face. I need to know about his mark. Ask her."

The command in his voice was clear, as was the frustration. Matt understood it well as he touched Christy's mind, finding a choking whirlwind of terror.

"Sweetheart, calm yourself."

"Calm myself? Matt! Sebastian's hurt!"

"I know. Mario's done something to the whole area. I can't move. Cam needs to know about Mario's mark. What can you see of it?"

"His mark?" Confusion sounded through her words, but

she was slowly getting it together. Matt only hoped it would be in time. For now, the mage was stalking her, moving closer as she cowered on the ground, seeming to enjoy her fear.

Matt saw her head move. She wasn't immobilized, thank heaven. He could have cheered when she got to her feet and faced Mario, but he also feared for her.

"The mark on his face is glowing, Matt. It's pulsing."

Matt relayed the information to Cam, who was still weaving patterns with his fingers. He seemed lost in concentration and barked back a single question.

"Which part of the pattern is glowing brightest, honey? Cam needs to know. And anything else you see."

"The sixth line, Matt. There are nine lines in all. They're all interwoven like Celtic knot work on the edges, but the center part lines up. The largest is at the base of his eyebrow, the smallest at the top. The sixth from the bottom is pulsing really strong. The bottom one is also brighter than the others, but not as bright as the sixth."

Matt passed on her words, cringing when he saw the mage close in on Christy. She looked so vulnerable, so defenseless as she waited for the attack that would surely come. He only hoped the training they'd been doing with her over the past days would help her stand strong.

It felt eerily familiar to be cowering before a man, hoping he wouldn't kill her. And the warm, loving presence that was Sebastian was gone from her mind. Christy didn't know if he was even alive, though she knew it would be hard to kill an immortal with nothing more than a flying shipping container. Still, that impressive little magic trick had scared the crap out of her!

She had to believe in her heart that Sebastian was just unconscious. The alternative was unthinkable.

"Be strong, sweetheart. Cam is working on something, but he's affected by the paralysis too. He can move, but only his hands, and not fast. You need to buy him some time to bring that spell down."

Matt's voice in her mind was a lifeline. It reminded her she wasn't alone anymore. Even with Sebastian's fate uncertain, she had friends all around. She just needed to keep this bastard busy while they worked. Only with their help could she get to Sebastian and find out if he would be all right. That was all that mattered now.

She segregated the fear and put it away. She'd had ample practice of late, hiding from things she didn't want to face. Pain, fear, longing for a more normal life. All those things she'd separated out while she'd put up with increasing problems in her home life and marriage.

That experience stood her in good stead now. She stood opposite the man, watching him watch her. He seemed to be sizing her up and the sneer on his swarthy face said he found her lacking.

Never again, she vowed. She'd never cower before a violent man again. She wouldn't play dead and she would defend herself to her last breath. She knew how now. Thanks to Sebastian. And Matt and Hiro, of course. She'd only known the men a short time, but they'd each touched her life in significant ways. Sebastian had given her new life and a reason to want to live it to the fullest...with him.

"How dare you?" Christy went on the verbal offensive, wanting to give Cameron the time he needed. "This is the second time you've attacked me and I don't even know you! What is your problem?"

His black eyebrows rose at her tone. She'd surprised him. That was good. Maybe.

"My problem, *señorita*, is you and all your little supernatural friends that would oppose our plans for this realm."

"Good girl," Matt crooned in her mind. *"Keep him talking. Cam says he's close. Just a few more minutes."*

"I have no idea what you're even talking about. Make some sense, will you? In case you didn't know, all I want is to get a divorce from the abusive slimeball I married and get on with my life."

"Don't you mean your death?" Mario moved closer, smiling in an evil way as he began to move his hands in a mesmerizing pattern.

"I'm not dead."

Mario sniffed disdainfully. "So you believe, but I will remedy that shortly."

"Don't let him wave his fingers around like that. Cam's doing something similar over here and I think it's the way they weave their spells. I bet if you can disrupt his hand motions, you might disrupt whatever it is he's planning to throw at you." Matt's advice was given in an urgent tone. Christy bided her time, waiting for Mario to move within range of her best roundhouse kick. *"Stop him, Christy. Stop him, now!"*

Christy let loose with a kick that took the mage by surprise. She heard a crunch and knew she'd broken at least one of his fingers and probably some of the bones in his palm, all thanks to her sturdy, pointy-toed flats and *Sensei* Hiro's tutelage.

"Christina?" Sebastian's voice sounded in her mind and the relief she felt knew no bounds.

"Sebastian! Are you all right?"

"My head hurts like the dickens and I can't move, but otherwise I'm okay. What happened?"

"Matt said this Mario guy did something that immobilized him and Cam too, to some extent. Cam's still working a countermeasure and I'm supposed to keep Mario busy until he gets it done. I kicked him and broke his finger, Sebastian. And probably some other bones in his hand."

"Good for you, sweetheart."

"You might think so, but it was really gross."

The warm chuckle in her mind and loving caress of his thoughts went a long way towards shoring up her flagging courage.

"Where is he now?"

She eyed the man, standing a few feet away, breathing harshly.

"He's giving me the stink eye from about five yards away. He's hurt, but he's still standing."

"If he hasn't fled, he'll come after you again, love. Be wary."

"Oh, I'm watching him like a hawk, don't worry."

"Dammit! I wish I could move!"

"Me too. I love you, Sebastian. No matter what, I'll always love you."

"And I you, my sweet. Forever."

Mario chose that moment to launch his next attack, but she was ready. Barely.

"Die, bitch!" Mario screamed, clutching his injured hand to his chest, while in his other hand, a sparkling fireball formed out of thin air. He lobbed it at her, but she was able to spring out of the way like a cat, diving, rolling, and landing, crouched on all fours. Mario launched another fireball, but she sprang out of the way again, rolling toward him, coming up in a fighting stance right in front of his startled face.

She took the opportunity to punch him in the stomach and when he crumpled inward, she grabbed his uninjured hand and twisted it up behind him, trapping him in an arm bar position. She couldn't allow him to lob more fireballs, so as gross as it was, she used the move Hiro had taught her to break his arm at the elbow. The crunch was sickening, but she had no alternative. It was either that or be burned alive by one of his magical fireballs.

Christy thought she was going to puke. She'd never forget the sound of that arm breaking as long as she lived. She let Mario go and stumbled away, revolted by what she'd been forced to do. A wave of nausea made her clutch her stomach and for a split second, the mage was forgotten.

"Hold fast, love," Sebastian counseled in her mind. *"I'm coming."*

"Sebastian?"

She saw him then, out of the corner of her eye, struggling as if his limbs weighed hundreds of pounds each, but still, somehow, making his way out of the remains of the shipping container behind Mario. But he was moving too slowly. He was fighting the immobilizing magic, but would be a sitting duck if Mario discovered his presence.

"Matt? How is Cam coming with that countermeasure?"

"Almost there."

"Tell him to hurry, Matt. Sebastian is awake and out in the open. He's fighting it, but he's very vulnerable right now."

"Dammit!" Matt broadened his communication to include Sebastian. *"Stay put, man, until Cam frees us completely."*

"Sorry, Matt. No can do. My lady needs me." Sebastian

sounded as if every word were a struggle as he fought against the magic trying to hold him in place.

"She needs you to stay alive, you idiot. Stay put! Cam says he'll punch through any second now."

Christy kept her focus on Mario. The man was still standing, mouthing words under his breath in some foreign language, and Christy feared what he might be calling.

"Oh, no you don't." She ran forward and launched herself in a flying kick, meant to knock him out, but ran into a kind of invisible wall that sent her flying backwards. Only the animal grace imparted by Matt's blood allowed her to land without breaking bones. As it was, she knew she'd be sore for days from her jarring contact with the ground.

But her distraction served its purpose. She saw the sixth line of Mario's tattoo stop pulsing and fade to match the other lines. That strange phenomenon was followed by a little pop of magic in the air and then Sebastian was moving normally. Well, normally for him. He was across the distance from the shipping container to Mario in a blurring display of speed.

His hands had morphed into razor-sharp talons the likes of which didn't exist in nature. With them, he neatly sliced the mage's neck from behind, before the other man even knew what hit him.

Sebastian threw him down hard, discarded like an old rag doll, and morphed his talons back to hands as he came to her, picking her up off the ground and tugging her into his arms.

He rocked her as she clung to him, touching his blood-stained face and inspecting what she could see of the damage. He'd been hit hard in the temple, which was undoubtedly what had knocked him out.

"Oh, my love," he whispered, kissing her hair and clutching her close, "I was so worried."

"Me too." She hiccupped, remembered fear clogging her throat.

Sebastian held her with his back to the man on the ground, but she could see Mario's body, twitching. He wasn't dead!

Things happened quickly then. A streak of tawny fur tore across the yard and tackled Mario as he rose to his knees, muttering dark words of magic. The glow of his facial tattoo increased and the cougar slowed, but refused to be stopped.

Matt had the mage by the throat, but Mario refused to fall. Then Cameron stepped out into the open and for a moment, Christy saw his whole body glow with otherworldly light. In the blink of an eye, Cam was dressed in ethereal armor as he strode forward to face Mario. His hands moved in intricate patterns and one by one the marks on Mario's face diminished and then popped out of existence. The glowing tattoo unraveled as it died, the intricate knot work of twining vines of energy retracting and winking out of sight.

Then the light of life itself left his eyes as Matt's strong, cougar jaws ripped out his throat. Mario fell, finally, lifeless to the ground while Christy hid her eyes against Sebastian's shoulder. She'd seen and done enough for one night. Never before had she witnessed or committed such acts and just thinking of it made her feel queasy.

"Courage, my love." Sebastian was there, with her, knowing her thoughts and ready to help her recover. If not for him, she could never have done any of this. If not for him, she'd already be dead. He was her life, her world, her universe, and she would be strong for him.

They stood together and faced what would come next.

Cameron stood over the body, still working the last of his spells while Matt trotted off. He reappeared a moment later, dressed once more in his jeans, though he was still buttoning his shirt as he walked toward them.

Chapter Fourteen

Mario Gonzalez lay dead on the ground, his lifeblood pooling around him, returning to the Earth from which he came, so many years before. Christy clung to Sebastian, holding on to her lover as if for dear life.

Others came out of the darkness to check on them. Matt met his fellow *were*, moving in from the perimeter. He spoke short words with Hastings and learned that every *were* who'd been placed on the perimeter of the grounds had been incapacitated by whatever spell Mario had woven.

Hiro and Ian reported the same had happened to them inside the warehouse, though Ian had been able to move a little more than his younger colleague, Hiro. That the human mage had been able to so easily disable so many beings of power over such a large area was troubling, to say the least.

Matt went to Christy and Sebastian, knowing from his connection to them that the storm was past for now. They pulled apart as Matt walked up. Cameron flanked them as they stood around Mario's lifeless body.

"This one's outstayed his welcome in the mortal realm." Cameron looked with satisfaction at the dead mage. "I sense the balance returning, and that's a good thing, but we'll need to do something with this." He gestured to the body.

Sebastian stepped forward. "Marc and I discussed this before he left." He nodded to Ian and Hiro, who also stepped forward. "We want to be sure he can't come back." A significant look passed between the men and Matt knew the vampires meant to sever the man's head and remove his heart, then burn him and scatter his ashes to the four winds. Matt personally thought it was a bit of overkill, but he didn't want to see this evil asshole resurrected any more than they did.

Hastings moved closer. "We can help."

"Ian and I can carry him aloft in shifted form," Sebastian said. "If some of your winged brethren would follow, we could use their help to scatter the remains as far and wide as possible."

"Done." Hastings moved off to organize his people.

"And you'll want to be doing this in a sacred space," Cameron added thoughtfully.

Sebastian nodded. "There's a stone circle in the foothills we can get to quick enough by air."

"I see you've thought it all through." Cam bowed his head, though his gaze never left Sebastian's. "Your leader has my compliments. He's a thorough man. I look forward to fighting at his side one day, should it prove necessary."

"I'll pass that along," Sebastian said. "For now, we'd better get to work. Matt, will you see Christy home? And please let the *were* know they are welcome to stay at our place. I think we should stick together after such traumatic events. At least for a while."

Matt stepped up. "I'll tell them." He gave Sebastian a brotherly hug, pounding him on the back. "I'm glad you're okay."

"Same here, friend. Thanks for sticking by us and helping my lady when I was unable." Matt was a little shocked to see the vampire's eyes fill with emotion. When Sebastian would have said more, Matt stopped him.

"We can talk later. For now, I'll take care of your woman. You take care of the bad guy, and do a thorough job of it. I shudder to think of any of us having to face that bastard again."

"Amen to that." Sebastian left Christy with a quick kiss and went to work with Ian, both vampires shifting quickly to bird form. They were huge California condors in shape, but in strength they were mightier than ten men. They each took hold of an arm and a leg with oversized talons and flapped great wings that lifted them into the air. They were awkward, but got the job done.

Matt marveled at the vampires' ability to shift into just

about any form they wished and selectively alter parts of their anatomies for whatever task they needed to do. That wasn't something *were* could do, but then, for all their power, the vampires paid dearly. Matt couldn't imagine never eating his favorite foods, or feeling the sun on his skin...or his fur. It was the vampires' greatest weakness.

Matt watched as the vampires flew out of sight, followed by a flight of various kinds of flying *were*. Most were raptors, with Hastings in the lead. Cameron spoke in quiet tones with Christy, then turned to Matt.

"Things should be all right now, for a while at least." Cam clapped him on the back, hugging him to his side for a brief moment. "You did good tonight, boyo. It was an honor working with you."

"Thanks. Same here." They shook hands and the fey warrior stepped back.

"With all the magic flying here tonight, it's a sure bet the enemy knows where I am. I'll teleport myself to the stone circle, just to make sure they've got a handle on things. Dealing with a mage of such power—even in death—is not an easy task. I'll set them on the right track, then 'port to Sebastian's house. Take Hiro with you and get some of your *were* brethren to guard your backs as you make your way to the estate."

"Will do. We'll be all right, Cam. Go do what you've got to do."

"Good man. Be safe, my friends." Cameron sent Christy a smile and a small nod of respect.

Then with a flash of light, he winked out of existence.

"Man, that is some cool shit." Matt marveled aloud at Cameron's abilities. When he turned his attention to Christy, she was looking fragile again. Poor mite had been through the wringer and then some in the past weeks, not to mention this hellacious evening.

Matt simply held out his arms and Christy walked into them, resting her cheek against his chest and hugging him.

"Thanks, Matt." Her voice quivered. "When I couldn't feel Sebastian in my mind, I almost lost it. If not for you..."

"Ssh, sweetheart. I'm glad I could help. You and Sebastian are very special to me. I want you both to live long, happy lives together and tell my descendants about me long after I've passed on."

"Don't talk about death, Matt. Not even remotely. I can't face any more tonight." She sniffled and burrowed closer. "Just take me home. I need to clean up and so do you."

"Yes, ma'am." He kissed the crown of her head. "Your wish is my command."

They walked around back to where they'd left the cars out of sight, picking up a small group of *were* along the way. Many of the land-based *were* wanted to decompress together after the harrowing events of the night and had already decided to act as guards during the next day or two at Sebastian's estate, just to be sure. His spacious grounds had the added attraction of being one of the few places *were* could run free and still be close to the city.

Hiro drove Sebastian's car from around front, and waited for Matt and Christy to hop in with him while a few carloads of *were* got in front and behind in an impromptu caravan. Hastings had given orders to his people, organizing them into watches. Some stayed behind to keep surveillance on the warehouse area in case any of Mario's associates came nosing around. Matt was glad, once again, to have the military-trained *were*hawk on their team. Hastings was on top of every aspect of the operation and always seemed to think three steps ahead.

Steel went back with them to the estate as well, having witnessed only a little of what went down in the warehouse compound. Like the *were*, he too had been immobilized by Mario's magic.

The mystery remained as to why Christy had been spared. Of all of them, she was the one Mario had gone there to kill. Why leave her able to move and immobilize everyone else?

Matt realized the answer almost before the thoughts finished forming. Like any sick predator, he'd wanted to play with his prey before killing it. The man had positively enjoyed Christy's fear in the moments before she got herself together.

He'd probably banked on the idea that with her past, she'd be easy pickings, regardless of the skirmish they'd had on the patio of Atticus and Kelly's home. Maybe Mario figured that on neutral ground—away from the serious protections around a vampire's lair—he'd have an open shot at the young woman who'd only been turned weeks before.

Lucky for them, he'd thought wrong, and his miscalculation had been his defeat. Underestimating Christy had been his first mistake. Underestimating her friends had been his last.

Matt felt satisfaction as he remembered the feel of the man's throat under his jaws. When he was in cat form, he reveled in the kill. More so, when it was as justified as this one had been.

The ride back to the estate was uneventful. Christy kept silent, staring out the window as Hiro drove. Matt sat with her in the backseat, in case she should need him, but she seemed to be holding up well. Just knowing that Sebastian was all right went a long way toward her equilibrium, he knew. The two depended so greatly on each other already, he marveled at the relationship.

Marveled and envied. Matt didn't ever think he'd be lucky enough to find a woman who could share his life. Many cats didn't. Chances were good that one of his brothers would find a mate and take care of siring the next generation. As the youngest, Matt didn't expect that task would fall to him, though after seeing Christy and Sebastian together, he wouldn't mind finding a partner to share his life and his love, if he should be so blessed. That was a rather startling revelation for a cat shifter who'd always been on the prowl. After seeing his friends and experiencing their love, it looked like his prowling days might just be over.

It took over an hour to get from the warehouse district to the estate. They pulled up and some of the *were* guards went ahead to be sure things hadn't been disturbed on the grounds or in the house before Matt and Hiro escorted Christy inside.

She went into the first bathroom they came to and cleaned up. When she emerged, she looked better, though tired. Matt led her into the living room and settled her on one of the soft couches. She seemed a little out of it still after the tumultuous events of the night. Not surprising, really, for a woman who'd only recently found courage to fight. Tonight had been brutal for her, considering her background.

Matt left her there with Hiro and went to clean himself up. He stopped in at the large kitchen and found a few of his *were* brethren had started cooking. He had to grin at that. Trust the *were* to want to chow down after a night watch. Matt found tomato sauce and pasta cooking on the stove. Nothing like carbs to reenergize.

But he decided to wait a while before eating anything heavy, grabbing a granola bar off the counter instead. His stomach felt a little off and now that the adrenaline high had faded, fatigue was setting in. It wasn't usual for him, but then, nothing about this night had been normal. Matt put the unsettling weakness up to the trauma of the battle and thought nothing more about it.

Christy appreciated Matt giving her some space. It was tough to come to terms with the things she'd seen and done that night. Thinking about it during the long ride home and now, sitting with Hiro in the living room, she was damned proud of the way she'd stood up to Mario.

It was a far cry from the way she would have reacted just a few short weeks ago. And it was all thanks to Sebastian. He'd saved her life and brought in Matt and Hiro to give her strength and knowledge. She owed all three men for her transformation, but most especially Sebastian. Without him, nothing else mattered.

Hiro sat silent sentinel across the big room, his quiet ways comforting. He watched over her without intruding on her thoughts, the *sensei* seeming to know instinctively when she needed to think things through.

"I haven't thanked you." She spoke into the silence, meeting Hiro's gaze as he stood from his meditative pose and took one of the chairs opposite the couch she'd chosen. "Your training went a long way towards saving my life tonight. I'm in your debt."

"You saved your own life, Lady Christina, I merely gave you the knowledge. You were the one who took it inside and let it guide you when there was need. You did us all proud tonight. Especially yourself."

The smile he gave her went straight to her pride. Such simple praise had never been directed her way during her married years and she'd only realized since waking up in the hospital, she'd missed it terribly. Hiro was a kind soul, a gentle man with a big heart, but he was also a tough task master. He didn't give praise easily and his words meant all that much more because of it.

"Thanks." She spoke in a careful way, afraid to let emotion overwhelm her. After the ordeal they'd been through, she felt more fragile than she liked.

Matt came into the room, munching on a granola bar, breaking the mood. He sprawled on the couch near Christy and put one foot up on the coffee table.

"Make yourself at home." Hiro chuckled and Christy followed suit.

"After the night we just had, I think I'm entitled to put my feet on the furniture, don't you?"

"Oh, you're entitled to more than that, my friend." Sebastian's voice came from the patio entry, where he drew the glass door open and stepped through.

Christy popped off the couch and went to him, hugging him in greeting as the others followed behind their host. Ian was there, with Hastings, Cameron, and a few other *were* she'd met in passing.

A dutiful host, Sebastian poured drinks for them all. He gave Cam the precious, two-hundred-year-old Scotch he favored and poured deep red wine for himself, his vampire brethren, and his lady. The *were* drank their choice of beers and liquors Sebastian kept on hand for guests, and chowed down on the various snacks stocked in the small bar at the side of the room. Some followed their noses to the kitchen for a meal with their fellows, who were cooking up a storm for the always hungry *were*folk.

"Everything's settled then?" Hiro asked as he greeted his colleagues.

Sebastian nodded once as Ian answered for them both. "He's never coming back."

"Praise the Lady for that," Matt said from the couch, succinctly summing up all their feelings on the matter.

"I still can't believe how powerful that mage was." Sebastian shook his head. "Cam, you did some amazing things tonight and I can never thank you enough."

Cameron gestured with one weary hand and collapsed into an overstuffed chair. Sebastian tucked Christy into his arms and sat on the couch beside Matt. The *were*cougar's head rested against the back of the leather sofa, his eyes heavy-lidded.

"The pattern on Mario's face was the key. The most important bit was the nine lines Christy described—signifying the nine realms to which Mario's magic was connected. I'm sorry to say, he was more powerful than any mage I've met before in this mortal realm. Few have connections to more than three or four other realms, but our boy Mario had a direct link to what I like to call the sixth level of hell. If I'm not much mistaken, that sixth line represented his link to the place where Elspeth is exiled. For a certainty, he was using Elspian magic of a kind not seen here for many generations." Cam sighed, not liking the implications for the future. "Since Mario was mortal, I assume that base line—the longest one and next powerful—was his link to this realm of his birth. The Lady only knows where those other lines led. I fear to think on it." Cam shuddered in his seat. "Once I was able to sever those two strongest links, the rest collapsed. It was a tricky piece of magic, and not my neatest by any means, but it did the trick. This time." His mouth set in a grim line.

"It was like nothing I've ever seen." Matt eyed him with both awe and suspicion.

"That sort of magic is not of this realm. For that matter, *I'm* not of this realm, laddie." Cam winked. "It's a case of fighting fire with fire. Otherrealm magic often can only be countered by similar means. That's part of what I do here, playing about in your world. When I find out about evil from other places infiltrating here, one of my duties is to track it down and eliminate it, but I'm sorry to say, without your link to our Christina, all my magic would have been for naught this night. I've never faced an opponent like this one and I fear he's not the last we will see. Tonight proved—as nothing else could—that we'll all have to work together. On my own, I could not have taken Mario down." Silence met that stark announcement. "His spell immobilized everything except his prey. It even worked to keep me glued to my place, though I could move more than anyone else because of my ties to other realms beyond Mario's reach. Still, if I'd been facing him alone, all he would've had to do is walk behind me where I couldn't see him and stab me in the back. He wouldn't even have to do it magically. A simple knife would've worked at that point. I've never felt so powerless in all my long life."

Cameron saw his words sink in. He'd meant his warning to sober them and judging by the looks on their faces, it had. He knew he had to impress upon them how important it was to keep their temporary alliance going.

Sebastian broke the uncomfortable silence. "Your words are troubling, old friend, but well taken. I think we've started something here, with this group of friends we've gathered together. I take your warning to mean we should probably expect to work together more often if Mario is just the tip of the evil iceberg we've yet to fully discover."

"As usual, you see through to the heart of the thing, lad." Cameron lifted the crystal glass and drained it. "This alliance between your kind and the *were* must continue. For my part, my few fey brethren in this realm are already allied with the *were*, we'd extend that to those bloodletters who are willing to work with us for the duration of this threat, as well."

Sebastian nodded, his face grave. "I've always been a friend to *were* and fey. We'll have to talk to Marc about formalizing relations, but I don't think he'll have any objection. He understands the threat we all face, though I don't think any of us realized until just recently how dreadful the danger truly is."

An hour or two before dawn, the informal gathering broke up. Most of them sought guest rooms to grab some much needed rest while the rest of the *were* took turns guarding the estate. Sebastian was grateful for their vigilance and willingness to lend a hand. He was wiped out from the adventures of the night, and in desperate need of some alone time with his new mate.

He led her to the large master bath in the underground chambers where they would sleep away the day in each other's arms. But first, he very much needed to clean up, and to pamper his lady. He needed to do so, to reassure himself that all was once again well—at least for now.

He drew a bath in the oversized tub while Christina undressed, lacing the warm water with lavender bath salts he had specially made with pure essential oils. There was nothing like the scent, and he loved the feel of the refreshing mixture of sea salt and cleansing lavender oil on his skin. It was something from his old life in England that he'd never been able to forget or cast aside.

His mother had grown lavender and used the essential oil from the plant for all kinds of things. She'd been an amateur herbalist and had taught her son many things about plants and their uses. Now, hundreds of years later, Sebastian used those same recipes, learned at his beloved mother's knee, to have different creams and lotions made up for his personal use—and now for Christina's.

In his day, lavender hadn't been strictly a women's scent, and he still loved it. Certainly, he didn't think he'd ever countenance going about smelling of roses or gardenias, but he knew some dandy recipes for things he would order at the first opportunity for Christina. He longed to spoil her in every way and protect her all their lives, however long that proved to be.

"Come, my love, the bath is ready."

He knew he didn't have to speak the words. Christina was in his mind at all times now, as he was in hers. It had been strange at first, until they'd learned how to manage the information overload. They'd worked over the past weeks at segregating each other's thoughts to discrete areas so things were less confusing, but when they wanted to, they could open the channel wide and share everything they felt and thought with each other.

The best possible time for such deep sharing was in passion and they did so often, but each time it was special. Still new, their relationship was the deepest part of each of their souls. They were truly One, never to be parted, which made him feel both safe and utterly terrified of losing her.

The past hours had been a trial almost beyond bearing. Putting Christina deliberately in the path of danger had gone against every fiber of his being, but Sebastian knew it had to be done. When Mario had changed all the rules of their encounter and knocked Sebastian flat on his ass, he'd never been more frightened.

As he'd blacked out from the massive blow to his head, his last horrified thought had been that Christina must now face the monster alone. He could have wept then, if he could have remained conscious. As it was, when he finally woke up he couldn't move, and the inability to see what was going on from inside the mangled container had sent terror streaking through him.

Until he heard her voice in his mind. The link that nothing short of death could destroy, had reassured him and alarmed him at the same time. Knowing his love was in mortal danger, facing a mage the likes of which they had not bargained for, all alone, terrified him. There was little in the world that could scare a vampire of his age and power, but his mate brought that uncomfortable feeling all too close for comfort.

"You're so good to me, Sebastian." Christina ran a gentle finger along his chin as she turned, dropping her silk robe. She climbed into the tub before he could waylay her, but she had his full attention. He could tell from the flirty look in her beautiful eyes and the connection they shared, that she was as needful of their joining as he was. It was nearly a physical ache. He needed to touch her, to be close to her, like he needed his next breath.

Sebastian shucked his clothes and stepped into the giant oval tub, settling behind her. She was tucked into the V of his thighs, her luscious bottom resting against him. For a moment he let the scent of lavender and Christina waft over him as he rested his chin atop her head and folded his arms around her middle, hugging her close.

"I love you more than life, Christina. I couldn't go on without you."

"Same goes for me, Sebastian." He couldn't see her expression in this position, but felt the tremors in her small body and the anguish in her mind. "When you pushed me out of that container and it went flying...and then you weren't in my mind..."

She hiccupped and Sebastian soothed her, rubbing her skin and murmuring soft sounds of comfort. "It's all over now, my love, though I just about lost it when I realized you had to face that bastard all on your own. I never wanted that to happen. I'm sorry I failed you." Deep shame filled him. He'd failed to protect his mate for those agonizing moments. It was something that made him feel less of a man and incompetent to be trusted with her precious life.

Christina turned in his arms in the slippery water and cupped his face. "No, Sebastian. Stop that right now. You've done nothing but shelter me and protect me from the moment you came to the hospital. You prepared me for any eventuality, though I know you would have died before deliberately putting me in the position we were in tonight. None of us—not even Cam—could have known Mario was such a threat. This was something new and unexpected. You should be proud you planned ahead and taught me how to take care of myself. I know I couldn't be more grateful for your foresight." She leaned forward. "And you were there, with me, when it really mattered. You saved my life again, Sebastian, and I haven't fully thanked you yet."

She leaned closer, rubbing her slick breasts against his chest, locking lips with him and deepening the kiss. It was heaven, having his lady in his arms, safe and sound.

"My love, you honor me with your words and your love." He stroked her cheek, tangling their legs beneath the water in the huge tub.

"As you honor me. Sebastian." She lifted away to look deep into his eyes. "I know your heart. I know your soul. I know *you.* You're the man I will spend the rest of my life with, however long that proves to be. Any time with you—whether an hour or a century—I'll count as precious. Just as you're precious to me in every way."

If Sebastian were a weepy sort of man, he would've cried at the way her heart shone in her eyes and conviction rang in every syllable of her words. But he'd been born a British nobleman, so he showed his appreciation for her without words or overt displays. He kissed her with all the passion locked inside, turning her in the big tub to straddle his thighs. Her heat enveloped him as he drove inside her, taking his time but leaving no doubt of his claim on her body, her soul...and her love.

Now that she was his, he would never let her go, even if he felt unworthy. He'd strive to be better than he was and with her to guide him and inspire him, he'd do his best to be deserving of her love forevermore. For he couldn't let her go. It just wasn't in him. He wasn't that strong.

He stroked within her welcoming heat, the scented water sloshing around them in undulating waves heady with fragrant steam. He felt enveloped both by her luscious body and by the comforting embrace of the water—the recipe that scented it a thing from his past, the woman in his arms, the best part of his future. It was a melding of old and new that was both symbolic and very real, cleansing in more than just the obvious way. While the salted water cleansed their bodies, the breakthroughs within cleansed his very soul, old, dark and sorrowful as it had become over the centuries of his quest.

Only now did he realize what he'd been searching for all that time. Her. He'd been searching for Christina—the One who would complete him and make him whole once more.

He rocked within her, knowing it would take little to bring her over the edge of ecstasy with him. It would be the first of many peaks he would bring her that night, in what time they had left before dawn claimed them.

Sebastian stroked upward while Christina writhed atop him. Some of the water swished out of the tub, but he didn't care. They'd worry about cleaning it up later. For now, he could only concentrate of the feel of his woman, loving him.

He reached up and licked the point of her pulse with his tongue, his teeth descending as his excitement grew. He felt her petite fangs against his skin. The feel of her scraping the delicate points over his neck drove them both higher.

With gentle strokes, he positioned the bite, judging the exact moment to press down and sever the skin, allowing the warm juice of life to flow onto his tongue. It tasted sublime. The wine of the gods, made just for him.

Christina bit down on his neck and the sensations multiplied as they went from him to her and back again many times over. They were sharing every thought, every feeling, every sensation as they shared their bodies and their blood. They were One.

Her core gripped him and he rode the feelings higher. When she cried out and began to pulse around him, Sebastian at last could loose the tight reins he'd held on himself, shooting into her hard, fast and complete, as just a few sips of her blood coated his tongue. Between mates, that's all that was needed to sustain each other's magic and life. Blood and sex, and the deepest kind of love in all the realms.

Christina wrung him dry and sapped his energy, all the while replenishing it with her love. The fireball of power went between them, filling their souls and renewing their immortal lives. They would be this way, together, forever now. For eternity.

Chapter Fifteen

When Christina and Sebastian rose the following evening, the house was quiet. Most of the *were*folk had gone home, though a small contingent of Hastings' agents had set up a surveillance schedule to prowl the grounds of the estate. Sebastian made arrangements to hire Hastings' firm, though protection was only a side business for the busy private investigator. Still, the man had to earn a living for himself and his people and Sebastian had plenty of money to pay them with. Plus, Hastings' people were well trained in security, and had their natural *were* talents to call on. They'd also seen firsthand the threatening evil of the *Venifucus*, and knew Sebastian and Christina on a personal level. They were friends now. Comrades in arms. Sebastian trusted them to look after him and his lady, as well as the estate. It was a good deal all the way around.

Cameron was keeping tabs on Steel, but the mortal had been thanked and allowed to go on his way. The reports he would've handed in to his superiors at the *Altor Custodis* were now in Sebastian's safe. They'd be burned in the presence of Marc and Ian, as soon as the Master returned. Ian was keeping an eye on the former *Altor Custodis* agent and Christina's doctor friend as well—during the evenings, of course.

Sebastian had been in touch with Marc, but it sounded like he was enjoying his excursion in the countryside with his new wife. They hadn't had much of a honeymoon, so this little sojourn was apparently filling the gap. Marc didn't sound like he was in any hurry to return home, but then, the danger had passed...for now.

Cameron was waiting in the living room with a grim look on his face when Christina and Sebastian came up from their chamber. Sebastian took mental stock of the house and grounds. Usually he could pinpoint every creature in his domain. Right now, there were two *were* patrollers on the perimeter, Cam here in the living room, and Matt was still upstairs in one of the guest rooms. Everything seemed all right, but Cam's expression was troubled.

"What's wrong?"

Cam sighed. "The young cougar bit off more than he bargained for, I'm afraid."

Christina moved into the room. "What do you mean? Is Matt okay?"

"He's upstairs, resting. He's been in bed all day. I checked on him earlier, but there's little I can do for this kind of malady." Cameron shook his head, his eyes grave.

"What's wrong with him?" Christina was upset. Sebastian could feel her worry through their bond.

"It was the blood, wasn't it?" Sebastian asked, fearing the answer.

The fey warrior nodded.

Sebastian touched Christina's shoulder. "Remember how I went after Mario? With my hands. Not my fangs." She nodded. "When someone is that evil, right down to their core, even their blood is tainted. It's like poison to one of us."

"But Matt bit him. Oh, no! Is it as bad for *were* as it would be for us?"

"Not quite that deadly," Cam drew her attention, "but still poisonous. It's something he'll have to work out of his system, but it could leave him impaired."

"He looked so tired last night, but I thought it was just from the stress. I should've known something was up. He's usually so full of life and energy." Christina turned back to Sebastian. "Isn't there anything we can do?"

The silence stretched.

"There is one thing." Cam spoke in a low, serious voice. "Evil can only be overcome with goodness, purity of heart, valor, and...love. You care for him. He's bonded with you, for Lady's sake. You, Christina, could help purge the poison from his blood, both with your vampiric gifts and the love you hold in your heart for him. I know it's not the same as the bond you share with Sebastian, but what you both feel for Matthew is good and true. Most importantly, it could heal him. If you're willing."

Christina looked confused as she turned to Sebastian. He opened his mind to her completely, sharing images of their first joining, when Matt had given her his blood, so she might grow strong enough to face her fears. Matt's blood had given her the agility to dodge Mario's attacks. He'd later helped her learn how to use the cat's grace and treated her with respect, and yes, a kind of love.

He shared their minds in a small way. He was a part of them, though not in the same way Sebastian and Christina were joined. Still, he was there, in their minds and hearts, not to be denied or left to suffer.

"We can help him," Sebastian said. "If you're willing." In their minds he showed her images of the three of them together. He knew when the spark ignited in her blood. They'd been good together. Healing Matt in such a way would be no hardship at all.

When it came down to it, Sebastian wouldn't share his One with anyone—except Matt. He'd been more than a brother to them, seeing both of them through danger and standing strong by their sides. He'd even been poisoned to save them. They could do no less than help him now. And if the road to health was paved with pleasure, then they'd just have to put up with it.

Sebastian sighed and Christina grinned.

She reached up and kissed him. "I love you, Sebastian."

Matt was aware when the door to the guest room opened, but he couldn't find the energy to do much more than crack open his eyes. He was unsurprised to find Sebastian towering over him, with Christy at his side.

"What are you still doing in bed, friend?" the vamp asked.

Matt shrugged. "I just need some rest. Shouldn't you guys be sleeping? What time is it?"

"Cam said you slept all day, Matt." Christy sat on the side of the bed, her beautiful eyes full of concern. "It's after dark."

"You're kidding."

"I'm afraid not." One of her soft hands pushed his hair away from his brow. Her touch was magic. "Matt, you're sick and I think we can cure you."

Matt's mind whirled in a foggy mist. Christy's touch acted on his senses, her tantalizing scent reaching out to fire his blood. He remembered how sweet she'd been to fuck and how much he liked her—even loved her, in a very special way. But he hadn't been invited back to her bed since that astonishing three-way when his mind had been touched ever-so-slightly by the joining of theirs.

"Sweetheart, you're with Sebastian now. I know you two are joined."

"Yes," Sebastian answered, drawing his gaze, "we are. And we will be for all eternity. But we're also connected—slightly—to you. We care for you, Matt. We don't want to see you suffer for having helped us."

"And you think...this...will help?"

Sebastian nodded. "That's what Cameron said, and I trust him to know more about magical matters than any other being I know."

"The old busybody." Matt cursed. "Don't listen to him. I'll be fine with a good night's sleep."

"Matt, you've slept more than thirteen hours already." Christy sounded worried. She was such a sweet woman. He envied Sebastian for having her in his life. "Let me help you."

"You don't have to do this."

"We want to." Sebastian's eyes flared and Matt couldn't tell if it was with ire or passion. In his weakened state, he couldn't work up the energy to fear either. "Don't we, Christina?"

She moved closer, stroking his cheek. "We do." One of her hands rested over his heart. "Matt, you gave me your strength when I most needed it. You saved my life. Let me give a little of that back."

"Let you?" Matt had to laugh. "I'd be a fool to say no, but I'd happily be the fool if it meant coming between you two in any way."

"Only in the best possible way, brother."

Matt was caught by both the unmistakable heat in Sebastian's gaze and the words he used. Sebastian had never called him brother before. Such words had significance among both *were* and bloodletters. They weren't used lightly.

"Are you sure about this?"

"Kiss him, Christina. Show him how sure we both are."

Christy leaned forward and brushed her lips over Matt's. He remembered her delicious flavor and felt the immediate spark of her energy seeping into his body. When her tongue tangled with his, he felt stronger. He also felt the bond between them flare to life—the bond that linked all three of them.

Sebastian hung back and watched from beside the bed, much as he'd done that first night. But Matt could sense the other man's passion building, just as he had on those other occasions when he'd been with Christy. Only this time, the passion wasn't one of unrequited yearning, but rather that of the flourishing love between Christy and Sebastian. It was a powerful thing. A sacred thing. A beautiful thing to witness and even more special to share in, if only for this moment.

Christy claimed all of Matt's attention, settling over him, her breasts brushing against his chest, her thighs straddling him. They were both clothed, but the small barrier of fabric only heightened the sensations.

With each kiss, Matt felt himself rising out of the fog that had enveloped his mind. Still, the whole encounter had a dreamlike quality, like something he wished for but knew he could no longer have. Yet, here he was. Even more importantly, here *she* was, in his arms, kissing him with real affection.

"Christy," Matt whispered as she pulled back and tugged her stretchy top over her head. Her breasts were bare beneath, a beacon to his hungry gaze. "You're beautiful, sweetheart. So beautiful."

She smiled and moved away, standing at the bedside. Matt was confused as he saw two hands come around her waist from behind. Then he remembered. Sebastian.

The vampire wasn't pulling her away. On the contrary, he unbuttoned and unzipped his lady's jeans, and pushed them down her long legs along with her lacy underwear. Sebastian's hands guided her toward Matt again and she undressed him as if he were a child. Matt didn't mind one bit. He still felt weak, but he enjoyed the feel of her delicate fingers running over his skin, undoing his buttons, unzipping him. All the while he watched her sway, the gentle bouncing of her breasts enchanted him. He reached out to hold her when he was finally as naked as she, touching her smooth skin and caressing her nipples with eager hands.

"Kiss him, Christy," Sebastian coached from the bedside. "Let him sip from your mouth. Any fluid from our kind—except blood—will strengthen a *were*'s natural healing."

Christy wondered what vampire blood would do to a *were*cougar, but left the question for another time. Things were getting too hot and heavy between her and Matt to let logic interfere. Just knowing Sebastian was there, watching, approving, coaching...it made this act of love all that much sexier.

Making love to Matt was no hardship, though in truth, all she needed in her life was Sebastian—now and forever. But Matt was a special case. He'd been there at the beginning of their relationship and she knew they both hoped he'd be around for a long time to come.

Christy had felt deep, numbing fear when Cameron said Matt might never be the same after biting the evil mage. If there was anything—*anything*—she could to do help him, she'd do it. Giving him pleasure while he pleasured her in return was little enough to ask, except that she knew it was hard on Sebastian.

She'd felt a little twang of fear until she'd searched his mind. He'd helped her come to terms with her own mixed emotions on the topic. They were joined so fully at times, they shared thoughts, emotions, and even opinions. They both loved Matt for the special friend he was. They didn't want to see him impaired when they might be able to help him.

And so here they were.

Christy opened up her mind enough to know that Sebastian was more than enjoying watching Matt lick her nipples. She shared the feel of it with Sebastian in the shared playground of their minds and knew he was growing more aroused by the second. She'd have to get as much of her essence into Matt as quickly as possible because Sebastian wasn't going to wait long to claim her. Nor could she wait for the possession she'd come to crave.

Christy reached down to stroke Matt's aroused cock, wanting him to enjoy every moment of his "medicine". She kissed him, enjoying the control he let her have for the first time over their kisses. She wasn't used to taking the lead in lovemaking. If Matt had been his usual self, he'd probably be too much of an Alpha to let her call the shots for long, but she was enjoying this short interlude immensely.

She turned on the bed to straddle his face while taking his thick cock between her lips. A moment later she felt that long *were* tongue of his lapping at her clit and swirling its way up her passage. Her body was on fire with the sensation. *Were*folk—at least cougars, judging by Matt—had talented tongues.

"Is he drinking your honey, Christina? Lapping at your cream like a good little cat?" Sebastian's eyes locked with hers from a few feet away. He'd pulled a chair over to the side of the bed, sitting, watching with a perfect view of all the action. "Does it feel good?"

She moaned and let him feel through their link a fraction of the need Matt was firing in her blood. Matt groaned too.

Sebastian was startled enough to send out a quick mental probe. Matt's link with them was stronger than ever. It seemed to grow with proximity and they couldn't get any closer than they were now. Well, not unless they were both inside Christina at the same time.

Which could be arranged.

Sebastian thought through the wicked possibilities. They'd done it once before, of course, but only once, and that episode had been overshadowed by the monumental occasion of their joining. Sebastian had always been adventurous sexually and he was glad to find his mate was open for new experiences as well. He could read how excited she was at the ideas running through their shared mind. Excited, but still a tad shy, to be sure. Just the way he liked her.

They could spend centuries together exploring all the different ways he wanted to take her, the ways he wanted her to take him, and all the possibilities in between. They would have a glorious life together, but none of that would be possible, of course, if the *Venifucus* had their way. Matt was a vital part of keeping them all alive. Every supernatural life was precious, but Matt's even more so for the goodness he'd already proven was in his heart, and the valor he'd shown in battle. He was a selfless man, with a pure soul. And apparently, a very talented tongue.

Christina writhed over him, her body undulating in sinuous moves that made Sebastian's cock stand at attention. Matt was also hard and benefiting from the wet warmth of her mouth. How Sebastian envied the young *were* at that moment, but the beauty of it was, he knew he'd be feeling her mouth again soon—and that he could do so any night for the rest of their long lives together. He could spare the *were*cougar who'd saved their lives this moment in time.

Christina met Sebastian's gaze as she went down on Matt. He'd never seen anything sexier. She was the most sultry, tempting, yet innocent seductress he'd ever had the good fortune to meet. Without even trying, she had him harder than a flagpole.

"Suck him, love. Make him come." Sebastian couldn't help the order that spilled from his lips. Christina might think she was in charge of this little show, but he knew how she liked to be dominated sexually. Her pupils flared with excitement at his words, proving he was right.

She redoubled her efforts and Sebastian could smell the increased excitement in the air. Matt needed her honey. It was one of the few ways she could pass some of their healing to him without putting him in even greater danger.

And they both needed to get off. The energies were still murky from Matt, but getting stronger. Vampires fed off the sexual energies of their prey. Sebastian could gauge a mortal's level of health from the pulsing of their energy in a situation like this. He'd had centuries to perfect his observations and a quick glance told him Matt was still suffering the effects of the tainted blood.

It was a testament to Matt's strength that he hadn't been in even worse condition. Such evil blood could have killed a vampire—or turned him into a demon—in short order, had he been foolish enough to drink from Mario. Matt was caught in a haze while his energy was sapped by the contagion, but with each lick of Christina's tasty cream, he grew stronger.

He needed to come—repeatedly—for the taint to leave him altogether. And so did Christina. For Matt. And for them all.

"Make him come now, baby. Now," Sebastian ordered.

Christina applied her lips and tongue, hollowing her cheeks as she scraped her nails lightly up Matt's thigh. The *were*cougar groaned and tensed, his hips lifting as he came in rapturous spurts inside her greedy mouth.

She would gain from this joining as well. Not as much as she had from those first, most important encounters but still a significant, if temporary, boost to her abilities.

Matt's energies seemed to clear substantially as he quieted down, still licking at her pussy with lazy strokes. Sebastian crooked his finger and she climbed off the *were*cougar and walked over to him.

"Now me, baby." He cupped her neck, leaning forward to graze his fangs over her pulse, nipping lightly before drawing back. "I want to feel those lips on me."

Christy knew Sebastian wouldn't be able to wait long. Truth to tell, neither could she. Matt had fired her senses to a fever pitch, but he still wasn't quite himself. She could feel his energies, and though she wasn't quite as good at interpreting the signs as Sebastian, she knew from her mate's thoughts that Matt was indeed getting better, but wasn't quite all the way back yet.

But thoughts of anything else were pushed away as she bent over the love of her life, taking him deep in her mouth, the way she'd learned he liked. She worked him, sliding wetly over him, teasing him, tantalizing him. She heard motion in the room but dismissed it, so intent was she on her task.

Sebastian's hands tangled in her hair, guiding her motions, softly petting. She knew she was driving him wild and she liked the sensation.

She gasped though, when a long, hot tongue insinuated itself into her pussy from behind. Matt, of course. Dimly she registered the movement she'd sensed had been Matt getting off the bed and kneeling behind her. His mouth feasted on her pussy as she sucked Sebastian, a chain of pleasure affecting all three of them.

She knew Matt gained from tasting her and kissing her. Not only did her healing abilities pass over to him, but the sensual magic that was common to all vampires made Matt feel things most other men would never experience. The "vampire mojo" as he called it, guaranteed every interaction with one of their kind could be as pleasurable as the vampire in question wished it to be. In this case, there was no question, Christy wanted Matt to feel as good as possible, so she let loose with the sensual magic she otherwise kept restrained.

She knew she succeeded when Matt purred. Cat that he was, the purr shook his whole body, resonating from deep within, and translated to the lips kissing her so intimately.

Christy went off like a rocket, coming hard against Matt's suctioning mouth. Sebastian, his thoughts tangled with hers, came with her, spurting into her mouth as she drank him down.

It was one of the most amazing completions they'd ever shared. Thanks to their furry friend and his innate catness. That purr was something she'd never quite forget.

Sebastian bent over her, his limbs still trembling from the incredible climax. His eyes danced with laughter as he looked down the length of his woman's curvy back to see the *were*cougar still lapping at her folds with feline content.

Sebastian caught her eye and winked. "Nice, kitty."

Christina's laughter was musical and uplifting. "You have no idea."

She stepped forward, petting Matt's head to hold him in place, otherwise, out of it as he was, he would have followed her anywhere. She kissed Sebastian before turning to Matt and giving him the same salute on his glistening lips.

"Take him in your hand," Sebastian instructed, watching as Christina followed his order without demur. "Walk him backwards to the bed. He needs to sit." Again, she did as he asked and Matt followed where she led. He was coming back to them in slow stages. Sebastian kept tabs on the *were*cat's progress, testing his energies with short forays of his own every few minutes. Matt's essence was still shrouded in a miasma that weighed him down, but it was starting to dissipate the more he was exposed to the love and light that came from their joining.

In this one special instance, the vampires were feeding the needy *were*cougar with their energies almost as much as the sexual energy between all of three of them fed the bloodletters. It was an odd occurrence, to be sure, but these were strange circumstances and even stranger times.

Christina guided Matt to sit on the bed. Sebastian watched them as she tugged on Matt's cock with gentle fingers that knew just the right pressure. She kissed him with genuine affection but Sebastian knew her heart as well as his own. She loved Matt in a very special way—much like the kinship Sebastian felt with the big *were*cat—but nothing could rival or ever threaten the soul-deep bond they shared. Sebastian was secure in the knowledge that while a small part of her heart would always have Matt in it, the main portion of her love would always be Sebastian's.

Christina trailed nibbling kisses down Matt's chest as he leaned back. When she bent lower to take his aroused cock in her mouth again, Sebastian couldn't resist either the view or the temptation. He went to his lover, claiming her pussy from behind.

He pushed into her with a slow, deliberate motion, testing her readiness, though he could feel the excitement in the part of their minds they shared. Fully seated, he waited just a breath to pick up the rhythm she was using on Matt. Synching their movements, he took over the work of driving them all toward climax.

If they could all come together this time, it might create enough sensual energy to pull Matt out of the fog completely. Sebastian kept a close eye on the *were*cat and Christina, as he drove into her, forcing her to swallow and release Matt's cock in the rhythm Sebastian set.

He sped up as he felt their climaxes approaching. After three centuries as a vampire, Sebastian was expert at gauging the sexual peak of his prey. Though his days of seeking sexual energy from anyone other than his mate were at an end, he still had the expertise to guide this little tableau and he used it to their best advantage.

Sebastian pushed into her with short digs, designed to rub her in just the right way while she sucked Matt's cock, her clever hands fondling his balls. Sebastian felt them all racing toward the edge and with a few crisp motions, he sent them all flying straight over the cliff, soaring with each other for long moments, then coasting downward together to make a soft landing on the Earth far below.

Sebastian pulled out and collapsed back in the chair. Christina went with him, to settle in his lap, curling into him in her languor. Matt lay back on the bed, his legs dangling off the side, his lungs laboring as he tried to catch his breath. Sebastian watched his friend through heavily lidded eyes. The energy in the room was thick, pure and filled with goodness. If anything could overcome the evil taint in Matt's body, this was the thing—the one thing in the universe that evil couldn't defeat—love.

Christina succumbed to sleep and nuzzled into Sebastian's chest while he sat watch, waiting to see if this last effort had wrought any significant change in Matt's condition. The air in the room was thick with the swirling energies they'd created between them so it was hard to read Matt as closely as he wished, but when the *were*cougar recovered from his climax, Sebastian would have his answer. He hoped it was the right answer. He desperately wanted Matt to be his old self again. The idea that he might suffer permanent damage from the encounter with Mario hurt Sebastian. He loved Matt like a brother and didn't like the idea of him being hurt by coming to his and Christina's rescue.

Matt blinked a few times before sitting up. His gaze met Sebastian's and the vampire was glad to note the glazed look was gone. Matt seemed more clear-headed than he'd seen him since the battle.

"Are you back with us, brother?" Sebastian deliberately used the term of kinship that meant so much more among their peoples.

Matt ran a weary hand through his shaggy hair and sighed. "I think so. Dammit, Sebastian, I feel like I've been walking in a dream. How long has it been?"

"Almost twenty-four hours since you saved our lives and got poisoned for your troubles. I should thank you again, by the way, since I don't think you've really been with us since Mario's blood got into your system."

Matt shook his head. "I spit it out. He tasted foul. I remember spitting as much as I could and then dragging my tongue along the side of the building for good measure. Even that tasted better than filthy Mario."

"Still, some of his taint got into you. Cameron was worried enough to send us to you when we rose this evening."

Matt nodded toward Christina, sleeping on Sebastian's lap. "You truly didn't have to do this, but I can never thank you enough. Looking at it clearly now, I don't think my natural ability to heal would've saved me from this poison. It kept getting worse instead of better. That's never happened to me before."

"It's that way with evil. Once it takes hold, it grows roots and spreads. But we stopped it in time. It seems well and truly gone."

"Thank the Lady for that." Matt's eyes were as serious as Sebastian had ever seen them. "And thank you, Sebastian. For saving me. And for..." He gestured toward Christina again, his eyes going soft as he gazed at her. "For both of you being willing to share this..." He seemed to be at a loss for words as he waved one hand in the air, indicating the room, the bed, and them. "With me."

Sebastian smiled, knowing their friendship would continue as it had, and be even stronger for sharing both danger and caring. "How much do you remember?"

"Pretty much all of it, but it has a hazy, dreamlike quality."

Sebastian couldn't resist teasing his friend. "She made you purr in human form."

"You're shitting me. I thought that part must have been wishful thinking."

"I'm afraid not." Sebastian smiled at Matt's stunned expression.

"You know how rare that is, don't you?"

"I've heard things, but I wasn't entirely sure."

"Let's put it this way. My sire passed on only one piece of advice to me and my brothers where females were concerned. He said if any of us ever found a female who could make us purr, we should marry the girl before she could get away."

Sebastian's arms tightened around Christina as she snuggled into his chest. "Sorry, Matt. This one's mine."

"I know. That's the hell of it. Damn. It's gotta be that vampire mojo you all have. The only other time in my life I ever came close to purring was with Althea Williams. Remember her?"

"Do I ever. She was quite a woman. And quite a bit younger than me. Rumor has it she's barely a century. I didn't know you'd bedded her. How in the world did that come about?"

Matt sighed. "It's a long story."

"And I'd love to hear it," Christina chimed in, her eyes still closed, "but I'll thank you not to be talking, or even *thinking*, of other women after what we just did to save your miserable hide. Ungrateful cat."

"Oh, sweetheart," Matt said with some guilt, falling to his knees at her side, "you know I didn't mean—"

"She's teasing you, brother." Sebastian squeezed her ribs, tickling a giggle out of her as she opened her eyes. "My woman has a mischievous streak, I'm afraid."

Matt sat back on his haunches and sighed. "Damn, girl, you had me scared there for a minute. But I hope you know how grateful I truly am for what you did for me. I really like your kind of medicine."

She leaned forward and placed her hands on his shoulders, drawing him close for a quick kiss. "I'm glad you're okay." There were tears in her voice as she whispered of her happiness.

"Me too." Matt brushed a strand of hair back behind her ear as she sat back. "Thank you both for caring enough to save me."

"Just returning the favor, my friend." Sebastian cuddled Christina close as Matt went back to the bed. They were all tired after the excesses of the previous hours, but it was a good kind of tired.

Sebastian scooted Christina off his lap and they both stood. She gathered their clothing and donned her top while handing

Sebastian his pants. In short order they were both presentable.

"There's plenty of food in the kitchen," Sebastian said on his way toward the door. "Hastings' people restocked earlier today, I heard."

Matt's stomach rumbled at the mention of food and they all laughed. Christina glanced back and blew a kiss toward the *were*cougar before heading out the door. Sebastian lingered with his hand on the knob.

"You're part of us, Matt," he said, finding it hard to express the thoughts in his mind, the feelings in his heart. "What you did...when you took down Mario...that's something I will never forget. Ever."

Matt didn't speak, but as their eyes met, Sebastian knew the other man understood. Theirs was a bond deeper than mere friendship. For as long as any of them lived, the bond forged in danger and tempered by fire would stand strong between them.

Sebastian left and Matt showered and dressed. He went first to the kitchen, where one of the *were*hawks had made a rare roast. Matt chowed down and soon felt much better. Except for the disturbing idea that Christy had made him purr.

Cameron came into the kitchen as Matt was digging into a bowl of gelatin for dessert. The fey turned a chair around and sat opposite him, staring at him until Matt was forced to look up.

"What? Do I have Jell-O on my nose?"

Cam barked out a laugh. "No, laddie, but Sebastian mentioned you might be troubled."

"And you thought you'd stick your nose in? Cam, your advice is what led to this little...difficulty."

"You're very focused on noses for some reason." Cam fingered the tip of his own nose for a second before his eyes cleared of laughter. "But I'm glad to see you looking better, my lad. That taint was nasty stuff and I was at a loss as to how to lift it."

"So you sent them to me. Dammit, Cam!" Matt shoved the dish and spoon aside.

"Now you can't tell me you regret it." Cam's knowing

expression demanded no less than the truth.

"Of course not," Matt swore. "But the whole purring thing. Fuck! That wasn't supposed to happen. Not with Christy."

Cam sat back and eyed him. "Lad, I've known more than a few of your kind in my times in this realm. I've run across this problem before and take it from me. This is not the problem you might think it is."

Matt didn't believe him, though he wanted to. He sat back and watched the other man, waiting for him to elaborate.

"It's true, the purr is rare for you *were*cats. Sebastian told me what your father said and your old man was right—for the most part. The thing is, in recent centuries, *were* and bloodletter haven't interacted much, so you don't realize that your reaction to Christy's new power is fairly common. In fact, I'm surprised it didn't happen in your earlier encounters. My only guess is that she wasn't as comfortable in her power at first and you weren't as susceptible as when you were so weak from the poison."

"So you think it was to be expected?"

Cam nodded. "More than that, I think you can rest easy. The purr will help you determine your true mate, but such things don't count when you're talking about mixing *weres* and vamps. Among other *were*cats or even with mortals, you might find a woman who can bring out the beast in you, even in human form. Such a woman would be potential mate material and I'll admit, it's rare, but it is possible."

"I didn't think I'd ever want to find a true mate, Cam," Matt admitted in a moment of candor. "Not until I witnessed the bond between Christy and Sebastian. But now I wonder if there's someone out there who could complete me the way they complete each other."

Cam's eyes clouded while the silence stretched. He blinked and came back, smiling with his customary cunning. "I'll tell you this, laddie. There is someone out there who could make you as happy as our vampire friends, but you'll have to be smart enough to recognize her when you see her." Cam stood and pushed the chair back under the table as he grinned. "She'll lead you a merry chase, but I think you'll do all right. You'll just have to expect the unexpected. Not everything is as it seems."

Cameron left and Matt cursed even as he pulled the bowl of gelatin back in front of him. Muttering, he spooned up more of the dessert. "Damned fey always speak in riddles." The faint smile that curved the corners of his mouth didn't fully express the light feeling in his heart. For the first time since witnessing the joining between Christy and Sebastian, Matt had hope for his own love life.

He sat in silence for a while, mulling over Cameron's words, when the back door opened. Hastings walked in and slapped a folder stuffed with papers on the table as he hooked a chair and sat down on the opposite side of the table.

"Glad to see you up and around, Matt."

"Thanks. Me too." Matt swallowed a sip of coffee and sat back. "So where did everyone go? The place looks like it's emptying out."

"My team is going on shifts. Sebastian's asked us to help with security here. We're also going to be working with Atticus at the winery. This mess has brought a lot of business my way, but I can't say I'm pleased by the necessity. Still, the work is good to have. Vamps pay well." Hastings wore the smug grin of a business man that almost made Matt laugh. The raptor had killer instincts no matter what the playing field.

"Where's Steel?"

"He took off already, but we had a talk before he left. He's going to be investigating his handlers in the AC from here on out. Any jobs he takes for them will be strictly for show and as far as they're concerned, all of Kelly LaTour's friends are still mortal and he has no idea what happened to their boy Mario." Hastings snagged a mug from the counter behind him and poured a cup of coffee for himself. "Steel is going to work with us to figure out what's going on over in the *Altor Custodis* and just how deep the *Venifucus* threat goes."

"Sounds dangerous."

Hastings sat back, his eyes going cold. "It is, but Steel can handle himself. He's just the kind of man we need on the inside."

"I'll drink to that." Matt raised his coffee cup and Hastings joined in the toast. Steel had impressed quite a few of them with his skill and strength under fire, not to mention his deep and true remorse for what had happened to the people he'd investigated in the past. Matt knew the former Navy SEAL would work hard to make up for his mistakes, though he'd have to live with the guilt for a long time to come. Still, he was a worthy ally and Matt was glad Steel was playing on their team now.

At sunset that same day, Christy woke in Sebastian's arms.

"Good morrow, my love." Sebastian stroked her hair as he gazed deep into her eyes.

"Have I told you yet today how much I love you?" She knew, looking up at him, that this was the man she would spend the rest of her life with, though the possible length of that life still boggled her mind. He'd changed her life so drastically, and all for the good. It was hard to think now about the person she'd been just a few weeks before. How could a man like this want such a weakling? The idea still made her pause.

"I knew you were special the moment I saw you at that wedding, Christina. You should be able to read that much in my memories. I have no doubt we were meant to be together." He leaned in to nibble at her throat. "I cursed the fact that you were married and had plans to wait for you, no matter how long it took. Eventually, you would be mine. I had faith."

Amazingly, she could feel the truth of his words. Just as she'd dreamed of him when the nights were long and lonely in her troubled home, he'd held hope that someday she'd be free and they would be together.

"I dreamed of you, Sebastian, so many nights."

"I know." A wicked light entered his eyes. "But I bet you never counted on some of the things I demanded of you. Can you ever forgive me for springing Matt on you so soon after your trauma? If there'd been any other way, I would've taken it, but that first meal was crucial."

She smiled up at him. "I understand your reasons now, but I will admit, it was hard to take at first. I mean..." She felt heat rise to her cheeks as she remembered those first encounters. "I had all this new, sexual energy pushing me to do things I'd never done before, though I had fantasized about some of them. Some of the things we did though, I never thought of in my wildest dreams." She laughed with embarrassment and a growing sensual thrill as Sebastian's fingers trailed over the sensitive skin of her abdomen.

"I knew Matt would treat you right and push your boundaries. I'm glad it worked out, though I was worried you might hate me. Or that you might prefer Matt to me. Of course, then there'd be one less *were*cougar in the world today." His dry tone made her gasp with scandalized laughter.

"Sebastian!" She pushed at his arm, knowing he was only teasing about doing away with his friend, though she could feel the very real fears he'd harbored before they'd been joined. "Do you think Matt will be okay now?"

"He'd damn well better be. I don't like sharing." He tightened his arms around her, snuggling her close.

"Don't you?" She blinked up at him, teasing him with the thoughts she could read in his mind. "That's not what you thought last night."

"Well," Sebastian cleared his throat, playing along, "perhaps I should rephrase that." He moved quicker than lightning, laying her flat on the bed while he loomed over her. His eyes were hot with desire, his body warm over hers. "You're mine, Christina. Forevermore. You are my sun, moon and stars, my days and most importantly, my nights. I'm a jealous man, my love, and I won't be so generous with anyone other than Matt. And even then, not often. He needs to find his own mate, but until he does, we can't ignore the fact that he's joined to us." He leaned closer. "To do so would be cruel, and even I will admit, the possibilities are...intriguing."

The fire in his gaze made her squirm. "Sebastian, I don't think—"

"Good." He leaned in to kiss her. "Don't think." He kissed her again. "Let me worry about Matt and his role in our lives. Given time, I think it'll all work out, my love. You'll see. For now, I just want to claim my mate again. And again. And again. I want you to never forget that I'm the man you will walk into eternity with."

"I could never forget that, Sebastian. I may be your days and nights, but you're my future. My forever. I love you,

Sebastian." She strained upward and kissed him, looping her hands around his neck to draw him down, over her. She put all her love into the kiss and the long, languorous loving that followed. They were One in mind, heart and body, as they would be forevermore.

Epilogue

A few weeks later, Christy and Sebastian walked into the courthouse just after sunset. Sebastian had used his influence—both political and magical—to get time with a judge willing to see them at night.

The *were* lawyer, Morgan, represented Christy in the action they'd brought against Jeff. Sebastian had paid a little private visit to Jeff and once again used some of his vampiric power to convince the man that fighting them in court would be detrimental to his health. The bully backed down with a whimper and didn't contest the divorce proceedings. Sebastian had even procured a lawyer for Jeff, to be certain there would be no doubt in anyone's mind that the proceeding was legal...and final.

Once the papers were signed, the couple went home to celebrate all night long—privately.

They celebrated again a few months later, with their friends, at an elaborate wedding held at Sebastian's estate. All of Christy's college friends came to the wedding, some of them already part of the supernatural world, some only just becoming aware of such things, and one who knew nothing at all...yet.

Jena was part of the middle group. She knew about vampires, but had no idea that most of the rest of the handsome men and women at the party were *were*folk. She saw them eating, so she knew they weren't vamps, but as a doctor she noticed differences about them. They all seemed in robust health with hearty appetites. And they were all muscular, lithe and drop dead gorgeous—the men and women alike. She couldn't stop staring at them, wondering what made them stand apart.

"Curiosity killed the cat." A deep voice spoke from behind her and Jena whirled to face the man she'd met earlier that evening, before the ceremony in the moonlit garden.

"Mr. Sinclair, isn't it?" She knew damned well what his name was. It was burned in her memory, as was the image of the most handsome man she'd ever seen in person.

"Call me Ian." He lifted a delicate glass filled with blood red wine to his lips, holding her gaze as he sipped from the exquisite antique crystal. "I noticed you were sizing up the company here tonight. Not such a wise thing for a woman in your position."

"I was doing no such thing." She was trying not to let him see how he affected her, but feared she was doing a lousy job. She'd never been good at dissembling. "And exactly what do you mean by *my position*?"

"You know about us now," he said in low tones, moving closer. His words only confirmed what she'd already guessed. He was one of them—a vampire. God only knew how many centuries a man had to live to get that sexy. His tone was seduction itself, but she did her best to resist. "And now that you know, you'll be watched. Probably for the rest of your life."

"Is that a threat?"

Even his shrug was sexy. "We will protect our secrecy by any means necessary. Too many lives are at stake to let one mortal endanger us all."

"I can understand your position, but surely you know I would never betray my friends, three of whom are now like you. I'd never hurt them or the men who've made them so happy." Her gaze turned to the dance floor where Christy, resplendent in her designer wedding gown, danced in the arms of her new, beloved husband. Next to them were Kelly and Marc, beaming with a love that was almost tangible, and on the other side danced Lissa and Atticus, just as blissfully happy. Never would Jena jeopardize the happiness of her best friends, no matter what they had become.

A warm hand touched her shoulder.

"Dance with me."

It wasn't a request, but regardless of the presumption, Jena found herself powerless to resist. She took Ian's hand as he led her out onto the dance floor and stepped into the dream.

Author's Note

Find Ian and Jena's story, *Forever Valentine*, in ebook or in the *Caught By Cupid* print anthology, available now at Samhain Publishing.

About the Author

A life-long martial arts enthusiast, Bianca enjoys a number of hobbies and interests that keep her busy and entertained such as playing the guitar, shopping, painting, shopping, skiing, shopping, road trips, and did we say... um... shopping? A bargain hunter through and through, Bianca loves the thrill of the hunt for that excellent price on quality items, though she's hardly a fashionista. She likes nothing better than curling up by the fire with a good book, or better yet, by the computer, writing a good book.

To learn more about Bianca D'Arc, please visit www.biancadarc.com. Send an email to Bianca at bianca@biancadarc.com or join her Yahoo group to join in the fun with other readers as well as Bianca at http://groups.yahoo.com/group/BiancaDArc/

What do you do when you've got a hillbilly tiger by the tail?
Or maybe the question should be: what wouldn't you do...

Here Kitty, Kitty
© 2007 Shelly Laurenston

Nikolai Vorislav likes his single life just as it is. Simple, relaxing and quiet. What he doesn't need is some foul-mouthed Texan hellcat living in his house, eating his food, flirting with his idiot brothers and shooting holes in his home with his granddaddy's gun. But those long legs, dark eyes and lethal tongue are making Nik insane and he fears he may be caught in the sexiest animal trap ever.

Angelina Santiago doesn't know how she got from Texas to North Carolina in a night or how she ended up in some hillbilly tiger's house wearing only a sheet. What she does know is that she doesn't like good ol' boys with slow, sexy drawls who can't seem to stop rubbing up against her. Yet in order to protect her friends, Angie has to stay with a cat who seems hellbent on finding all sorts of delicious ways to make her purr.

Available now in ebook from Samhain Publishing.

Enjoy the following excerpt from Here Kitty, Kitty...

A soft knock at the door almost had her diving out the window.

"Angie, sugar. Open the door."

She almost screamed, "Are you fuckin' nuts?" But, instead, she took another shaky deep breath, and pulled the door open.

The hillbilly stood there, a brown blanket wrapped around his hips.

"Can I come in?"

She was staying in his house and he was asking her if he could come in.

Only in the South.

Angie nodded, not sure if she could create an intelligent sentence if she decided to speak, and stepped away from the door. She went and sat down on her bed, then jumped back up again.

Sitting on bed...not good.

Nik closed the door and slowly walked over to her. When she stepped back, he stopped.

"You okay?"

She finally spoke, unable to hold it in any longer. "In less than twenty-four hours, your mother has seen me break a man's nose, hit him with a chair, and molest her son. No, I'm not okay."

Grinning, Nik took a step toward her. She jumped back, slamming into the bed. She held her arm up. "Stay!"

He laughed. "Aw, sugar. That only works with dogs." Then he was right there. Right in front of her. She put her hands down at her sides to prevent herself from rubbing that amazing body all over.

"It's not a big deal. Really. My momma don't care."

"I do. That woman probably thinks I'm a whore. A dangerous, psychotic whore."

"Naw. Daddy has twenty-eight stitches where Momma mauled him one time. Trust me. In my family, this is nothin'."

He couldn't believe how beautiful this woman was. She wore no makeup, her thick hair still damp and tangled from their roll on the floor, her clothes a simple T-shirt and shorts. Yet to him she was ten times more beautiful than she had been the night before when she'd gotten all fancy. At some point, he'd tell her never to wear makeup again. She didn't need it. It actually stole some of her natural beauty. And she was a natural.

One of his hands held the blanket. The other reached up to touch her face. She took another step back. Or, at least, she tried to. But the bed got in her way.

Nik waited until she stopped moving, and he lightly touched her cheek. To his surprise, she didn't swat him away this time. Instead, she closed her eyes and made that sexy little whimpering sound.

"Okay." Her eyes snapped open and focused on him. "Let's get this over with."

"Get what over with?"

"You. Me. Let's just fuck and get it over with."

She had to be *the most* entertaining female he'd ever met in his damn life. Where the hell had she been hidin'? Were all the women in Texas like this?

"What?"

"Look, hillbilly, I want you. You want me. Let's just bang this out and go on about our day."

Nik shook his head slowly. "No."

She frowned, then nodded in understanding. "I see. You don't want me."

"Sugar, you must be kidding." He grabbed her hand and wrapped it around his cock, the blanket the only thing between them. "Feel that? You did that. You *keep* doin' that to me."

"Oh." She stared down at where her hand connected with his body. Then those beautiful brown eyes snapped up to his. "So what's the problem?"

"There will be no banging out anything." He stepped even closer to her. "When we do this—and we will do this—I don't plan to rush a goddamn thing. We're not something to 'get over with'."

She stared up at him, brown eyes wide. "We're not?"

Since she seemed quite content to keep a healthy hold on his growing erection, he moved his hand back up to her cheek. He brushed the smooth skin with the tips of his fingers—and she let him.

"Nope. We're not. We're going to take this slow and easy, sugar."

"We are?"

He pressed his body against hers, her hand caught between them. "Oh, yeah. We are."

"Why?"

And she meant it. She had no idea why he wouldn't just throw her down on the bed, come, and go on about his day. That Nik had no intention of rushing anything where Angelina Santiago was concerned. This was a woman you savored. Enjoyed. Fucked. Hard, long, and as often as possible.

No. She'd have to forget about "banging out" anything.

He had other plans. Bigger plans. And they all involved her coming all over him.

"Because, sugar—you make me purr."

She had men say many things to her over the years. Some nice. Some sweet. Some thoroughly disgusting. But no one had ever told her she made them purr. And she never knew it would have the kind of effect on her it did.

Angie wrapped her hand tight around his cock and squeezed. Nik closed his eyes, leaning down until his forehead rested against hers.

"Damn, darlin'. That was plain mean."

"I don't like to wait, hillbilly." She really wanted to beg. She wanted to scream, "Please don't make me wait!"

But, dammit, a girl had her pride. Didn't she?

He smiled, even though she got the feeling she might be killing him. "But you're gonna wait." And it was an order. A delicious order she felt all the way to her toes. "You'll wait for me."

In the big scheme of things, it wasn't like she really had a choice.

"Damn cat."

He chuckled, his free hand playing along the bottom edge of her T-shirt. The air changed around them. Going from playful to serious in a heartbeat. He tugged on the shirt.

"Pull your shirt up."

Normally, she'd ask what the fuck for. But they both knew that wasn't going to happen now.

Unwilling to release his cock anytime soon, she gripped the end of her shirt with her free hand and brought it up over her breasts. She'd never had time to fix her bra, so they were bare, the nipples hard.

Nik tucked the blanket he wore into itself, so that it stayed on his hips. Then he took both his hands and ran them up her ribcage, his fingers gliding along her flesh.

Nik's big fingers circled her breasts and both she and Nik let out a shuddering breath. She no longer found his hands on her annoying. Not in the least. She had the distinct feeling she could easily get used to this. Used to him touching her, fondling her, making her squirm.

He gripped each of her nipples between thumb and forefinger. Her squirming intensified, the ball of her right foot pushing into the floor.

He rubbed his lips against hers, but he didn't kiss her. She wondered if he was afraid to. Afraid he wouldn't be able to stop.

With a deep sigh, he released her breasts, and grabbed hold of her bra. Gently, he re-hooked the lace over her, took the T-shirt from her hand and pulled it back down. He still had his forehead against hers and she watched him struggle with his decision to pull away.

Finally, and with obvious reluctance, he stepped back, unwrapping her fingers from his hard cock.

"We're not doin' this now." He brought her hand to his mouth, turned it over and kissed the inside of her wrist, right below her palm. He ran his tongue along the veins. Once he had her squirming again, he stopped.

"Slow and easy, sugar. That's what the South is all about."

"I'm beginning to hate the South."

GREAT CHEAP FUN

Discover eBooks!

THE FASTEST WAY TO GET THE HOTTEST NAMES

Get your favorite authors on your favorite reader, long before they're out in print! Ebooks from Samhain go wherever you go, and work with whatever you carry—Palm, PDF, Mobi, and more.

Samhain
publishing
ltd